With best w

The Fortune Hunter

A novel by

Jan Pollard

Strategic Book Publishing and Rights Co.

Strategic Book Publishing and Rights Co.
12620 FM 1960, Suite A4-507
Houston, TX 77065
www.sbpra.com

ISBN: 978-1-62857-697-9

Book Design: Suzanne Kelly

For Louisa and Angela, with love.

CHAPTER 1

It started a long time before Anna had met him, and had she known about it she would never have married him, but then who does know the person they marry until it is too late.

***

Harry had always been a difficult child; one minute giving the appearance of a kind and thoughtful boy, when it suited, and the next minute an evil little monster; the perfect opposite of each other, like a two-sided coin. His parents could do nothing with him and being wealthy sent him to a prestigious boarding school as soon as he was old enough, hoping they could sort him out. But Harry, being Harry, went from bad to worse as he grew into manhood, leaving a trail of misery and destruction behind him as he spent his inheritance in a riotous orgy of self-indulgence until there was hardly anything left. That was where Anna comes into the story but to find out what happened you will need to read the book to the very last page.

By the age of ten Harry knew that his father, Percival Langford, might have been in line for a title and the wealth that came with it, had it not been for his older brother Walter, who had married in his late sixties a young and flighty actress who had given him a son, Rupert, before running off with a much younger man. Rupert of course would now inherit the title of Lord Charlesworth on the death of his ancient father which would put Harry third in line, and that did not suit Harry.

Rupert and Harry although close to each other in age were like chalk and cheese. Rupert was often bullied by his peers as, like his father, he suffered from myopia and wore unattractive round spectacles without which he could see very little. He was a studious boy and kept to himself rather than join in with boys of his own age, who gave him the nickname, Professor Owl. Harry however was strong and athletic and could hold his own amongst his peers. Harry was afraid of no one and was the biggest bully in his form and the leader of the pack. Fortunately for Rupert they went to different schools, but Rupert dreaded the school holidays and the cruel tricks which his cousin, Harry, thought up each year to frighten him.

Every summer holiday the cousins spent together at The Old Priory, the Langford's home on the Essex/Suffolk borders where there was a large impressive garden, a tennis court and a swimming pool for the boys. The coast was not too far away and a comfortable beach house overlooking the grey North Sea, and a hut at Frinton were also at their disposal. There was a well paid staff, to look after the boys' every need and they had each other for company. Once they were a bit older then holidays abroad would be arranged and skiing trips and sailing lessons would come into the picture, or so their parents thought without knowing that Rupert would no longer be around to share such delights.

Harry's parents spent the summer at their country retreat in the south of France, far away from their son and his problems. Harry never missed them and they had given up on him since he had been expelled from his last public school. Next term he would be attending a school in the Essex countryside where there were no rules of any kind; even attendance at class was up to each child. The development of the individual, without restrictions, was the aim of this school. Harry was looking forward to the new term for the first time in his life but before that happened Rupert was coming to stay, and Harry had plans about that.

***

The garden at The Old Priory boasted a lake and on this particular holiday Harry decided to build a raft. As Rupert had just finished reading Robinson Crusoe he found the idea more appealing than some of Harry's previous ideas and joined in with enthusiasm. Once completed to the boy's satisfaction the raft had been launched with Rupert being encouraged to be the first on board.

'I have made you the Captain,' said Harry, in case Rupert might show some sign of being nervous, as they launched the unstable raft of logs.

Once Rupert had grasped the mast to steady himself Harry had pushed it off into the deep water of the lake and Rupert found himself alone, with no means of steering his craft. Fumbling around to get his balance Rupert lost his spectacles and panicked. His surroundings became blurred and he fell onto the logs, unable to do anything to help himself. Worse still, Rupert had never learned to swim and the water seeping between the roughly tied logs frightened him. He called out to his cousin to help him but that was the last thing on Harry's mind as he watched from the lakeside. When Rupert had rolled into the water and sunk without trace then Harry ran back to the house to call for help, but it was too late by then and Rupert had drowned.

'I told him not to go on his own,' insisted Harry, 'but he wouldn't listen. He wanted to be the first. We were playing at being Robinson Crusoe. He really enjoyed making the raft – I shall miss him. We had some good times together – especially on this holiday.'

As nobody had witnessed the sad event then Harry's explanation of events had to be believed although those who knew Harry and the unkind tricks he used to play on his cousin were in two minds about it. There was nothing anyone could do to alter the situation and a verdict of accidental drowning was decided upon.

A few months later Rupert's father died; a broken man at the loss of his son and heir. Harry's father became the new Lord Charlesworth with a large inheritance to go with the title and Harry became the heir apparent, much to his satisfaction. An unfortunate car accident in the south of France killed both Harry's father and his step-mother, the Lady Letitia, leaving Harry in sole possession of their estate and a title.

The Old Priory had been his childhood home and he continued to live there, selling off his other properties as he grew into manhood and his debts piled up until one day he found he was left almost destitute and the sale of The Old Priory became a necessity – and that was when Anna came into the story.

CHAPTER 2

Even before she had opened the back door to her house in The Rows, Mollie could hear raised voices and sudden bursts of laughter. Who were these people? She recognised her daughter Anna's voice and Josie's squeals of delight. Whoever these people were Anna must have invited them. It was odd. Anna had few close friends although everyone who knew her liked her. She couldn't have been home long from her secretarial course at the college, and Josie would have just arrived back from school.

Gingerly, Mollie pushed open the door into the small front room and saw a group of strangers raising their glasses to toast Anna. Was it champagne they were drinking? Mollie's mouth fell open with amazement. Whatever was going on?

Josie saw her first. 'Mum! Mum!' she shrieked. 'Anna has won the lottery, and she's going to buy me a horse. A horse, Mum! I've always wanted a horse—always, but Dad said—.'

'Be quiet for a minute, Josie, and settle down. Let me talk to your sister.'

'It's true, Mum. It really is; I can't take it in either. I was looking for the bill for my shopping and pulled the lottery ticket out of my pocket at the same time. It was weeks old but still valid. When I got home I phoned the number and look what's happened.' Someone placed a glass of champagne in Mollie's hand.

'Lucky girl your daughter, Mrs Hamilton—she's won ten million—a record win. It was a roll over week.' Mollie felt faint with shock and the champagne slopped onto the carpet.

'Sit down, Mum. I know. I couldn't take it in either.' Anna helped her to a chair and sat on the arm beside her. 'No more worries. No more debts to pay off. You needn't go to that Bingo hall any more hoping to win a fortune. We've all we need and more beside.'

'But I like going to Bingo, Anna, you know I do. Why, I won fifty pounds today.' There was a great burst of laughter in the room at this statement. Mollie felt peeved. Fifty pounds meant a lot to her. It was all right for these people to laugh. They were used to dealing with large sums of money and she had never had much in her purse. 'Time we were going, folks,' said one of the men, sensing a change in the atmosphere. The two men and the woman who had brought the cheque drove away. An older man with a kind face remained behind—a local man, but not one anyone knew by name.

'Don't I know you?' asked Mollie. 'Are you local?'

'Mr Appleby,' replied the man, introducing himself. 'I'm a partner in the firm of solicitors in the town square. Your daughter asked me here to represent her during the hand over of the cheque.'

Mollie nodded. People were only too quick to drop everything when there was a lot of money about. It was none of her business anyway. Anna held the purse strings now.

'Well, I'll be off now,' said Mr Appleby, as Anna came back into the room. 'Ring us anytime if you need us, but I think you should come into the office to-morrow, if possible. I will ask the bank to send a representative if you wish. There will be investments to be discussed.'

'Of course; I'll be there at ten, if that's convenient.'

'I'll expect you then,' said Mr Appleby, taking his leave.

'They'll all be at your beck and call now, Anna. Money opens all the doors.'

'He's a kind man, Mum, and a genuine one I feel sure. He'll be there if I need advice. I feel really scared having all that money to spend.'

'Have you resigned your course at the college?'

'I hadn't thought of that, Mum? I'd nearly finished it anyway. I'll 'phone them now.'

The family settled down, chatting excitedly, to await Reg's arrival. He had been a good electrician but now he spent his days looking for work once his firm had closed down, ending each day by visiting the betting shop or the pub. His redundancy pay would soon come to an end and he had tried not to think about how they would manage when that happened. The little Anna brought home helped but once Amanda had left home to live with her photographer boyfriend they had felt the pinch. Amanda had earned good money working as a receptionist.

'Perhaps Amanda will come back home now. I've missed her since she left to live with that Justin of hers. Your Dad has never got over it. There's been no talk of a wedding as yet,' said Mollie, going over a frequently discussed subject which was close to her heart.

Anna smiled. Her parents disliked Justin who was making a folio of Amanda's photographs. Amanda had visions of becoming a photographic model and certainly had the looks for it, but you needed to catch the right person's eye to get noticed.

'Your Dad says that Justin's taken photos of her in the nude, so he can sell them to those dirty magazines and make lots of money,' grumbled Mollie.

Anna had heard this argument many times before and sighed.

'Our Amanda's a big girl now, Mum. She can do what she likes and good luck to her. You wouldn't like Justin any better if she did marry him, would you.'

'I suppose not love—but it seems all wrong to me. Perhaps you'll find a handsome young man to marry you, Anna, now you're so wealthy.'

'Perhaps, Mum. We'll have to wait and see, but first I'm going to buy us a wonderful house which we all like, so we can move out of the Rows.'

'And I'm going to have a horse, aren't I Anna.'

'Yes, love, I haven't forgotten.'

'And a stable to put him in?'

'Yes, Josie—all in good time.'

'You'll have to learn to ride first,' said Mollie, thoughtfully.

'Anna will pay for me to have lessons, won't you Anna, now you're so rich.'

'Don't you forget it's Anna's money, Josie. You'd spend it all in the first few minutes, you would. We've heard enough from you for a bit. Go upstairs and get on with your homework.' Josie made a face at the prospect but decided not to complain in case her sister changed her mind about the horse. Soon the sounds of music filtered down the stairs from Josie's bedroom; a sure sign of homework being done, as Josie could only work if surrounded by noise.

'I'll give Amanda a ring at work. 1 know they don't approve but I can't keep it until she gets home.' Anna telephoned the hotel where Amanda worked. Fortunately she was on duty at the reception desk.

'I shall be in trouble if the manager twigs that I'm taking a personal call,' whispered Amanda, urgently. 'Is something the matter?'

'Not really. I've won the lottery, that's all—ten million pounds.'

Amanda screamed. 'You're joking!'

The hotel manager looked up and glared at Amanda.

'I can't talk now,' she hissed, 'the manager has his eye on me. I'll call in after work'. The 'phone went dead.

'Amanda's calling in after work, Mum. Perhaps she'll come back home once I've bought a big house for us all to live in. Maybe some of this money can help her to find a good agent for her modelling.'

Mollie looked at her daughter with pride. She was as good as she was beautiful and deserved to find happiness for herself one day. When Reg returned home the house was in total confusion. No meal was waiting for him on the table and his womenfolk seemed to have taken leave of their senses. Amanda was there, which was unusual, talking about leaving her Justin and returning home. About time too, thought Reg. He only used her as a meal ticket as if she was some commodity.

'I've been given a month's notice by that rotten manager,' said Amanda, grimly.

'It doesn't matter anymore,' said Anna, smiling. 'You can find a better agent now, and use the top photographers.'

Reg stared in amazement. 'That costs money—and where is that coming from may I ask?'

The family burst out laughing. Anna gave her father a hug and told him the news. It hit him like a thunderbolt, but once he had taken it in, Reg ran to the door like a madman, shouting that he was going to tell them all at the pub before they read it in the newspapers.

'No, Dad, please don't.' Anna called after him, but her father had already gone on his way. Now the news would become public knowledge, which was not her intention. Despite the euphoria surrounding her Anna felt a niggling sense of concern. Her family were working class and knew nothing of the lives of the rich and powerful. How would they all adapt, and would the money bring them the happy carefree lives they all craved, or would it bring them unexpected problems.

Whatever the future held, the excitement was about to begin.

CHAPTER 3

After Reg had left the house Anna insisted that the whole family packed up and moved before the reporters arrived. Mollie and Josie set off with bulging suitcases in a taxi, to stay with Mollie's friend in the next town, and Anna returned with Amanda to her flat on the outskirts of Chelmsford. A note was left for Reg telling him where they were in case he wanted to avoid the newspaper reporters who would soon be on his trail. The next day Anna contacted every estate agent for miles around to find a new home as soon as possible, and set off to view all the suitable properties. It took her a week to find The Old Priory, a large turreted building, with wisteria covering the front elevation and set in a landscaped garden of great beauty. The cook/housekeeper and her husband, the head gardener, lived in The Lodge house with their nephew, Josh, who was also employed on the estate. They were willing to work for the new owner if required. It was almost too perfect, thought Anna, as she viewed one beautiful room after another.

'Why is it being sold with everything complete?' she asked the estate agent, after her initial look around the property.

'Death duties,' explained the agent. 'Lord and Lady Charlesworth were killed in a car accident in Brittany, and their son cannot afford to keep on the family home. He has a flat in Belgravia, but the rest of the property has to be sold.'

'Poor man,' said Anna, feeling pity for the new heir. 'How dreadful to lose his parents and his home all at once. I can't imagine anything worse.'

'That's not all,' continued the agent. 'There are two holiday homes abroad which are being sold by our overseas branch.'

'How very sad for the family.'

'Yes, indeed—I think I should mention that we have had two other enquires about The Old Priory—one from a company who want it for a conference centre.'

'That would be terrible,' said Anna. 'They would ruin it. It should stay as a home and not lose its character.'

'Terrible, quite terrible,' agreed the estate agent, 'but it's good for our business. This property is most unusual.'

'I love it,' said, Anna. 'Everything about it appeals to me. I want it to be a family home again, and I hope, when my family see it they will love it as much as I do.'

When the family came to view The Old Priory they were as enthusiastic as Anna. Josie found two stables in the courtyard, which filled her with a great longing to be taken to choose her promised horse, although Mollie pointed out that riding lessons must come first. The kitchen with every conceivable gadget and a large Aga, warmed Mollie's heart, and Reg found a well equipped workshop which would keep him happy for hours. Amanda discovered a self-sufficient wing of The Old Priory exactly to her liking, where she could come and go as she liked while she pursued her ambition to become a model, using the money her sister had generously settled on her.

Anna looked at their happy, excited faces and felt pleased for them. In The Old Priory they would each have their own space although that might take a bit of getting used to. Her lottery win had come just in time to solve the problem of where to live. The letter from the Chelmsford Highways Department had come as a total shock to Reg. The Rows were being bought up to make way for a ring road round the town. As their house belonged to Reg he was to receive compensation, but as things were in the property market Reg knew that buying another house would be beyond his means, and there was no hope at his age and without a job of getting a mortgage. Anna had asked them all to come and live with her at The Old Priory and they were only too happy to join her. They would stay together as a family as they always had done. For some time now The Rows had been too small for all the family. When the old houses were to be demolished was still in doubt but they were to be boarded up to prevent vandalism while a new roundabout was built.

Once the family had settled into The Old Priory their lives took a different turn. Josie was sent to a prestigious girls' school, much to her annoyance. Her accent was different and she was often picked on by the other girls. The comprehensive had been good enough for her sisters and she had to leave her friends behind. All of Josie's schoolmates envied her new horse, a beautiful palomino, and they were only too pleased to be invited to ride, and to use the indoor pool. No one could compete with such luxury, yet Josie felt as if she was an outsider and often wished she could return to the comprehensive school in town. She envied her sister Amanda, able to travel to the world of fashion houses in pursuit of becoming a famous model. Perhaps when she was older, like Amanda, she could do that too. Twiggy never spoke with a posh accent and look how famous she had become.

Reg and Mollie set off on a world cruise, visiting all the places they had never expected to see in their wildest dreams. And Anna—what about Anna, the owner of an unexpected fortune? Every slight acquaintance from the past was only too pleased to know her now and angled for an invitation to see The Old Priory and the grounds. But Anna had never made any close friends and kept quietly to herself and spent her time opening cupboards and drawers to discover the contents. She took down each book in turn from the folio editions, so carefully arranged on the library shelves and dusted them. Hardly any appeared to have been read. In the china cabinets she lovingly touched the Dresden china figurines and the Meissen ware. She had never seen anything so beautiful or delicate before, and it all belonged to her. She felt as if she was living in a dream from which she would never awake. She looked through the photograph albums and wondered about the people who had once lived here. A handsome young boy and his attractive sister often featured in the photographs. They must have lived here once, she mused. In matching silver frames there was a beautiful bride and her husband, and a handsome young man standing by a painting. She had asked the housekeeper about them.

'Well, that's Harry,' said Mrs Hardy. 'He's the present Lord Charlesworth, since his father's recent death. He's an artist and mostly paints portraits—society portraits, if you know what I mean. And that's his sister, Fleur, on her wedding day. She married Hugh Flambard, the son of the MP. They live in Surrey. Would you like me to pack the family photos away, Miss Anna? They can't be of any interest to you .'

'No thank you. I like to see them there. They belong to this house. Sometimes I think they are still living here, and I am just a visitor.'

'A visitor! Well you won't feel like that for long, I feel sure.' The housekeeper smiled wryly to herself. Miss Anna was a strange girl to be sure.

One afternoon, Anna was surprised by an unexpected visitor. 'Lord Harry Charlesworth, Miss Anna,' announced Mrs Hardy, as she ushered him into the long drawing room. Anna had heard the bell in the distance, but had taken no notice. Callers usually came to the back door and were seen to by Mrs Hardy.

'Lord Harry,' stammered Anna. She recognised the dark curly hair and the handsome features from the photographs scattered around and was quite taken aback to see him in reality. The photographs were a pale reflection of the real man, with his ready smile and his bedroom eyes, summing up her potential as a future conquest.

'Oh, just Harry, if you don't mind. I haven't got used to the title as yet.' Anna shook hands nervously. This suave stranger unnerved her initially. She felt as if she was standing naked in front of him, he had such a hypnotic presence.

'So you are the new owner of The Old Priory. How have you settled in? I see you have left everything as it used to be, when I sadly lost my parents.'

'I love it, just as it is,' said Anna, regaining her self-composure. 'It was a family home and I want it to stay that way.'

'How quite extraordinary—I am amazed—I really am. I see the family photos are still here. Would you like me to take them with me when I leave?'

'Oh, no—please leave them, unless you wish to have them of course. I feel as if they are a part of the house and its memories.'

Harry gave her a sidelong look. She was a remarkably beautiful young woman with a natural grace and a lack of sophistication, which he found refreshing, compared to the young women with whom he usually associated.

'Can I get you a cup of tea or coffee?' asked Anna, wondering why he had come.

'How kind of you—coffee please. But that can wait. I must explain why I am here, taking up your time like this. I left some of my easels and canvases in the top room which I used as a studio, and I really would like to collect them if it is convenient.'

'Of course you can. I saw them piled up against a wall in what I thought was one of the attics. You are most welcome to them. I had heard you were an artist.'

Harry smiled. 'May I help myself, if it's not too much trouble.'

'Not at all,' said Anna, opening the door. 'You know your way, I feel sure.'

While he had gone Anna arranged for coffee to be served and dug out the old photograph albums from the bottom drawer of the chiffonier where she had found them. If Harry had time perhaps he would tell her the history of the people in the old albums. She was interested to know the history of the family who had once lived here. Mrs Hardy was amazed when she came to clear away the tray to find the two young people sitting together on one of the settees and laughing happily as Harry described some amusing event from the past. Before he left he promised Anna that he would be back in a few days time to take her out to lunch. Anna was delighted by the invitation.

'There is only one thing missing here,' Harry told her as they walked to the door, 'and those are the flowers. My stepmother filled every room with the most beautiful flowers from the garden. They made The Old Priory into a home, and the scent in all the rooms was wonderful. Do you like flowers, Anna?'

'Of course, but I have no experience in arranging them. I've never had a garden before.'

'Well, you have one now, so you have no excuse. You'd be good at it with a bit of practice.'

Harry smiled and waved as he set off in his silver Porsche. His introduction to the new owner of The Old Priory could not have been more satisfactory. He had read the report in the daily newspapers of Anna's fantastic lottery win, and once he realised she had bought The Old Priory, his interest became personal. Now he had met her and discovered how charming and unaffected she was, it should be simple enough to bring her round to his way of thinking. He had been pleasantly surprised when meeting her for Anna was a natural beauty with a perfect complexion and long ash blonde hair which tumbled over her shoulders. She had the bluest of blue eyes and a look of innocence, which appealed immediately to a man of Harry's inclinations. She would soon be his adoring slave if he played his cards right. He had no doubt of it. He was feeling well pleased with himself as he drove the Porsche back to his flat, and then to the garage from which he had rented it, to carry all his easels.

'Won the lottery, have you?' asked the mechanic, to whom he handed the keys.

'You could say that,' said Harry, smiling broadly.

CHAPTER 4

Josh put down his hoe when he saw Anna coming towards him across the lawn. She hadn't set foot into the garden in all the weeks she had been in residence in The Old Priory. His aunt had told him how intrigued she was with the house and its contents.

'You'd think she had never had anything before in her life the way she turns everything out,' his aunt had told him. 'She's so gentle and careful, even the smallest thing is precious. You can't help liking her. A sweet, natural girl she is, but she has no idea about running a big place like this. Good thing we are still in employment here, or I don't know what she would do.'

Josh had met Anna briefly when the family had taken up residence, and later when the horse had arrived he had been asked to help Josie care for the animal and muck out the stable. He polished Reg's new Jaguar but mostly spent his time gardening and helping his uncle with the estate work.

'I wonder Josh, if you could spare a few minutes to take me round the garden? I need some flowers for the house and perhaps you can help me to choose some. That is if you don't mind.' Josh smiled at her, a friendly, cheerful smile. If he didn't mind indeed! He wasn't used to such consideration. His late lordship referred to him as Hardy, the same as his uncle, although that was not his real name and they had been expected to jump to attention when spoken to.

'I would be delighted,' said Josh. 'I'll fetch a trug and some secateurs.' The trug, when Josh returned, turned out to be a long wooden basket made of willow with a handle. 'Just right for flowers,' explained Josh. 'Shall we start with the long borders—there are quite a selection of flowers there. June is a good month for flowers.'

As they walked along Anna felt very much at home with him. He told her the names of the different species and explained about the lilies, of which her late ladyship had been justly proud.

'Hybrids we call them,' explained Josh. 'We cross fertilize them to get all these exotic colours, but keep the pollen off your hands and clothes. It stains badly.'

As Josh cut some lilies for her he explained how he had worked at The Old Priory with his uncle since leaving agricultural college. 'It's my life, Miss Anna, working here. This is an old garden. The flowers were grown to arrange in the house, and the vegetables were for the family and the staff. No supermarkets in those days. We only grow a few vegetables now and what we don't use here are sold and the money put back in seed.'

By now they had reached the rose garden, a delight to all the senses, and Anna began to pick some of her favourites. 'The old musk roses have the best scent you'll find. Lady Charlesworth used to float the heads in bowls of water. She liked her flowers to look as natural as possible and picked the ones she liked best, rather than make formal arrangements.'

'You seem to have known her well.'

'Oh, yes. She was a really kind person and treated us well. Let me show you the wild garden. This was kept for the butterflies mostly but the goldfinches love the teasels so we never cut them down. You see those holes in the dead elms?' Anna nodded. 'Green woodpeckers still come to fetch the insects from them so we keep them standing, as long as they are safe. Gertrude Jekyll designed the water garden. We unblocked the channels and planted blue and yellow irises in the pools. It all leads to the lake. Have you seen the lake yet?'

Anna had to admit that she had only seen it from the upstairs windows.

'Come on. I'll show you. I think it's the nicest part of the estate. Kingcups grow round the edges in the spring, and wild ducks nest in the reeds. They bring their offspring into the garden when they think it is safe. My aunt calls them and they waddle up to the back door to be fed.'

As he spoke his sunburnt face lit up with enthusiasm for his subject, and his earnest blue eyes smiled down at her. Anna felt at ease with him. He was obviously a genuine person in whom one could have complete trust. His hair had been bleached in the sunshine, like his faded denims and his old shirt, and they suited his open nature. Anna liked him immediately.

'Lady Charlesworth remembered me in her Will, but I heard that there will be no money left when the estate is settled. It was a great surprise to me, I can tell you'

Anna was impressed. Josh must have been highly thought of by his late employer. 'I was brought up here, you see,' explained Josh. 'My adoptive parents lived at The Lodge. My father was head gardener and my mother was the housekeeper. My uncle and aunt took over when my parents emigrated and I stayed on here, with them. I've never lived anywhere else.'

'No wonder you have such a feeling for the garden.'

Josh smiled—a wide, sunny smile which went with his happy nature. 'I played in this garden as a child, sometimes with Lord Harry, when his Lordship was away, but we never really got on.'

'Why was that? I've just met Lord Harry and he was charming.'

'He was the heir apparent and I was a nobody, so I always had to be the loser.'

Anna shrugged. Children were often unkind to one another. Lord Harry was the epitome of good manners and she had been enchanted by him.

'It's my ambition to own my own nursery garden and export my hybrid lilies—but that won't be for a long time yet.'

'Oh, I hope not. Whatever would I do without you?' Josh paused for a moment. Her words had taken him unawares.

'Thank you, Miss Anna. We had wondered how we were to keep things going as you had shown no interest in the garden up to now—if you beg pardon for my mentioning it.'

Anna felt humbled by his remarks. He was quite right. She had shown no interest in the land outside The Old Priory and it was time she put her mind to it. It was time she came down to earth, and faced up to the responsibilities of owning an estate. She couldn't leave it all to the agent, however good he might be.

'Please work as you used to in the past, Josh. I want things to run well. The garden is beautiful, and a credit to you and your uncle. If there is anything you need you only have to ask.'

'Thank you, Miss Anna. We shall enjoy working for you, I feel sure.'

'And no more of the Miss Anna, please. Anna is fine by me.' Josh grinned. His aunt was right about her. She was a lovely person. He watched her walk into the house with her flowers and found it hard to take his eyes off her. She seemed to glide across the grass she was so graceful. He longed to get to know her better, but that might be difficult, although he was determined to try. Winning all that money didn't make an ordinary girl all that different did it? He wished he had met her before that had happened. He might have stood a chance then. So she found that bastard Harry, charming, did she? Josh sighed and went on with his hoeing. She had a lot to learn.

Mrs Hardy showed Anna a small scullery, with a sink and a worktop, which Lady Charlesworth had used to arrange her flowers. In a cupboard there were containers of all shapes and sizes. Anna set to work with secateurs and piles of oasis to see what she could make of the flowers she had picked. She was determined to make a success of it, and hoped Harry would approve of her efforts when he called to take her out as promised. Pleasing Harry was all she could think about right now and her heart sang at the thought of seeing him again.

CHAPTER 5

There were two messages left on the answer phone. One from Harry to say he would be collecting her that morning to take her out to lunch as promised, and one from Amanda to say she would be arriving from Paris for the weekend.

The first put Anna in a flap. She had nothing suitable to wear for a date with Harry. Her clothes were inexpensive of necessity, and she could hardly appear in denims and a top. If only she had a decent outfit. She had never bothered much about fashion because she had never had enough money to spend on herself like her sister. Amanda had an eye for fashion and usually looked smart. Now she was so wealthy there was no excuse to look dowdy and Anna decided to do something about it once Amanda was back home. She would know where to shop, and would give her good advice. But Amanda wasn't here right now and Anna had a frantic search through her wardrobe. She had forgotten to listen to the messages left on the answer phone yesterday so it was her own fault. Harry's invitation had taken her unawares and left her no time to go shopping. A plain blouse and matching skirt was all she could muster, and then she remembered Amanda's black leather jacket which she had always envied. Amanda had left it behind and fortunately it was a good fit, as were her long black leather boots. Anna felt rather strange wearing her sister's clothes but she had no choice, and vowed to go shopping for herself as soon as possible. Meanwhile she washed her hair. It needed cutting and shaping but there was no time for that. She had neglected herself in her excitement at discovering everything about this beautiful place, of which she was now the owner.

Harry looked at her with undisguised disapproval as she came down the stairs to greet him. He had expected her to look stunning like a fashion model, in expensive clothes. A beautiful girl like Anna should have style.

'I didn't realise you were into black leather. Anna,' he remarked, coldly. 'An amazing transformation, I must say.'

'Oh, but I'm not. I had nothing suitable to wear, so I borrowed this jacket and the boots from my sister.'

'Nothing to wear, my dear! With all your money! Why you could buy up a fashion house, if you wanted.'

'I intend to go on a shopping spree, Harry. It's just that I've been so busy here I haven't given it a thought. Sorry.'

'Think nothing of it. I came to see you, but most of the girls I know would have thought of nothing else but buying clothes by now. Come on—your chariot awaits.'

A red sports car was parked in the driveway. On the passenger seat lay a huge bunch of red roses, to match the car.

'Oh, Harry! Are they for me? No one has ever given me red roses before. They're lovely. Thank you.'

'Well, I didn't buy them for Mrs Hardy, fond as I am of her.'

Anna laughed, and kissing him lightly on the cheek she took the roses indoors. He hadn't mentioned the flowers she had so carefully arranged for his benefit and she decided not to say anything after he had given her this wonderful bouquet. 'I love this dear little car,' said Anna, as they drove out of the gate. 'Is it another one of yours? 1 shall have to learn to drive. Then I will buy one just like it.'

'Consider this as yours, my dear. If you like it so much I will leave it here for you.'

Anna was overcome. What a wonderful, generous person he was. She blushed with pleasure and looked up at him, adoringly. 'Josh can drive me back to London and then return it to you. How about that?'

'I'm sure Josh won't mind. Oh, it's a wonderful present, Harry. What have I done to deserve it?'

Harry smiled at her, but his eyes were as cold as steel. She had done nothing as yet. 'You love The Old Priory, don't you Anna? It means so much to me that you love my childhood home and I know you will take good care of it.'

'I'm so glad I bought it. I would never have met you otherwise. Please come Harry, whenever you want. You will always be welcome.'

Harry gave her a grateful look and took her hand in his, as they sped along the country lanes. He doubted that she had ever had a relationship before. Innocence shone out of her trusting blue eyes. He would have to court her gently and not force her, if he was to get what he wanted. Like an untrained filly she would eat out of his hand if treated gently. The car sped past the old mill, where he had intended to stop for lunch, but Harry decided to take her to a pub, some long distance from The Old Priory. She looked so different from his usual glamorous companions that he had no wish to be recognised in her company. A quiet meal in a dark corner would suffice on this occasion. Anna would expect nothing better he felt sure. He was right. She had eyes only for him and the surroundings meant little to her.

'What about your family?' he asked, as they ate their tuna salad.

'My parents have gone on a world cruise, and plan to be back in time for my twenty first birthday, in August. They're having a wonderful time it would seem.'

'What! You'll be twenty-one in August! How marvellous. We must arrange a party for you at The Old Priory—just like the one we had for my sister Fleur's wedding, two years ago. It was a great success. We had two huge marquees on the lawn, one for the disco and the other for the food. There were hundreds of guests enjoying themselves.'

'It sounds lovely Harry, but I hardly know hundreds of guests to invite. I'm sure Amanda could bring people from the fashion world, now she works for a top agency in Paris, but we're not the kind of family to go in for huge parties.'

'Leave it to me. I could bring lots of guests—that is, of course, if I'm invited.' Harry laughed. 'I'm only joking, my sweet. Don't look so downcast. You have just what you want.'

'It's a lovely idea, but I shall have to think about it. It's such a big undertaking, I wouldn't know where to start.'

'Leave it to me, my sweet. Leave it to your Uncle Harry.'

Anna made no reply. It was all going too fast for her. She would ask Amanda when she next saw her and see how the family felt about it, but she didn't like disappointing Harry when he was so keen on the idea. Harry made no mention of the party as he drove her home. No need to hassle her, but it would suit his purposes well. It would give him the opportunity to meet up with many of his wealthy friends who relied on him to provide the drugs they craved. That side of his life was more lucrative than painting portraits of society women. At The Old Priory, Anna threw her arms round him and kissed him warmly. He held her tightly in a brotherly hug, 'You are the nicest person I have ever met, Harry, and the car is the best present I have ever had. I can never thank you enough.'

'Think nothing of it, my sweet. Consider it an early birthday present.' Harry showed nothing of the annoyance he was feeling. It was a nuisance to lose his sports car, but it was all in a good cause, or so he hoped. From now on he would have to rent a car to get about in or use expensive taxies. He climbed into the passenger seat beside Josh who was waiting to drive him back to London. Seeing the happiness on Anna's face as she waved him goodbye made Josh squirm. What was Harry doing back here at The Old Priory, and how well did Anna know him, he wondered. Not well enough for a nice girl like her to get involved with that individual. The Hardy family had been only too glad to see the back of Harry Charlesworth and his wild ways. It had been like a breath of fresh air to have Anna and her family around the place, and now Harry was back, worming his way into Anna's affections. Knowing that he was to drive Harry's sports car back to The Old Priory made him think something was going on between them, and he didn't like it one little bit. The journey to London was made in absolute silence and Josh didn't relax until Harry got out of the car and he was back on the road home.

Amanda arrived home that weekend and was stunned to hear that the expensive car standing in the drive had been a present to her sister from Lord Charlesworth.

'But he's drop dead gorgeous,' exclaimed Amanda, examining his photograph. She found it hard to believe that such a person had found her unfashionable, quiet sister, attractive enough to give her such a wonderful present. 'Is he rich, Anna?' asked the ever practical Amanda.

'I don't really know. All the property had to be sold to meet the death duties on the estate apparently, but he might have money of his own. He is a lord of the realm, after all.'

'That's nothing to go by. Some people who inherit titles work in mundane jobs. They could be road sweepers or office clerks.'

Anna laughed. 'I don't believe you, Amanda. Harry is very clever. He paints portraits of wealthy people so he must earn a lot of money doing that, and anyway why should that bother me—I've more than enough for myself. He's taken me out and will be coming again soon.'

'Ooooh! I say! Mixing with the high and mighty now,' teased Amanda. 'Well, you'll be needing some new clothes and that's a fact, if you're keeping company with his sort.'

'I was going to ask you about that, Amanda. I'd like to come to Paris with you when you go back, and perhaps you could help me to choose a wardrobe.'

'I'd love to. I'll take you round the fashion houses. How about Dior for a start? We'll shop 'til we drop, as the saying goes. What fun! I know my way around now, and I've met a lot of the photographic models. We'll soon have you looking like a lady so your Harry will be proud of you.'

Anna blushed. 'He's not my Harry—just a good friend.'

Amanda gave her sister a searching look. Not just good friends for much longer by the look of it. She felt sure that Anna had fallen deeply in love for the first time in her life.

CHAPTER 6

Amanda's apartment was in the Rue de Sauvigne in an unfashionable quarter of Paris. Anna was surprised after leaving the dingy courtyard at the entrance and following her sister up the narrow staircase to the top floor, to find three comfortable rooms, a bathroom and a tiny kitchen.

'I share with two other models, Louise and Cecily,' she explained. 'Usually the place is in a mess, but as they are both abroad on assignments I have done my best to tidy up a bit in your honour.'

Anna looked around her. 'I think it's all wonderful, the posters and the fans on the wall and the shawls covering the chairs. It's all so—.'

'French?'

The sisters laughed. 'Well, enjoy it Anna, and stay as long as you like. It suits us. It's close to the metro and the market and cheap enough for us to rent as a base.'

Anna unpacked her case and found Amanda making coffee in the kitchen. They sat facing each other at the tiny table, sipping from the large bowls of coffee as Amanda explained her plans for Anna's visit. 'First of all Anna, we're going to visit Dior, to get you fitted out. I've told them you are coming and that you will be good customer. Money opens many doors you will find. They have booked two models to show you a selection of their clothes so you can choose what you like before being fitted.'

'That's not necessary, surely!'

'It saves a lot of time; no off the peg for you anymore. It's haute couture from now on.'

At the showroom Anna sat on an uncomfortable gold chair and watched as clothes for all occasions were brought for her consideration. With Amanda's help she chose a new wardrobe; skirts and trousers in soft suede with pure silk tunics for the country, elegant outfits for the town, coats and dresses for all occasions, including a magnificent dress for evening wear, covered in sparkling rhinestones.

'I shall never wear that,' said Anna, horrified. 'It hardly covers anything. Whatever would Mum say!'

Amanda burst out laughing. 'What does that matter, for goodness sake; it's fashionable to show what you've got these days. You'll look marvellous in it. Just you wait and see.'

'But it costs thousands of pounds, Amanda. I can't imagine spending so much on one dress.'

Amanda sighed. 'You can afford anything you want, you noodle, and not miss it. You know you can.'

Anna had to agree with her, but she wasn't sure she would ever wear such a revealing dress, however grand a party Harry might escort her to. Still, if Amanda was so set on her having it, then she would agree to buy it. After making arrangements to have the clothes delivered, the girls set off to buy a selection of Italian bags and shoes, and to have a make over at a beauty salon. Anna was transformed into a beautiful woman. Her long fair hair had been cut and shaped and highlighted, and the expertly applied make up had brought out her best features.

'I look so different, Amanda. I hardly recognise myself.'

'You look fabulous, Anna, believe me. We'll have a bite to eat at a pavement café and then I'll show you a bit of Paris. Tomorrow I'm taking you to see a fashion show. Dior gave me two tickets for the front row, on the strength of your order. You'll enjoy that. It's fun. I know some of the models and can introduce you to them afterwards.'

'But I've bought enough clothes to last me a life time,' objected Anna. Amanda shook her head. 'You aren't expected to buy these, just to look at the new designs. Fashions change, Anna, but I don't think you ever will.'

'Is that such a bad thing?'

'Depends doesn't it. You'll have to look the part if you're going to be a lady. You can't rely on breeding or a posh education because we didn't have any, so you'll have to make up for it in other ways.' Anna gave this some thought. Her sister was worldly wise and she could see the sense of this. Suddenly, living up to owning a huge fortune was becoming something of a liability unless she became a recluse, and that wasn't her intention. In fact it was quite the opposite. She had the opportunity to live a full and exciting life and she intended to do so. Amanda was making a new life for herself, making new friends and travelling to exotic locations and enjoying every minute of it. She had an outgoing personality, unlike her sister, but Anna was determined to learn from her. This visit to Paris would open her eyes to a different world and already she felt excited by the experience.

The two girls sat on the steps of the Sacre Coeur and looked out over the city. 'The night life is all around here,' explained Amanda. 'There are some splendid places to eat. My favourite is in the Place Pigalle. We'll go there tonight and maybe we will see someone famous. The food is marvellous. I often go there to eat with my friend Pierre'

'Am I going to meet him while I'm here?'

'No; it's not a serious relationship as such.' Anna asked no more questions. Her sister's life was her own business. 'Before we eat I thought you might like to go to a show so I've booked tickets for the Moulin Rouge. Will that suit you?'

'It sounds wonderful.'

'Come on then. It's time we made a move.' Anna loved the fast moving show and the exotic dancers. She had never seen anything like it before except on the television and then it had been edited.

'It's really for tourists to give them a taste of Paris, but it's well produced.'

'I loved it,' said Anna. 'That evening gown I bought this morning will seem over dressed after this.'

Amanda laughed. 'What did I tell you! Well, come on. I booked a table so we'd be sure to get one.' The girls took a taxi to the restaurant where they were given a good table. Amanda was well known there, her friend Pierre being a rich banker.

As they began to eat their hors-d'oeuvres Anna caught sight of Harry sitting in the far corner with a beautiful dark skinned girl. She pointed him out to her sister. 'Harry is sitting in the corner over there,' said Anna excitedly. 'There's someone with him. Do you know who she is?'

Amanda glanced over her shoulder. 'Why, that's Leonie,' she whispered.

'You know her then?'

'Of course, so do most people here. She's the most famous model in Paris. She's known as the black panther for the way she glides across the catwalk. You might see her tomorrow.'

'I'd like to know what Harry's interest is in her. He didn't say anything to me about coming to Paris this weekend.'

'You didn't tell him you were coming either, did you?'

'I didn't know for sure if you would be here until the last moment.'

'Well then. I expect he knows a lot of beautiful women. He's young and good looking and a lord, so he must mix amongst the cream of society.'

'Of course.' Anna looked glum. She must be one of many yet he had made her feel as if she was special to him. Did he usually give his girlfriends an Alfa as a birthday present as if it meant nothing to him? Perhaps she had misunderstood his intentions, if so she had a lot to learn about the aristocracy.

Amanda looked hard at Anna. If Harry's interest was in Leonie, then what was it that had attracted him to her sister. A terrible suspicion was forming in her mind, but for Anna's sake she kept it to herself.

'He's so handsome,' breathed Anna, gazing at Harry from afar as if she was a starstruck teenager. 'And he's been so kind to me.'

'He certainly has,' agreed Amanda, watching the pair at the other table who were completely absorbed in one another. 'I wouldn't interrupt their tete-a-tete if I were you. You are the last person he would expect to see right now. He must have many friends, so just forget about it.'

'I wonder what they're talking about,' pondered Anna, as she toyed with her meal. 'They seem to have a lot to say to one another.'

'Enjoy your food, Anna, and forget he is here. You can surprise him when you next see him and tell him you saw him in the same restaurant that I had taken you to, for a meal. Mind you, he might think you were spying on him. On second thoughts I don't think I would say anything if I was you. I might be able to find out a bit more about his friendship with Leonie from the other models, so don't say anything.'

Anna nodded. She had no wish to upset Harry.

Amanda hurried the meal along before Harry was ready to leave. He was still deep in conversation when they left and Anna would have been very surprised had she know that the subject of the conversation was herself, the new owner of Harry's old home.

After a restless night in a strange bed and disconcerting thoughts about Harry, Anna dressed herself in a smart trouser suit, ready to do some sightseeing. Amanda had promised a visit to the Eiffel Tower where the observation platform at the top would give Anna the best views of Paris. That was to be their first port of call.

Their taxi took them through the Latin Quarter beside the river, sparkling in the morning sunlight. They took the lift up the Tower and wandered across to view the gold dome of Les Invalids.

'You're so lucky to live here Amanda. It's such a wonderful city.'

'If you hadn't won all that money, Anna, you would still be at college and I would be on the reception desk in the hotel, making bookings. It seems like a lifetime away to me.'

'It was fate I suppose. I can't really believe it myself.'

Amanda hailed a taxi and asked for the Rue de Rivoli. They crossed over the Seine and found themselves amongst the great hotels and the fine, expensive shops. 'You can always stay here in a hotel when you feel like a trip to Paris, if I am away. It's very central and the hotels are luxurious. There's so much to see and do, you could spend weeks visiting everything. I love living here.' The girls found a pavement café for coffee and canapés until it was time to watch the fashion show. Anna would have much rather continued to watch the world go by from her seat but Amanda was adamant. It was an honour to be given two front seats by Dior and they must take up the offer. The more Amanda was seen the better, as far as her career was concerned. Anna sighed. She was always the one to give in to her more dominant sister, and they set off to find the venue for the show. Despite herself Anna was fascinated. The enthusiasm shown by the audience and the cries of approval when the models appeared wearing more and more fantastic designs, surprised her. Her sister was in her element. This was her world and where she felt most at ease. Anna thought some of the models looked bored and sulky.

'They look so unhappy, poor things,' she remarked. 'I'm sure they don't enjoy wearing all that weird makeup and those peculiar hairstyles.'

'They work hard. It's no joke being hauled out of one garment and into another. They party a lot and only get a few hours sleep when they are working. The world of modelling is a dark area these days. It's difficult to avoid the drugs scene, and the drink. It's champagne, champagne all the way, especially during a show. Sounds OK but it takes its toll and some of them get hooked and need treatment. The designers need thin models to show off their clothes so the models get younger and younger. They are just kids when they start and are vulnerable.'

'You don't use drugs do you Amanda?'

'Nothing for you to worry about, honestly—I've had the odd puff just to be sociable but nothing else. I shall never become addicted like some of the models.' A dark and sinuous model appeared who seemed to glide along the catwalk, wearing a fake leopard skin creation. 'Leonie,' breathed Anna. A huge burst of applause greeted her arrival and some of the audience stood up to applaud. It was then that Anna thought she saw Harry, framed in a doorway. She stared in his direction but he only had eyes for the model on the catwalk. 'Isn't she beautiful!' whispered Amanda. Anna turned towards her sister for a split second and when she turned back Harry had disappeared.

'I'll take you behind the scenes afterwards, and maybe you can meet Leonie.'

'No thanks. I'd rather not. I don't want to meet her, and if Harry's there I don't want to see him either.'

'Why should he be?'

'Because I saw him a moment ago. I'd rather go, Amanda, if it's all right by you.' As they left by the exit a Rolls Royce drew up by the kerb with a chauffeur behind the wheel. In the back seat sat Harry. Leonie ran across the pavement from a side exit and was ushered into the car. 'He didn't recognise me,' said Anna, miserably.

'You look like a million dollars, that's why,' said Amanda. 'No wonder he didn't recognise you.'

By the end of the week Anna was glad to board the 'plane home. Amanda had walked her off her feet thinking it would take her mind off Harry. They had visited the great palaces of Versailles and Fontainebleau and trudged round the formal gardens, but Anna's heart wasn't in it. There were so many unanswered questions in her mind she found it difficult to take an interest in anything however hard she tried.

'Forget him, Anna,' were her sister's last words, as she saw her off. 'He's just not worth it.'

Anna considered her sister's advice on the flight back, and once she arrived at Stanstead Airport and saw Josh waiting at the barrier to meet her and drive her back to The Old Priory she was so pleased to see his welcoming smile that her heart lightened considerably.

'I didn't bring the Alfa as I hadn't got your permission to use it so I hope you won't mind coming back in my old shooting brake.'

'To tell you the truth, Josh, I would prefer it. I can't imagine learning to drive a fast sports car; later on perhaps, when I'm competent, but not to start with.'

'Then perhaps I'd better begin teaching you on my old banger.'

'Would you really? I'd love that.'

‘Then we’ll begin to-morrow, if that will suit you.’ Anna could think of nothing she would like better, and it was arranged there and then. They chatted together amicably, and once the gates of The Old Priory came into view and she was home again, she had ceased to worry about Lord Harry and his friendship with the beautiful Leonie.

CHAPTER 7

Anna and Josh sat inside the George Hotel, facing each other across the ring marked table in the bar. There was no one else inside; the other customers were outside enjoying a drink in the attractive gardens which overlooked the estuary. It was a very hot day and Josh had suggested that it might be cooler to sit indoors, although, if he had been truthful, he really wanted to have her company to himself. Before they returned to The Old Priory after Anna's driving lessons it had been customary for them to stop and have a drink together. Anna paid Josh what she owed him for the driving lesson and Josh returned the compliment by buying the drinks; a glass of wine for Anna and a pint of bitter for himself. Today was the first time Anna had attempted to drive the Alfa. The L plates had been removed from the old shooting brake and attached to the Alfa after two weeks of lessons, and Anna was feeling proud of herself.

'We should celebrate,' she said, lifting up her glass. 'I never thought I would feel this competent. You've taught me well, Josh. My father would never have been so patient. I'll surprise him when he gets home.'

'When will that be?'

'They'll be back in three weeks. Josie can't wait to show them how well she rides now. Her whole world revolves around that horse. It helps to take her mind off school. She really hates it there.'

'Poor Josie; I know how she feels. I couldn't wait to get to Agricultural College. As long as I'm outside working I'm happy. Growing things is what I'm best at.'

'I didn't like school either. I was so shy—just the opposite to Amanda. I was never any good with boyfriends although plenty flocked round. They used to call me the ice maiden, but I'm not really like that at all. I became a nanny after a nursery course and left when one of the children's fathers made advances when his wife was away. I've just finished a computer course and hoped to work as a secretary once I'd finished the secretarial course. It seems funny now but maybe the course will help me to understand the running of the estate.'

Josh was surprised at her honesty with him, but that was one of the things he liked about Anna. It showed in her open, sweet face and her trusting blue eyes.

Today she was wearing her old jeans and a blue check shirt and looked so young and unassuming that he longed to take her in his arms and kiss her. That feeling had almost become too much for him in the close confines of the car, and at times it was a struggle to remember his position as her employee. Anna had shown none of her feelings towards him, even if she had any, and if he stepped out of line he might lose his job and that would be a disaster. On all these jaunts he changed into a clean shirt and trousers so as not to offend her, which amused his aunt as Josh was not one to care overmuch about his appearance.

'Why do you live with the Hardys, Josh? Have you no family locally?'

'My parents are in New Zealand. 1 had just been accepted for a place at the college when they emigrated, so I decided to stay. My uncle had worked for Lord Charlesworth for years and when he mentioned that I would be looking for a job eventually I was offered the position as under gardener, and I've been at The Old Priory ever since.'

'Have you enjoyed it?'

'Most of the time. Lady Charlesworth was very easy to get on with but her husband had a short temper. He had been an Army officer and he was a tartar for discipline. We had to be on our toes when he came to inspect our work. My uncle used to say that even the leeks stood to attention when he passed by.'

Anna laughed. 'And what about you?'

Josh smiled. 'Oh, we did too. I was really scared of him at first, but I got used to it. He would shout at his wife in front of us which annoyed me, but she seemed able to cope with it. She was happy in a world of her own, amongst the flowers.'

'And what about their children?'

'They weren't here much. The family had a home in France and there was a shooting lodge in Scotland. Fleur was like her mother; a gentle, kind girl; very horsey, like Josie. Time to go I think, Miss Anna.'

Anna got up and they walked back towards the car. It was obvious that Josh did not intend to talk about Harry. As they drove through the gates of The Old Priory Anna could see a dark green car parked in the driveway.

'Looks as if I've got company,' she said. Josh got out of the Alfa and walked back to The Lodge to change into his work clothes, and Anna opened the front door. There was nobody in the entrance hall and nobody in the long lounge, where visitors were usually entertained. She went into the kitchen to find Mrs Hardy, but the kitchen was empty. A slight sound made her look round the door to the study and there was Harry, opening the desk drawers. He appeared to be unaware of her presence and Anna watched him with growing annoyance. As he closed the last drawer he turned to the door and saw her standing watching him.

'Oh, there you are, my sweet—I'm not being nosey—just looking for something I thought I'd left here. The drawers are empty anyway.'

'Harry!! You have no right to look through the drawers. What were you hoping to find?'

'Nothing in particular, my dear – just a little packet I thought I'd left here, but apparently it's been removed. I expect Mrs Hardy threw it out when you took over. She must have known it didn't belong to you.'

'A packet—a packet of what? Cigarettes?' Anna laughed scornfully. ' But surely you can afford to buy another packet?'

'These were rather special, my dear. More than I can afford at the moment. But if no one has seen them then there is no more to be said. I was hoping to ask Mrs Hardy but she isn't anywhere around. She let me in, told me to make myself comfortable until you arrived and then went out. You were so long that I thought I would look for myself. Please forgive me. I was only interested in my own property.'

Harry looked contrite, like a naughty boy, thought Anna. 'I see. Well I won't fall out with you over a packet of cigarettes.'

Harry breathed a sigh of relief. He must go carefully in future. 'Thank you, Anna. I'm so grateful. I've missed you during the last few weeks and I'm sorry I haven't been in touch. I had things to attend to.'

'I see.'

'So perhaps we can take up where we left off.'

'Where did we leave off, Harry?'

'Oh, come on, Anna. You know what I mean. I had begun to fall in love with you and I thought you cared for me a little.'

Anna said nothing. If this conversation had taken place before she had gone to Paris she would have been in her seventh heaven. Now she wanted some answers. 'Tell me where you have been, Harry. I heard nothing from you for weeks.'

'Finishing a painting—I have to work for rny living, you know.'

'May I see it? I really would like to.'

'No, I'm afraid not. The woman I painted has bought it.'

'A woman! Was she beautiful, Harry? Was she dark skinned?'

Harry stared at her. 'How did you know that?'

'I saw you with her, in Paris.'

'Well, well, you are a dark horse, Anna. I had no idea you had been to Paris recently. Why didn't you tell me you were going? I would have loved to have taken you there. Paris is for lovers.'

'A bit difficult for you, Harry; with Leonie around.'

Harry was stunned. 'I don't know how you know all this, but I can assure you it was simply business. The business is over now so please let's forget it. I came back to see you. You were always in my thoughts while I was away and I longed to see you again.'

He sounded so genuine that Anna relented a little. Perhaps she was wrong and had read more into his association with Leonie than she should have done.

'Come with me now and I'll drive you to Burnham-on-Crouch and show you the marina. I had a sea going motor boat there but I had to sell it when I was short of funds. I'd like to consider buying another one eventually, when I can afford it. A friend of mine has one for sale and I thought I would look it over. No harm in just looking. Would you like to come with me?'

'We mustn't quarrel, Harry. I'm sorry if I was a bit put out just now. Of course I'd love to come. I won't keep you a moment.' Anna ran upstairs and put on one of her more casual Dior outfits, and was soon back by his side.

Harry looked at her in amazement. 'I can see you've been shopping, my sweet. It's a transformation. You look stunning.' He bent down to place a kiss on her hair and immediately everything was forgotten. Anna clung to him with a passion she didn't know she possessed and Harry took full advantage of the situation, responding with an ardour he never expected to feel for her. For a few terrible moments he had thought his plans to acquire her fortune would come to nothing, but now he felt sure of success. As they set off in the Alfa, with Harry at the wheel, Josh looked up from the stable yard. The screech of the wheels as the car left the drive and the roar of the engine as the car gathered speed made him wonder who was driving. Surely it wasn't Anna. He looked round the corner to see the Alfa tearing down the road with Harry at the wheel and Anna sitting beside him. His heart sank as he returned to mucking out the stable. There was no hope for him now in her affections. He wished he could leave and find a job elsewhere but knowing Harry Charlesworth as he did, he felt he should stay and protect Anna should she need him, and he feared it might come to that.

CHAPTER 8

Anna looked at the Sea Princess with interest. This slim, streamlined cruiser had just about everything according to Harry.

'It's fully equipped, down to the last teaspoon,' enthused Harry; 'duvets in three luxury cabins, two showers, a modern galley and an elegant saloon. What more could one want, apart from the money to buy it.' Harry laughed bitterly. 'We had a boat similar to this one when my father was alive, but it had to be sold, like pretty well everything else.' Anna sympathised with him. 'One of my friends is down on his luck right now and has to sell his pride and joy. I only wish I could afford it myself. I promised him I'd come and see how the sale was going. The agent should be here any time now. I rang him before we left.'

'Why can't your friend come himself?'

'He's overseas at the moment and needs the ready—ah, here comes the agent. Wander along the decking, my pet. I'll join you in a moment.' Anna climbed aboard and up the steep steps to the fly bridge where she sat, overlooking the water. 'It must be a bit like driving a car,' she thought, as she looked at the wheel and the controls. 'The same feeling of power as you cut through the waves at speed. I think I would like that.'

It was a beautiful afternoon and the gulls swooped and dived across the river. A feeling of well being overtook her as she listened to the lapping of the water and the chink of the masts on the moored sailing yachts. The muted voices of the yacht's owners as they prepared to set sail floated across to her in the breeze. 'I could stay here for ever,' she thought, 'as long as Harry was with me.' She could imagine Harry taking the wheel as she sat beside him, and dashing through the waves to distant, romantic places.

'Hi, there,' shouted Harry. 'I've got the keys so I can take you all over her, and then I'll take her out for a bit, if you would like that.'

'I'd love that, Harry. Let's go now.' Harry smiled at her excitement. It was a perfect day for a trip up the Crouch and he had brought a hamper of food and a bottle of champagne. He stowed these in the galley and joined her on the bridge.

'I'll just untie her from the moorings. I won't be a minute.' As soon as he was back and the twin engines switched on, the cruiser moved gently away and up river. Anna felt the sea spray on her face as the boat gathered speed and she threw back her head to enjoy the experience. She felt exhilarated. Harry, who was enjoying every moment of their trip decided that this was the right moment to approach the subject of their future together. He had never seen her so happy and carefree. 'This is just a taster, my sweet. I shall soon have to turn her round and head back to the marina. The boat doesn't belong to me—I only wish it did—but I can't let the agent think I've stolen it. I tell you what, there's an inlet here where we can moor for a while and I'll show you the rest of the boat.'

'I wish it did belong to you Harry, then we could enjoy it together.' Anna closed her eyes and sighed with pleasure. She could have gone on forever. Harry looked straight ahead. His face showed no emotion whatsoever as he held his breath, waiting for her next remark. He did not have long to wait. 'How expensive is it, Harry? Very expensive?'

'I'm afraid so, my love. Four hundred thousand pounds, or near enough. It's almost new, you see, and has only been taken out twice before.'

'Let me buy it for you, Harry.'

Harry said nothing; his heart was thumping with anticipation. 'Please, Harry. I mean it. You gave me your Alfa sports car which you loved. I want to do something for you. Please let me.'

'Are you sure, Anna?'

'Of course I'm sure. It's because—' She was about to say it was because she loved him, but finished the sentence with—'I want to, with all my heart.'

'Then I accept, my sweet. You are the most wonderful girl in the world, and the most generous.'

'We'll go out in it often, won't we Harry?'

'As often as you like. Just say the word.' Harry placed his arm around her and took her down into the boat. With countless kisses and caresses he showed her the little galley, the saloon and the three cabins. In the most luxurious one he took her in his arms and began to undress her. Anna felt too weak with emotion to object as he fondled and kissed her. She lay back on the bed and gave in to his lovemaking. As he had thought, she was a virgin and untried in the game of love. It had been so easy to seduce her and he treated her gently as he made love to her. Anna clung to him afterwards as he lay beside her. 'You're shaking, my darling. The next time it will be easier, I promise you. Take a shower. It will relax you.'

Anna found herself still shaking as she dressed. It had all happened so quickly and unexpectedly. She loved Harry, there was no doubt about that, but he had never mentioned love to her. This could have meant nothing to him and that worried her. She was after all a willing, if inexperienced partner in the act, just carried away by her feelings for him. As she emerged from the shower she saw that Harry had unpacked the hamper and poured out two glasses of champagne.

'This is a celebration, my darling—to us, my sweet.' Anna clinked her glass against his. 'To us,' she whispered.

'I have something to ask you, my sweet; something very special. Can you imagine what it is?'

Anna looked at him solemnly over her glass and made no reply. There had been no mention of him loving her so she was unsure of his thoughts.

'1 want you to be my wife, Anna. Will you marry me?'

Anna shivered slightly. Perhaps it was the champagne. 'I love you too Harry, but we don't know each other very well as yet. It's so soon—too soon for me. I think I fell in love with you when I came across your photograph. It was love at first sight.'

'So what's the problem? Say you will marry me, Anna. Without you my life will have no meaning.'

'Yes. Harry. I will—but not just yet. Wait a little while for me, please. I want to get used to you and the idea first—becoming Lady Charlesworth and meeting all your grand friends will be a big step for me.'

'Just as you say, my darling, but don't leave it too long. I couldn't bear to lose you.'

'You'll never lose me, Harry— never. I love you too much.'

Harry took her in his arms and kissed her passionately. 'I love you too, my pet— you can be sure of that.' His words melted away the last of her worries. He really did love her after all.

She smiled up at him, safe in his arms. 'I can't wait to tell my family. My parents will be home in two weeks time. Not long to wait now.'

'Not long for sure,' thought Harry. He must get settled in The Old Priory before they arrived so there would be no difficulties with him marrying their daughter. 'Of course, they will want to be home in good time for your twenty-first birthday. A good time to announce our engagement, don't you think?'

Anna smiled. 'Why not—anything you say, Harry.'

'Time to get back, I think. Just look at that sky. It looks like a storm brewing up over there.'

The cruiser sped back to the marina. The water was whipped up by the wind and became choppy and Anna was thankful to return to dry land. 'Now be a poppet and put the hamper back in the car while I fix things with the harbour master and telephone the agent about the sale.' Harry handed her the car keys and the hamper. 'I'll be back as soon as I can.'

As Anna hurried towards the car park, Harry returned to the Sea Princess. There was something he needed to check. Once inside the boat he headed for the galley and removed the inside panel of one of the cupboards, and then took out yet another panel behind that. He felt inside and brought out a small white packet which he placed in his pocket before replacing the panels. So that was one the police hadn't discovered when they searched the boat. He could sell the contents to a dealer he knew and have enough to buy Anna a magnificent engagement ring as well as some marijuana for his own use. He had made one run in the boat with his friend Simon, to whom the boat belonged, but on the second occasion he had been unable to crew for him as he was in a drug treatment clinic at the insistence of his father. Simon had been caught shipping drugs and was now in prison serving a life sentence for smuggling. Harry had been shocked at the length of the sentence and had decided not to pursue this means of making money for the time being. The Sea Princess might come in useful at a later date once it was registered in his name, but the risk was no longer necessary now he had Anna as his future wife.

His father's Will disinheriting him had put him on the spot, until he had chanced upon Anna's huge lottery win from a newspaper report, and could see a way of making a fortune by other means. Fortunately, she had turned out to be an unworldly girl, and easy prey to his undoubted charms. Once she had bothered about her appearance she had a delicate beauty and also, as he had discovered, a perfect body. She had been nervous at first but she would soon learn how to excite him sexually. It was a refreshing change from Leonie and her animal sexuality. Leonie would never know how the dull little thing he had described to her in Paris had changed into this beautiful woman, whose charms he intended to enjoy until he was tired of her and had thought up a plan to inherit all those millions. Leonie would have to wait a while for him until he was free. Then he would buy her the Oriental palace he had promised her.

After organising the sale with the agent Harry walked back to the car where Anna was waiting.

'Forgive me, Anna, but I shall have to rush away. I have urgent business to attend to. The lease on my flat has run out and I have to move and find somewhere else to live. From next week I shall be homeless.'

'Oh, Harry. That's terrible! There's no need for that, surely. We shall be married before long and you will be living at The Old Priory then, so bring everything there now. You can paint in your old studio and have the room next to mine. It has a connecting door and I only use it as a dressing room. I have no need of it. My bedroom is enormous.'

'Big enough for two?' teased Harry.

'Plenty big enough,' laughed Anna, 'but it might not go down too well when my parents arrive home if they find you sharing my bed, although what we do when the door is shut is our own business. I don't want to upset them before we are married. They don't even know you exist, let alone know that I am engaged to you.'

'Do you think they will approve of me, Anna?'

'I'm sure my mother will. She won't believe it; such a handsome man and a lord at that, to be marrying her quiet daughter. But Dad will take time to come round to the idea. He will feel out of place with you at first. When my sister moved out to live with her boyfriend he was furious. He expected her to stay at home until she was married. He looked forward to giving her away at a huge wedding but it didn't come to that so she came back to live with us at The Old Priory until her job took her to Paris. Now she travels all over the world and we don't see her often. Josie goes to a private day school which she hates. Mrs Hardy gets her meals and Josh takes her to school and brings her back in the car. I'm always at home with her in the evenings until my mother can take over.'

'Best if she went to a boarding school I would imagine,' said Harry, who did not want all of Anna's family under his feet.

'She would miss her horse,' said Anna, 'so a boarding school wouldn't do for Josie.'

Harry could see problems looming once he took occupancy of The Old Priory, but he would have to put up with the situation to begin with. When they were married he would make it obvious to Anna that her family were no longer welcome. Once their long journey back to The Old Priory was over Harry dropped Anna at her door and transferred to the green Saab. Soon there would be no need to hire cars. If the price of heroin was high enough he might be able to buy a Ferrari as well as buy Anna a ring from Aspreys. He was so busy with his thoughts that he turned the car quickly in the drive and swept through the gates without even a wave to Anna, who stood for some time wondering what had come over him. He seemed to have completely forgotten she was there. It was strange behaviour from a man who had just proposed marriage to her and whom she had accepted so readily.

CHAPTER 9

'You would never believe what I've been asked to do.' Mrs Hardy was indignant. She was serving lunch to her husband and Josh in The Old Priory kitchen. Her husband looked up from his plate. It was rare to hear his wife sound off about anything. Normally, she was the most placid of women and took most things in her stride. This was a surprising outburst, especially as Anna had been such a considerate employer and was well liked by them all. 'I've been asked to make up the bed in the master's old dressing room and to clean it out.'

'Is that so surprising, my dear? Anna's parents will be here shortly and maybe they are bringing back some friends with them.'

'Oh, yes! There will be an extra visitor, and who do you think that will be? No-one her parents know, but someone we know very well.' She stood with her arms akimbo as a red flush spread over her face. She was seething with anger.

Josh put down his knife and fork and looked at his aunt with amazement. In all his life he had never seen her like this before. 'His young lordship; Harry is corning back home, would you believe. No doubt by Miss Anna's invitation.'

Josh grew red in the face. He pushed his chair back and stood up, angrily. 'She doesn't know anything about him,' he shouted. 'She's lost her reason asking him to come here.' He strode to the door, leaving his meal behind and slammed the door behind him.

'He's in love with her,' muttered Mr Hardy, 'Poor chap; no wonder he's so upset.'

'Surely not; you're wrong about that, Joe. He hardly knows her.'

'Don't you believe it, my dear. He gave her all those driving lessons, didn't he? A strong silent sort is our Josh. His type takes it hard. Things go deep with him.'

His wife became thoughtful. 'Now you mention it, Joe, I used to laugh at the fuss he made about his clothes before he took her out for a driving lesson.'

'Well then.'

'But he couldn't have expected her to fall for him, surely. She's a grand lady now; a millionairess.'

'That means nothing. She's the same as us. Money doesn't make you into a lady overnight. Josh likes her for herself. She's a lovely girl, beautiful, kind and considerate. That's why he's fallen in love with her.'

'And what about, Harry? Where does he fit into this?'

'He's been hanging about here lately… turns up in one of his grand cars to take her out. Gave her his Alfa, didn't he? And now he's moving in, you say. Fishy if you ask me, but there's nothing we can do about it. I wouldn't have thought he was her type.'

'It's a good thing her parents will be back soon. I can't see them putting up with the wild parties there used to be here before the old master put a stop to them. The clearing up afterwards was dreadful. Getting the carpets and the bed covers cleaned and finding syringes and needles in the bathrooms. I'm not going through all that again for anybody.'

'Maybe he's cured since he had that spell in a drug clinic. Mad as a hatter he used to be when he was on the hard stuff.'

'I found some of those weird things he used to roll and smoke in a drawer in the study when I was checking that all the private papers had been removed before The Old Priory was sold.'

'What did you do with them?'

Mrs Hardy sniffed. 'I burnt them of course, in the incinerator. Smelt dreadful they did.'

'It's no good worrying, my dear. Perhaps he's a reformed character since he's met Miss Anna. We can only hope so.'

Mrs Hardy, sighed deeply. 'I doubt it. I hope she'll see through him before its too late, poor girl.' From where she was standing she could see Anna making her way across the lawn to where Josh was using an axe on a tree stump. His muscles rippled with the effort and the sweat poured off him. He stopped for a moment and tore off his shirt, throwing it onto the ground. It was then that he saw Anna standing there, holding an envelope in her hand and turned to face her. She was taken aback by the anguish and pain in his eyes as he looked at her and the smile disappeared from her lips. This was not the time to give him good news.

'Josh!—I'm so sorry. Has something happened?'

'You could say that.' He turned his back on her and continued to split up the wood. Anna stood and watched him in silence. There was such fury in his actions she wished she could understand just what had caused him to be so upset. When he had finished he began to collect up the pieces, still with his back to her. As she hadn't moved he straightened up and faced her. 'Was there anything you wanted?' he asked, grimly.

'I can see this is a bad time for you, but I need another driving lesson before my test. I've just had notification about it. I take it next week.'

'Sorry,' muttered Josh. 'There is a lot of dead wood to be cut out of the spinney. I shall be too busy.'

'Oh, Josh. Can't you leave that for a few hours?' Her disappointment was obvious. 'I was so looking forward to you taking me. It wouldn't be the same with anyone else.'

Josh looked hard at her. 'Perhaps Lord Harry will take you, or you can find a driving school in town.'

Anna blushed deeply. It was obvious their friendship was over. 'If that's how it's to be, then. I thought you enjoyed our trips out as much as I did. I'm sorry you feel like this.' She turned on her heel and made her way back to the house. She liked Josh and thought of him as her friend and couldn't imagine what she had done to upset him so much. The hurt of losing that friendship went much deeper than she had expected. Because he was the strong, silent type she might have misread his feelings towards her. He had always been so kind and considerate she would never have hurt him deliberately. She longed to make things better between them and hoped that in time the problem would be resolved. As she went back into the house she felt lonely and rejected as if the joy of living in these beautiful surroundings had suddenly disappeared. Harry had been gone for over a week and there had been no word from him—no letter and no messages left on the answer phone. It was as if the past events had never happened. Even Mrs Hardy's happy chatter had ceased since she had told her that Harry would be returning to live in his old home. It was as if The Old Priory and its occupants were living under a permanent black cloud.

To pass the time she found a driving school in Chelmsford and took her last few lessons with an efficient instructor and passed her test without any problems. Afterwards, as she drove the Alfa home on her own, her thoughts were all of Josh. If things hadn't gone wrong between them she would be celebrating her success with him, but Josh was nowhere to be seen of late. He was keeping out of her way and that was beginning to trouble her. There was a sparkling new red Ferrari parked at the door when she arrived home. Harry had turned up out of the blue. Her spirits rose immediately at the thought of seeing him again. She would celebrate her success with him instead. She ran indoors and found him, surrounded by his luggage, talking to Mrs Hardy, who left discreetly as soon as Anna appeared. Anna clung to him with a cry of relief. 'Harry, my darling—where have you been? I missed you so much. Why didn't you call me? I've been so worried.'

Harry disentangled himself from her arms and gave her a chaste kiss. 'Stop fussing, Anna. It takes time to sort things out; packing up the flat, settling my business affairs and everything else. Let me get my belongings upstairs and then we can talk for as long as you like—how about some coffee, my sweet, while I settle in.'

Anna was taken aback by his apparent indifference to seeing her again, and the fact that he made no apology for not contacting her. She stood at the bottom of the stairs until he entered his room and closed the door, and then went into the kitchen to prepare coffee for them both. 'We shall be eating out to-night, Mrs Hardy, so there will be nothing more for you to do today.'

'Thank you Miss Anna—I'll be off then.'

'See you tomorrow.' Anna smiled politely. Mrs Hardy nodded her head in reply but did not speak. When she had gone, Anna took the coffee into the long sitting room and called Harry who came running down the stairs.

'I can't tell you how good it is to be back here, my love—home at last and you to wait on me.'

'I'm not here just to wait on you, Harry, so you can put that idea right out of your head.'

'I'm just teasing, my sweet. Come and sit here beside me. I have something for you.'

Harry put his hand in his pocket and took out a small box. 'Give me your left hand—there! What do you think?' He placed a large diamond ring on her wedding finger. The size of the diamond amongst a cluster of smaller diamonds took Anna's breath away. The light flashed a myriad of colours as it caught the largest diamond, and she moved her finger this way and that to admire the reflections.

'Oh, Harry. I've never seen anything so wonderful. I love it. Thank you—oh, thank you.' She flung herself across him with her arms around his neck and kissed him passionately. Harry was surprised at the depth of her feeling for him and found himself kissing her just as passionately. He would enjoy their relationship for as long as it lasted, which was something he had not expected when he had set out to court her. It was a bonus as far as he was concerned.

'So you see, my sweet, I didn't forget you. I had you in mind all the time I was away; and now, how about a proper thank-you.' He had felt the stirring of his sexual needs after their embrace, and lifted her to her feet. 'How about trying out that big bed of yours, my love'

Anna was only too willing. He really did love her, the way she loved him. He must have been too busy to remember to telephone her—that was all. How could she have ever doubted him. Harry carried her upstairs and undressed her without ceremony, pulling off his own clothes in his need to possess her. Anna was frightened by the ferocity of his passion. He had been so gentle the first time he had made love to her so as not to hurt her, but this was different. As he thrust himself into her, over and over again before his climax she had tried to push him away, but he was too strong for her, and his need was too great. Afterwards she was crying. She felt bruised all over.

Harry began to get dressed. 'You'll learn to like it in time, my sweet, but you can't expect an engagement ring that cost thousands and be the wife of Lord Charlesworth without giving a bit in return.'

'I'm sorry, Harry. I really will try to please you, but give me a little time to recover. Last time you were kind but this time you hurt me. Please never treat me like that again.' Her face was streaked with tears as she turned to him.

Harry went across to the bed and took her in his arms. 'I'm sorry, my love—truly sorry. I got carried away. I promise to be more gentle next time.' He took a handkerchief from his pocket and dried her eyes. 'Get dressed now, my sweet, and come downstairs. I want to show you my new car. It's a real beauty, just like you. We'll go for a spin and I'll show off my new fiancée to the world.' He smiled down at her, but there was no warmth in his smile for Anna. It was a smile of self-gratification for he cared little about her feelings.

Harry went downstairs while she bathed her bruises and dressed herself. She felt shocked by his insensitive behaviour and wondered if all strong, virile men made love in that way. Somehow she couldn't believe that her father treated her mother like that, although they were of a different generation. Her sister, Amanda, called them old fashioned when she went to live with her boyfriend. Amanda was worldly wise and had experience in such matters. She wished she could talk it over with her and get her advice. Did all men act like Harry when aroused? Where was the pleasure for a woman if they did? Her instincts told her that it could not be so.

Harry lounged in a languid fashion in one of the large comfortable chairs in the long sitting room. He rolled a joint and smoked it as he waited for her to come downstairs. The sex and the marijuana had given him a buzz. He felt in a good mood. He had been rough with her, he realised that, but it had only been a short time since he had left Leonie, and she liked it rough, and gave as good as she got. He must tone down his treatment of Anna and act the part of a loving suitor or she might change her mind about marrying him. He would have a stunningly beautiful wife for a short time, who would provide him with a mildly satisfying love life until such time as he could part her from her money. He could always slip across the Channel for a few days on some excuse, where Leonie and the heroin were waiting for him in Paris. That is where he had been the previous week. Living with Anna would have to be endured for a time, if he was to inherit her millions. Anna came downstairs, slowly. She intended to keep him to his promise to treat her with respect, or else she would return his ring.

Harry turned towards her as she entered the room. 'Ready?' he asked, cheerfully.

Anna nodded. He put his arm around her as they walked to the door. She dutifully admired the car and they set off in the direction of Cambridge. 'I passed my driving test today,' she said, quietly.

'Well done!' enthused, Harry. 'We'll celebrate that when we get to the River Restaurant.' He put his foot down hard on the accelerator and the car roared into life. 'Get there in no time,' he said. 'This is a marvellous car!' Anna knew he was driving too fast, but she felt too numb to care and did not reply. If she was to marry Harry he would have to prove to her that making love to her meant considering her feeling too, so the experience was one of mutual pleasure.

Harry slowed down and took her hand in his. 'Sorry, sweetheart,' he said, humbly. 'I'd missed you, that was all. Seeing you naked again was just too much and I lost control. It won't happen again, I promise you. Please forgive me.'

Anna gave him a wan smile. Despite what had just happened she couldn't help loving him. He was like a little boy who had misbehaved and was asking for her forgiveness. She raised his fingers to her lips and kissed them. Harry breathed a sigh of relief, and for once in his life he felt a pang of remorse at what the future held for her. If he had disliked her or she had been as ugly as hell it would have been so much easier for him to dispose of her once they were married. He hardened his heart and withdrew his hand from her soft fingers and replaced it onto the steering wheel, changed into a higher gear and sped towards Cambridge.

CHAPTER 10

Harry had made himself well and truly at home by the time Anna's parents arrived. His painting paraphernalia had been delivered by a removals firm, plus the pieces of furniture which had originally come from The Old Priory. These he intended to place in an auction for his own benefit. The money he would find useful as he had almost spent the amount he had gained from the unexpected drug haul from the boat. To wine and dine Anna in style cost money, and he needed to keep her happy until he married her. On no account was she to discover his pecuniary position or she might realise the reason behind his interest in her and call off the wedding.

Reg and Mollie found him a strange choice for their daughter. His aristocratic connections filled them with awe and a certain foreboding. They had nothing in common with him and preferred to keep to their own rooms in The Old Priory. The atmosphere had deteriorated into a frosty politeness between all parties when they met, and conversations became brief and of no consequence. The Old Priory, which they had loved when they had moved there seemed now to belong to someone else. Anna had changed beyond recognition. She dressed to please Harry, with style and panache. Her face was expertly made up and her hands manicured. She looked every inch a lady, which she soon would be, once she was married to Lord Charlesworth. Such a lot had happened since they had left on their world cruise, and it saddened them. Anna was still their loving daughter, but now she lived with Lord Harry he appeared to control her, as well as the life at The Old Priory.

'We're not wanted here any more, Reg. I don't feel as if this is home. We've always been a close family—couldn't be anything else, living on top of each other in the Rows—but I was happier there.' Mollie sighed.

Reg nodded in agreement. It had been Anna's wish that they had continued to live as a family, but things had moved on since they had returned from the cruise. 'He doesn't want us here. You can feel that every time we see him.' They had been amazed on their return to discover their daughter had become engaged to the previous owners' son. It had been difficult to take in knowing Anna. If it had been Amanda, then it would have been easier to believe. Anna had always been so shy and retiring and had never shown any interest in a serious relationship. Reg had taken an instant dislike to Harry on meeting him for the first time. He had been polite and formal but there had been no warmth in his greeting. In his beautifully cut trousers and expensive silk shirt Harry looked the perfect gentleman. When their daughter introduced him as Lord Harry Charlesworth, her fiancé, they had been flabbergasted. He was a very handsome man with an aristocratic bearing and fine artistic hands. His limp handshake did nothing for Reg who had a strong grip himself. Mollie had been enchanted at first to think of her daughter marrying a lord. This feeling of euphoria gradually wore off as she realised that there would be no place for her and Reg once Anna was married. She had always expected that Anna would have remained close to the family if she married. She had never shown any signs of independence like her sister, Amanda. This engagement had come like a bolt out of the blue and had disturbed them both.

'Let's find our own place, Reg. We can afford it. Anna was good to us when she won all that money so we have no more worries. Josie hates that school we found for her and wants to go back to the comprehensive. The Hardys have been wonderful to her since we went away, and Anna has taken care of her, but it's not like living in a real family. I miss my old friends at the Rows and I want to go back.' They were sitting watching the moorhens swimming in and out of the reeds. The lake was their favourite place on the estate, for here they could speak their innermost thoughts without being overheard. Reg had been feeling the same as his wife. They had frequently grumbled about the inconvenience of living at the Rows when they had lived there, but now they could only remember the good times; the neighbours who had popped in and out, the pub where Reg had enjoyed a pint with his pals, and the Bingo hall, where Mollie had won, and lost, her meagre earnings. 'I don't understand why he wants our Anna,' said Mollie. 'It can't be for her money. Look at all the things he's given her. That ring she wears, she told me, cost him thousands and the sports car is for her twenty-first birthday present. She seems happy enough but she's changed somehow.' Mollie spoke with regret. She felt a million miles away from her daughter these days and wished she could put the clock back.

'We haven't been back there since we moved, so why don't we take a look at the old place,' remarked Reg. Mollie was only too pleased, and they set off in their new Jaguar to the outskirts of Chelmsford where they had lived all their married life. Nothing had altered much as the car purred along, just a few shops had closed or changed hands, including the supermarket where Mollie had done her weekly shopping. There was a new roundabout and a new by-pass cutting across the small back road which had led to the Rows. Reg felt lost as he drove round looking for the old road, and then Mollie saw the terrace. The six houses stood in a cul-de-sac, all of them empty with boarded up windows. 'Perhaps it had been intended to demolish the Rows when they made the new by-pass,' said Reg, who could hardly believe what he was seeing. 'So that's why the residents were re-housed.'

'They're up for sale, Reg. Look at that notice there. Let's buy them back.'Mollie had made up her mind, and they set off immediately to find the estate agent and make an offer. To find two people so determined to buy the dilapidated properties made the agent's day, and a deal was soon struck. Mollie and Reg returned to The Old Priory much happier than when they had left it. 'Being cut off from the traffic it will be much quieter,' said Reg. 'We can make all six houses into one long house, with a patio at the back where the yards used to be and build a high brick wall round it all for privacy. While I see an architect you can choose the furniture and the fittings Mollie. That'll keep you busy for weeks. Then we will try and find all our old neighbours and make them welcome. It will be like old times.'

'I can go back to the Bingo,' said Mollie, happily. 'I've missed that.'

'Perhaps not, my dear; you might not be so welcome if you win a prize. They'll say that you don't deserve one now.'

'I hadn't thought of that. Oh dear! Well, I'll think of something. Perhaps if I give a prize each week they will still let me play.'

Reg laughed. 'You're a caution, Mollie.'

'What about Josie's horse, Reg? We can't leave that behind.'

'We'll find a stable for it, or I'll have one built nearby. We want her to be happy don't we?'

And Josie was happy. She had wanted to go back home to live, and when she heard that her horse would be stabled nearby and that she would be with her friends at the comprehensive school, she was overjoyed. She ran to tell Anna the news and Anna came to talk it over with her parents, agreeing with them that it might be for the best. She would miss them but she knew how much Harry wanted The Old Priory to be their home once they were married, and it solved a problem. Harry had been nagging her to speak to her family about it and she had kept putting it off. Upsetting her parents was the last thing she wanted to do, and now the matter had been resolved. She persuaded them to stay on at The Old Priory until the Rows were ready for occupation. Harry had made all the arrangements for her twenty-first, and they had to be there for that event which would take place in two weeks time or she would be deeply disappointed. 'Harry has so many friends and I shall know hardly any of them,' she explained, 'and we are announcing our engagement then.'

'Of course we will be there, dear,' said Mollie, in her motherly way. 'I wouldn't miss it for the worlds, and Josie will love all the fun.' Reg smiled, but he was not looking forward to the event. Harry's grand friends were not his type. He would much rather spend the evening at the pub with his old mates, and as for wearing an evening suit and a bow tie, the very idea made him shudder, but he would do it for Anna,

'I've just heard that Amanda will be coming, with her friend, Pierre,' said Anna. 'She's finished her photo shoot in Tunisia and is back in Paris. Look, there are photos of her in these fashion magazines.' Mollie and Reg eagerly turned over the glossy pages until they came to the centre fold and there was their daughter, supposedly leading a camel across the dunes, dressed in a flowing garment, with a burnous covering her head.

'She looks as if she's done that all her life,' said Reg, fascinated by the pictures of his sun tanned daughter. 'A real beauty is our Amanda.' Mollie turned over the page. 'There are more pictures here, Reg. She's with a group of children and with some nomads.'

Anna left them to discuss the magazine and returned to the house. She was relieved that her parents were moving on as her life would soon be very different once she was married, and Harry was getting anxious that they should tie the knot as soon as possible. He had taken care to tune his lovemaking down to suit her needs, and was getting tired of playing the considerate lover.Once their wedding had taken place there would be no reason for any more play acting on his part, and during the honeymoon, while she was still susceptible to his charms it was his intention to persuade her to change her bank account into both their names in as gentle a way as possible, without arousing her suspicions as to the real reason for his marriage to her.

CHAPTER 11

Anna came down the main staircase to greet her guests who had been arriving through the afternoon. A stylish company of models and dress designers, artists, and people from the film and television world awaited her. Harry felt proud of her as he watched her descend. She had come a long way since he had first seen her. Now she had poise and had learnt how to make the most of herself. She was wearing the dress of sparkling rhinestones which she had bought in Paris, and looked as stunning in it as Amanda had predicted. The assembled company were suitably impressed and clapped her entrance. Anna felt overwhelmed. She had never experienced anything like it before and thought she must be dreaming. To have found this marvellous house and Harry, with his title and his film star good looks, who wanted to marry her, and now the adulation of all these well known people, made her feel as if she was living in a fantasy world, and would soon wake up. Harry took her by the hand and introduced her to her previously unknown guests, all of whom presented her with beautifully wrapped presents. She passed amongst them in a daze, thanking them all individually.

'What did I tell you,' whispered Amanda, 'the dress was worth every penny. You're the belle of the ball.' Anna gave her sister's hand a squeeze. She was so grateful to her for helping her to prepare for her new life. Amanda had turned her into a stylish woman.

Once the introductions were completed, she stood by Harry's side, as if mesmerized, as he announced their engagement, and his friends proffered their congratulations. The champagne flowed and the party came to life. The guests moved between the two enormous marquees erected on the lawns, to eat and drink and listen to the famous group of musicians who played on a flower decked stage.At midnight Leonie appeared; her simple white revealing gown showing off her sultry dark beauty to perfection. Anna was amazed to see her. She had not realised she had been invited. Harry must have asked her to come after the guest list had been drawn up. Conversations ceased as she swept towards Anna to proffer her congratulations, as most of the people present knew she was Harry's mistress. Anna felt nervous in her presence. Leonie was used to taking centre stage and often had a demoralising effect upon people. Anna's hand trembled as she took hold of the silver knife and cut her magnificent birthday cake to the singing of Happy Birthday. As the waiters arrived with flutes of champagne for the guests, and the cake was removed, Anna turned to see Harry, his arm around Leonie's waist, ushering her into the marquee where the dancing was about to begin. She felt angry and humiliated but there was nothing she could do about it. Amanda, watching from a distance, worried for her sister. There was something sinister about Leonie's unexpected arrival. She had heard rumours recently about Harry's relationship with Leonie in the past, but had hoped that was now finished. Now she was not so sure. Before she left for Paris Amanda decided to warn her besotted sister of her fears, but she would not spoil her special day with such morbid thoughts.

A disco took the place of the musicians and the dancing became wilder and more manic. When it packed up some people began to take their leave but the majority looked as if they intended to stay until morning. Anna felt strangely alone in her own house, and sought out her family who had been watching the firework display and the laser lights as they lit up the night sky. The marquee was empty now and the dancers had disappeared but most of them were still somewhere on the property.

'We're taking Josie to our room tonight,' said Mollie. 'She can sleep on the sofa bed. It's getting out of hand here and your father and I don't want to leave her on her own. We can't find Amanda anywhere, so Josie must come with us.' Anna wished them good-night and Reg and Mollie made their way upstairs between some of the guests who were drinking and making love wherever they could find a space. Reg unlocked their bedroom door and they went inside and relocked it.

'No place for us outside there,' said Reg, who had been shocked by some of the sights he had seen.

'You can't blame Anna, Reg, for the way some people behave in public. They were Lord Harry's guests. He invited them, remember?'

Anna wandered through the gardens looking for Harry and found them almost deserted. Back in the house she found small groups of people sitting cross legged on the carpets in the long lounge, smoking joints. They seemed to be in another world and none of them recognised her. Some guests were asleep, curled up in chairs or on settees. They looked drunk or drugged, and one man had pulled down a curtain and rolled himself inside it. She heard the sound of a powerful engine starting up and ran to the door to see Harry driving away in the Ferrari with Leonie by his side. So he had left her to cope with a house full of guests whom she did not know, and who appeared to have settled down for the night. People were strewn everywhere, some of them only partly dressed. It was like a nightmare. She struggled upstairs stepping over people to reach her own bedroom only to find her bed was occupied by three couples, and from the noises coming from the other bedrooms similar activities were taking place. She knocked on her parents' door but they were deaf to her pleas, not realising who it was who wanted admittance.

A man approached her, pulling down her shoulder straps. Anna struggled to get away and almost fell down the stairs across the somnolent bodies littered everywhere. She reached the front door with difficulty and fled sobbing down the drive to The Lodge. Mr Hardy opened the door and took her in after her repeated knocking. She sat weeping in a rocking chair while Josh and his aunt tried to comfort her. They said very little about the events at The Old Priory for they had seen it all before.

'Can I stay, please,' asked Anna, 'until all these people have left? Harry has taken the car and I don't know when he will be back. I just can't cope on my own.'

'Of course, my dear; you stay as long as you like. Josh will be here, so no harm will come to you. When your guests have slept it off they'll leave – with thick heads I wouldn't wonder.' Mrs Hardy tucked a blanket round Anna and returned to her bed. There would be all the clearing up once the party guests had left and she needed her sleep.

'I'll never have another party like this again,' said Anna, 'never, as long as I live.'

'Don't you worry about it,' said Josh, kindly. 'In the morning things will look different, you'll see.'

As Anna dozed in the chair Josh went to the door and looked out. The Old Priory was a blaze of lights. It was almost five in the morning and Harry had yet to return. There was no sound from the house now and he imagined they were sleeping off the excesses of the previous night. He cursed Harry under his breath for landing her in this mess and then running off and leaving her. Surely, she would soon come to her senses and realise he was no good for her. He closed the door and came back into the kitchen. Anna was asleep at last, snuggled inside the blanket. A strand of hair had fallen across her face and she looked so vulnerable that his heart went out to her. He longed to hold her safely in his arms but he must wait until such time as she needed him, even if it took for the rest of his life. Josh climbed up the stairs and lay on his bed. There was no point in getting undressed. He usually got up around six anyway. There would be no more sleep for him. His thoughts troubled him. If Anna went through with this marriage it would become more difficult for him to watch over her, even from a distance. The roar of the Ferrari disturbed his thoughts and he hurried downstairs. Anna was awake.

'Harry is back,' she said, quietly. 'It will be all right now.'

'Stay for a while, Miss Anna. Don't go back yet. Let Lord Harry sort out his guests first. Once one car leaves the rest will follow. Then it will be time for you to go home.'

'But he won't know where I am, nor will my family.'

'Just wait a little while and then I will walk back with you. You only have to explain why you needed to come to The Lodge, and my aunt will speak to Lord Harry if you wish her to.'

While Anna was drinking a cup of tea she looked round the homely kitchen as she warmed her hands on the mug. It was a small room, like the kitchen had been at The Rows, with a place for everything and everything in its place. Tidy and efficient was Mrs Hardy, just like her own mother. She felt at home in these comfortable surroundings and wished she could stay. Returning to The Old Priory was going to be difficult, especially as she was determined to have an explanation from Harry as to why he had left her to go off with Leonie.

The cars gradually filled up with the previous night's guests and drove away and once they had all gone Anna returned home to discover her family desperately trying to find her. She started to explain her absence when she realised that her mother was in a state of shock.

'The ambulance is coming any minute now to take her to Broomfield hospital, but I don't think there is anything they can do.'

'Take who, Mum? …What's happened? ... Speak to me!'

'Amanda—it's Amanda. We can't wake her. Josie went in to see her this morning once everyone had left. She was so still Josie thought she was dead. When I saw her I thought the same—.'

Anna ran upstairs to her sister's room where her father was weeping at his daughter's bedside. She put her arm around him and tried to comfort him without success. Reg was inconsolable. Then she heard Harry's voice directing the ambulance men upstairs to Amanda's room. There was a brief discussion before they brought her downstairs on a stretcher. 'But what is it?' asked Anna, in a panic. 'Has she had a heart attack?'

'The doctor will tell you when we get to hospital. Are you a relative?'

'Yes, her sister. Can I come with my parents? I can drive them there.'

'Follow the ambulance. We must get her to Broomfield as soon as possible.'

Anna grabbed a coat to cover her dress and bundled her father and Josie into the Alfa while her mother travelled in the ambulance. Josh watched them go and wondered, hopefully, if Lord Harry had come to grief. His hopes were soon dashed as Harry came out of The Old Priory and got into his car.

'It's her sister, Amanda,' he called out to Josh. 'Tell your aunt I've arranged for a cleaning firm to come in today to sort out the mess. Take some time by the look of it. I expect she'd like to supervise them.' The car sped off and Josh was left wondering what exactly had happened.

When the family were allowed in to see Amanda she was a mass of tubes. She looked so pale and lifeless that Anna felt sure she was dead. The doctor was kind for he could give them no hope of a recovery. 'Your daughter is in a deep coma,' he explained to her parents. 'We are keeping her alive but she is virtually brain dead. I must ask you some questions so we can evaluate her condition more accurately. Was she addicted to any kind of drug that you knew about?'

'Oh, no,' said Anna, quickly, 'she told me that although many of the models took drugs to pep themselves up before a show, she only had the occasional puff herself to be sociable.'

'Ah, cannabis I presume,' said the doctor, taking notes. 'I think your sister had taken a designer drug. We shall need to track it down. She must have taken it last night. Can you tell us what happened last night?'

'We had a party,' said Anna, miserably. 'It was my twenty-first birthday. There were a lot of people there whom I didn't know – models, and people from the film world. Perhaps she was given something then. But it doesn't seem like Amanda. She certainly wasn't an addict.'

'Just one tablet can cause this condition,' said the doctor, 'especially if she had been drinking. It's a matter for the police, I'm afraid.'

Reg broke down in distress and Mollie wept with him. Anna felt angry. She was horrified to think this could have happened to her sister in her house. She thought back to her guests. Some had seemed respectable people but others had behaved badly. She had seen them for herself. Their sexual irresponsibility could have been triggered off by something they had taken.

Harry might know. He had often had parties at The Old Priory in the past. She would ask him when she returned home. She had rather a lot to ask Harry and needed to see him urgently. Anna took Josie home and dropped her off with Mrs Hardy for the day, leaving her parents at the hospital. She looked everywhere for Harry but Harry had gone out some time ago according to Mrs Hardy. He was never there for her when she most needed him. She decided to cut some roses to take with her to the hospital. She knew which were the old musk roses; the ones which filled a room with scent. Perhaps if Amanda could smell them it might trigger off a memory. Anna collected a garden trug and some secateurs and began to cut the flowers but her feelings became too much for her and she collapsed weeping onto the grass. Josh found her, crying as if her heart would break. He put his arms around her and lifted her to her feet, holding her close to him. Anna rested her head on his shoulder and found she was unable to stop crying. Josh stroked her hair and spoke softly to her to calm her. He led her to the stone seat in the rose garden and sat with her, holding her close. For some time they sat with his arm around her until her weeping ceased. He kissed her forehead gently and she drew away from his embrace.

'I'm sorry,' he said, thinking he had offended her.

'We are still friends, aren't we, Josh?' – I hated it when you were so angry the other day. What had I done to upset you so much?'

'Nothing – you had done nothing.'

'What was it then?'

'It was Lord Harry coming back here that upset me, if you must know.'

Anna was silent. There was some bitter enmity between the two men which must have gone back to their childhood, back to the days when Josh had spent his holidays with his aunt and uncle at The Lodge. And now Harry had won her heart and Josh resented it.

'I wish he'd never come back. Things might have been different then.'

Anna looked up at his handsome, sunburnt face, and into his honest blue eyes and saw the hurt he felt, but her feelings for Harry were too deep to change. Harry had taught her the ways of love and she had fallen for his dashing good looks and his elegant manners. She had learnt how to do the things he had asked of her to please him and from an inexperienced young girl she had flowered into a gracious, beautiful woman under his tutelage. She had come too far along the line with Harry to care about anyone else in that way. She was glad that Josh was still her friend. It had hurt her deeply when he had turned away from her – more deeply than she had cared to admit to herself – but Harry, her handsome, dashing lover, had stolen her heart.

'Forgive me for speaking my mind, Anna. I should never have spoken about Lord Harry like that. I hope you will be very happy together. I will leave my position here if you wish and look for another job.'

Anna felt remorseful. 'Don't go please Josh – especially on my account. You will find happiness too, one of these days.' She picked up her roses and walked quickly away without looking back. Josh had awakened feelings in her which had never surfaced before and which she must forget. Nothing would ever come between her and the love she felt for Harry. Her mind was full of concern for her sister and the agony of her parents suffering and she must get back to the hospital to share their vigil.

Josh was distraught. He could have wept himself after she had gone. All this time he had kept his feelings for her bottled up and now it was hopeless. Once Anna was Harry's wife he would pack up and go elsewhere. There would be other women in his life and other gardens he could landscape, but none would compare to The Old Priory garden and its owner.

CHAPTER 12

Amanda lingered on for two more weeks, kept alive by a life support system, without any hope of recovery. The family stayed by her side until the medical staff advised that her life support should be turned off. They were all in a state of shock as they returned to The Old Priory, especially Reg, who could not be comforted. Harry was waiting for them, having heard the news from Mrs Hardy on his return. When Anna told him that Amanda had virtually died the moment she had taken a drug at her party he was genuinely shocked. He hardly knew Amanda, having only met her briefly, but the fact that she had died after one of his parties could mean trouble from the police. He was a known drug addict and had been fortunate to get away with a large fine and a spell in a rehabilitation clinic a few years ago. If this information was to be unearthed it would be the end of his plans to marry Anna, and he would have to tread very carefully now the police were getting involved. He was careful to keep the hard stuff hidden away in Leonie's apartment in Paris, and only smoked marijuana at The Old Priory occasionally, out of the sight of the family. He had given out the 'poppers' to the guests whom he knew would appreciate them. Unfortunately Amanda's boyfriend had asked for a couple. He really couldn't be blamed if they had killed her. He hadn't been the one to give them to her. He never sold ecstasy to his friends. They were used to make his parties go with a swing. He was famous for his parties, and the sexual capers his guests got up to. He rarely took part but got his kicks from seeing how dependent his friends were on their need for his drugs. Anna's party had been a very mild affair compared to the usual orgy. He had been in two minds about handing out the pills on this occasion, but some of his guests had asked for them just before he discovered he would have to drive Leonie to

Heathrow or she would miss her flight to the U.S.A. Most of the guests would have left by the time he got back and Anna would have gone to bed, or so he had hoped, unaware of any untoward behaviour from his guests. He intended to clear them out on his return and to see that any incriminating evidence was removed. The death of her sister came as a bitter blow.

Once her parents had left to grieve together in their suite of rooms he could see that Anna was furious with him. It was a revelation to Harry who thought he could get away with anything as far as she was concerned.

'I deserve an explanation from you, Harry, and I intend to have one, right now. And I want the truth— do you hear— the truth, Harry!' she sobbed, angrily.

Harry was shocked by her outburst and went to put his arm round her but she shrugged him off. 'You're upset, Anna, and no wonder. Come and sit down and tell me what this is about. I'm sorry about Amanda, too, but there's nothing we can do to bring her back—try not to get so upset, my sweet.'

'Where did you go, Harry, when you left the party with Leonie? Why did she come here? I didn't invite her and I needed you here. Things got out of hand after you left.'

'My poor darling. You've been through a bad time—but, as to Leonie, there is nothing to tell you. I left a message with Amanda because I couldn't find you. Obviously, you didn't see her after I left, or you would have known all about it.'

'All about what, Harry?'

Harry shifted uneasily. A little time with Leonie on their own when such a disaster was happening would be difficult to explain. 'Let's leave it for a while, shall we. This is a bad time for everyone.'

'No, Harry. I want to know now.'

'Very well, then it's perfectly simple. Leonie telephoned to say she would like to come for a few hours only, as she was en route to the U.S.A. She wanted to meet you and to give us her good wishes. I didn't invite her because I had heard that she was abroad on an assignment, but the dates were changed at the last minute, and she telephoned when she arrived at Stanstead.'

'So why didn't you tell me?'

'It was a last minute thing and you were upstairs making yourself beautiful so I didn't get around to telling you. I was sure you would have no objection. There were lots of other models here.'

'But where did you go with her—before the guests had left?'

'I told you. I explained to Amanda. She needed to get to Heathrow quickly to catch her night plane. The Ferrari is fast and a taxi might not have made it in time. I had no intention of leaving you in the lurch on your special day. Please forgive me.'

'I understand what you are saying, Harry, but you should never have gone. It was our engagement party.'

'I know, sweetheart - I know. Nothing seems right at the moment does it—but I felt it would be unfair to ask Josh to turn out at that hour, and I expected to get there and back fairly quickly.'

'But those people, Harry—I couldn't cope. I didn't know them and their behaviour was disgusting—and in my bed, too! I never want to see any of them again.'

She was still trembling and at last allowed him to take her in his arms and comfort her.

'My poor little darling; try to forget about them—I can't think who they could have been, but when you invite friends of other friends their drinking habits are an unknown factor, and if they drink more than is good for them there isn't much you can do about it. What did you do?'

'I went to The Lodge. My parents had gone to bed and didn't hear me knocking on their door and I couldn't stay here.'

'Of course not, sweetheart. I can see I should have been here to turn them out. We must keep a tight check on who comes to The Old Priory in future. Some of them might have been gate crashers who slipped in later.' Anna hadn't thought of that possibility. She might be unfair blaming Harry for unwanted guests whom he hadn't invited in the first place.

Harry stroked her arm and kissed her hand. 'Feeling better now, sweetheart?'

Anna nodded. She still felt disturbed by recent events and wondered why Amanda hadn't passed the message on to her. Perhaps, she had lapsed into a coma before she could speak to her. A thought occurred to her.

'Harry?'

'Yes, my sweet.'

'Did you see Amanda's boyfriend when everyone left?'

'Can't say that I did, but I'm sure he was there. They all left together to catch the plane back to Paris. Somebody would have mentioned his absence—they came together as a group.'

'He won't know about Amanda, will he? Perhaps he thought she was asleep when he left.'

'Do you know his name?'

'Pierre—nothing else.'

'There must be an awful lot of Frenchmen called, Pierre. The news will get to him eventually no doubt and then he will keep a low profile if he has any sense.'

Anna nodded. They would never see Pierre again she felt sure. 'I haven't seen you, Harry, for the last few weeks. Every time I telephoned home you seemed to be out. I really needed to talk to you during this awful time—it would have been a comfort.'

'Sorry, love. I thought you would prefer to be undisturbed, and there was nothing I could do to help; but I'm here now, for as long as you need me.'

Anna nestled into the crook of his arm, glad to have him back home with her. 'What have you been doing with yourself while I've been away? Not too bored I hope.' Anna gave him no answer. Her time had been spent trying to comfort her family, surely he would have realised that.

'I missed you, sweetheart, but I played a lot of golf and visited the Snape Maltings to see if they had sold any of my seascapes at the gallery. Fortunately, they had sold a few so I collected some badly needed cash to tide me over.'

Anna sat up and faced him. 'How are you placed for money, Harry? I've never discussed the subject with you—I always imagined you had a private income and I didn't want to embarrass you.'

Harry laughed, without humour. 'I really couldn't talk to you about that, now could I – beneath one's dignity for a lord of the realm to plead poverty.'

'But you spent a fortune on my ring, and then there was the car.'

'The car is a status symbol, sweetheart, and your ring was for the dearest girl in the world who had stolen my heart. After that I literally had nothing.'

'Nothing but me,' said Anna, looking up into his eyes, adoringly. 'Oh, Harry, you poor thing.'

'You speak the truth, Anna. I really am a poor thing these days. I didn't intend to tell you until after we were married. I thought you might turn me down if you knew of my impecunious circumstances.'

Anna put her arms around him and rested her cheek against his. Her worries had been explained away and the old feeling of adoration for him stirred within her. 'You silly boy, I have plenty for both of us.'

'But I would have felt like a kept man, Anna, and that goes against the grain. Don't forget, I have a noble ancestry.'

'Well, I certainly haven't, so what is it to me if I share all that I possess with my husband. Doesn't it say something like that in the wedding service—that what is mine is yours, and what is yours is mine?'

'Oh, my darling—I don't deserve you. You are the sweetest girl.' Harry was overcome by her generous gesture and kissed her with real feeling. It had been easier than he had hoped for in his wildest dreams. He would be rich again and his immediate troubles were over. The telephone rang and Anna went to answer it. The hospital wanted to speak to her parents. They had the results of the autopsy so Amanda's body could be released for burial. Reg took the call. There was sufficient evidence to show that she had taken an overdose of amyl nitrate, commonly known as 'poppers', to stimulate sexual activity. Reg couldn't take it in. His daughter was a good girl, he kept repeating. She would never have taken drugs. That boyfriend of hers must have given them to her. He would willingly have killed him with his bare hands if he could find him, but if he searched the length and breadth of Paris he knew it would be impossible to locate him.

'Don't take on so, Reg. There's nothing you can do—you'll only make yourself more depressed,' said his wife, concerned about his sanity during the last few weeks.

Harry got up and put his arm around Reg, to comfort him. 'I feel just like you,' said Harry, with feeling. 'Drug dealers should receive the death penalty here, like they do in Shanghai. They are the scum of the earth.'

Reg shook his hand. 'You are a good man. I wasn't altogether happy about you marrying our Anna, I must admit. I thought the difference between the way you had both been brought up only spelt disaster, but I have been proved wrong. You will make her a good husband, I feel sure.' Both Anna and her mother felt embarrassed by his outburst. Reg was usually a man of very few words, and this was out of character.

'Thank you, Reg,' said Harry. 'I only wish my parents were still here to meet Anna. They would have loved her as much as I do.' In his heart of hearts Harry knew perfectly well that his father would have been appalled at his choice of wife, and even his gentle mother would have shown her disapproval in a polite, but obvious way. Anna would never have felt welcome at The Old Priory if they had still been alive—but what did that matter now. As far as he was concerned his marriage was one of convenience and would not last long.

Upstairs in their own apartment Mollie turned to Reg. 'I don't know what came over you, Reg Hamilton, speaking your mind like that. I thought you disliked Lord Harry—a snob of the first order, you used to call him.'

'I've changed my mind that's all. He's a good man and I'm glad I said what I did.'

Mollie sighed and wondered how Anna had taken her father's outburst, but Anna was close to tears. 'You were wonderful, darling, speaking to my Dad like that. He even gave us his blessing and I never expected him to do that.'

Harry smiled his usual sardonic smile. He was a terrible hypocrite but if it eased the situation then what did it matter. He was a plausible liar and always had been. 'After the funeral, Anna, I think it would be a good idea if we go abroad and get married quietly somewhere—more suitable under the circumstances don't you think?'

Anna was horrified. 'No, I don't, Harry. We will have to wait for a while—surely you understand that. I feel much too upset to even consider it as yet, and my parents would feel as if I hadn't cared about Amanda—and I did—I loved her very much. Losing her has broken my heart.'

Harry was disappointed at her decision and tried to sound understanding without showing his true feelings. It meant waiting around and acting the part of a caring lover so as not to upset the wedding plans. He felt like grinding his teeth in rage, while keeping a permanent smile on his face. After a while Reg and Mollie moved out of The Old Priory, taking Josie with them. The Rows were still being converted but there was enough room for them to live in a part of the property. Passing the room in The Old Priory which had once belonged to Amanda caused them so much grief that they wanted to live elsewhere.

Once they had gone Anna began to feel lonely and Harry only needed a little persuasion to get her to agree to a romantic wedding on the island of St Lucia.

CHAPTER 13

The hotel was set on a hillside sloping down to a secluded bay of glistening white sand, where Anna and Harry had decided to get married. They had taken a honeymoon suite with their own pool, overlooking the lush tropical gardens where orchids, oleanders, hibiscus and bougainvillea bloomed in abundance. Anna thought she was in paradise as soon as she set eyes on it.

During the statutory four days residence before they could be married they had plenty of time to explore. Anna swam well having practised nearly every day in the pool at The Old Priory, since she had lived there, and each day she swam in the clear blue waters of the sea. At Marigot Bay the yacht harbour attracted Harry who hired a local skipper to sail them round the island. At tiny hidden coves they swam ashore to laze on the golden beaches before returning to the boat to eat the local fish and drink rum cocktails. Anna, who had never learnt to water-ski, took lessons, while Harry played golf on the Cap Estate course. He preferred this to energetic water sports, and had no idea as to how expert Anna had become. The sea held no fears for her and she was enjoying herself. She loved snorkelling and watched the angel fish as they swam amongst the coral. She had tried to persuade Harry to come and snorkel with her but he preferred to go deep sea fishing for marlin and barracuda. While he was away Anna visited the colourful markets in the square at Castries, where she bought some local crafts to take back home to her family. She walked through the volcanic cave with the other tourists and bathed in the sulphur springs nearby. As she stood and watched the multicoloured water pour down the Diamond Falls she began to wonder why she had been left alone so much. She accepted that the things Harry liked were not her choice but she still felt let down when he made no effort to please her. She would never be able to play golf with him, he was just too good a player, but maybe, when they were home again he would find a professional to teach her. Playing golf appeared to be a social acquisition which she would have to master. She began to find his behaviour strange, as since their arrival he had cared little about making love to her in the enormous four poster bed, draped round with white muslin curtains. Their bedroom was delightful, filled with flowers, which over flowed onto the balcony. A huge basket of tropical fruit had been left for them and a bottle of champagne, with the compliments of the hotel. There was nothing for them to do but enjoy themselves, soak up the sun, and make love, but Harry seemed to have lost interest in her. 'We came here to get married, Harry. Nobody who saw us would think so. What's come over you? Do you want to call it off?'

'Sorry, sweetheart. It's just me. Think nothing of it—the mood will pass. It's probably the humidity getting to me.' His mind was preoccupied with a way to dispose of her after the wedding and making love to her bored him. She meant nothing to him now. Teaching her the pleasures and the pain of sex had provided him with a perverse satisfaction, but that was in the past. Every time he looked at her he imagined how she would look in her coffin, pale and beautiful and surrounded by flowers, while he acted the part of a grieving husband. It would all be over soon and then he could take up his old way of life with Leonie.

Just thinking about Leonie and the mutual passion they shared filled him with longing. He would bring her here one day and make love to her under the palm trees with the waves caressing their bodies, or in the forest with the parrots screeching above as she screamed with the pleasure he gave her. Leonie had come to The Old Priory to see his future bride and considered her an easy victim. Too trusting and too good was her opinion of Anna. Once married Harry must organise a fatal accident which would lay no blame at his door, but he still had to go through with this travesty of a marriage. They stood side by side in the small private bay they had chosen for their wedding as a

Justice of the Peace married them. The hotel had provided two witnesses. Apart from that they were alone. Harry wanted the wedding to be as simple as possible, with no photographs and no fuss. Anna was disappointed. She wanted a keepsake of her wedding day even if Harry wanted no memories of the occasion, and she had given one of the witnesses her camera.

Harry's bride looked beautiful in her pale pink shift dress with pink orchids in her long sun bleached hair. She held a bouquet of wild orchids which matched his buttonhole.

Harry wore black trousers and a black open necked silk shirt, with a black velvet blazer, which suited his black mood. He was not marrying her for love as Anna would soon discover. Then, as the waves lapped gently onto the palm fringed beach they were pronounced man and wife. Harry kissed his bride with a sense of relief. There would be no more suggestions from Anna about calling the wedding off. Afterwards the hotel provided champagne, a wedding cake, and a candlelit gourmet dinner, in traditional Creole style. In the evening a steel band played on the beach and limbo dancers entertained the crowd. Harry watched, fascinated, as a black girl moved her sinuous body under the rope. The lower the rope the fewer the dancers who could manage it until the girl was the only one left. The firelight from the beach glistened on her oiled skin and she looked more like a snake than a woman as she writhed and slid beneath the rope, with her dreadlocks sweeping the sand. Harry clapped enthusiastically and the girl looked in his direction and smiled. Anna wandered off to watch the dancers and soon found herself moving to the rhythm of the band. Harry gave the girl some dollars and suggested she came with him. Her thin, supple body reminded him of Leonie and he wanted to make love to her. In the darkness Anna did not see him leave. She was enjoying dancing with the happy crowd on the beach and, like them, soon got swept along by the rhythm of the drums.

The black girl led Harry to a deserted part of the beach. She was practised in the ways of love and was happy to satisfy his kinky demands as long as he paid her money. Harry obliged, willingly. As he began to leave her she called out to him. 'More dollars; more dollars, or I tell your wife.' Harry approached her angrily. He had paid her well for her services and had no more money on him. He took hold of her by the shoulders and shook her violently. The girl struggled and bit him on the arm to make him let go, but Harry, who was fast losing control of himself, threw her against the side of a boat drawn up on the beach. There was a crack as her head made contact with the wood and she lay very still. Harry was horrified and tried to lift her up, but it was obvious that the girl was dead. Her head fell back as if she had broken her neck. He let her body drop back onto the sand and hurried down the beach to where he had left Anna. This might complicate matters once the girl's body was discovered and they would have to leave St Lucia quickly before enquiries were made.

He had not been missed in the short time he had been away and in his black clothes he had not been seen as he followed the girl in the shadow of the palm trees along the dark sand. He looked for Anna amongst the beach party and soon found her, happily chatting to another couple who had come to the island to get married. Harry joined in the conversation. It was important that he had an alibi. Nobody would think that Lord Charlesworth had caused the girl's death. It was his wedding day, and naturally he had been with his bride all the time. However, he would ask the hotel to book them on the plane to Martinique the next day and to find them a good hotel for the rest of their honeymoon.

As they walked back to their honeymoon suite Harry shivered. Anna would expect him to behave like a lover, tonight of all nights, but it was impossible; he had brought no pills with him to pep himself up. If he hadn't missed Leonie so desperately it would never have happened, and now he had to explain to Anna that they were moving on and she would have to pack right away. It could be difficult. He knew she had been happy here and might not want to spend the rest of their honeymoon in Martinique. 'Did I tell you my darling that we are going to Martinique for the rest of our honeymoon? It's so close – just a hop across the water, but quite different in many ways. You must have seen most of St Lucia since we've been here.'

'What a lovely idea, Harry, but I wish you'd told me sooner. Men never think of the packing. When do we leave?'

Harry was surprised that she fell in with his plans so easily. 'Oh, in the morning I would think. I only have to check a few details with the hotel first thing.'

Anna smiled. Perhaps, he had waited until now for the honeymoon to begin in earnest, and they would enjoy themselves together, as husband and wife. She sat in the big bed, hugging her knees, and waited for Harry to come to her. He was such a long time that she lay down and fell asleep, exhausted by the evening's energetic entertainment. Harry had been sitting on the balcony watching the sky. It was looking ominous, with heavy black clouds gathering. If there was going to be a tropical storm they must leave quickly before the storm broke. By the time Harry went into the bedroom, Anna had fallen asleep, much to his relief. He lay some distance away from her in the enormous bed, and fell into a deep and troubled sleep.

They left St Lucia the next morning just as it began to rain and soon landed at Martinique, where a car was waiting to take them to the Novotel Le Diamant. The hotel was situated on a rocky cape at the end of the beach with a good view of the Diamant rock from their large bedroom. Anna was enchanted with the island and all it offered to the visitor. Flowers grew in abundance wherever she looked and from the hills she could see the glitter of rivers and streams, culminating into waterfalls which rushed into deep gorges. Harry rented a car to take them over the island as soon as they arrived, and on their first afternoon he drove along the coastal road to Coffres-a-Morts. From these limestone hills the last caribs had thrown themselves to their deaths rather than surrender to the whites. Harry had heard the story in the bar of the hotel. He had listened in to the conversation with interest and decided to take a look at the area. He told Anna they were going sightseeing that afternoon. As they had only just arrived there was no possibility that she had heard the story as yet. Pleased that he wanted her company Anna hoped this would set the scene for the remainder of their honeymoon. They set off cheerfully together until they reached the top of the limestone hills. Below them the sea crashed against the rocks, menacingly. Harry swung the car round until it pointed to the edge of the cliff and got out of the driving seat quickly, without putting on the brake properly. Anna felt the car move, slowly at first and then it gathered speed towards the edge of the cliff. She pulled on the brake as hard as she could and turned the wheel round. The car slid to a stop, and then she looked for Harry, but Harry was nowhere to be seen. Now she was frightened and got out of the car, only to see Harry running down the road. She shouted his name but he appeared not to have heard her. Anna climbed into the driving seat, started the ignition and gradually drove the car back onto the road. Harry was far in the distance and she drove towards him, catching him up as he ran frantically back in the direction of the hotel. She drove slowly beside him before, in his panic, he realised it was Anna at the wheel, and stopped abruptly. However had she pulled the car round from the passenger seat? It must have been a superhuman effort on her part. He had left as soon as it had begun to pick up speed and expected her to be at the bottom of the cliff by now, smashed to pieces on the rocks.

Anna pulled up. 'Wherever do you think you're going to, Harry? I could easily have been killed. You didn't put the brake on fully.'

Harry was out of breath. Being an absolute coward he had hated the idea of witnessing her death despite having been the person responsible for it, and had run away from the scene. 'Anna.—Oh, Anna,' he stuttered, amazed to see her still alive. 'As soon as I saw the car slide forward I knew it was only a matter of minutes before it went over the edge. There was nothing I could do to stop it. I was going to get help from St Pierre.'

'Get in, Harry. I'll drive. It was a stupid place to park anyway, however marvellous the view. I think the brakes on this car are a bit dodgy.'

'Maybe—I'll exchange it when we get back.' Harry was shaking with the shock of seeing her. It had been uncanny the way she had driven along beside him. He still found it hard to believe that she was still here. 'For God's sake stop, Anna,' he begged, as she drove through Fort-de France. '1 need a drink.'

Anna drove into the Place de la Savane and pulled up beside a small street cafe: 'I'm not surprised,' she replied, taking her trembling hands off the wheel. 'I think I'll join you.'

They sat for some time to recover. Harry looked as white as a sheet as he sipped his brandy and Anna found it difficult to hold her glass steady. The square was shaded by trees and filled with flowers and was a peaceful place in which to sit. Shopping streets led off from the square and hotels surrounded it. Anna decided to return at some time to look at the shops, but right now she only wanted to go back to the hotel and rest. It had taken a little time for the realisation to hit her that she had been so close to losing her life, and she was suffering from delayed shock. When they were ready they continued their journey to Le Diamant, with Harry driving. Anna went straight to their room to lie down, and Harry, who by now was getting over the fact that he had failed in his first attempt to kill his wife, went off to find the golf course, where he played an aggressive round of golf.

CHAPTER 14

Harry exchanged the hire car, with no questions asked, for a more expensive model. At last he had no money problems as Anna had changed her bank account into both their names to take effect from their marriage. This was her wedding present to him and had given him carte blanche to spend what he wanted within reason. The large amount of her fortune had been invested wisely and provided enough interest for her to be a wealthy woman for as long as she lived, without touching the capital. She intended to make a will in Harry's favour once they had returned home, but this was not altogether necessary for Harry to inherit a large portion of her estate if she died now. Her will would iron out a few difficulties, but Harry wanted to take advantage of the possibilities of causing her death whilst in the Windward Islands, where they were both unknown. He explained to Anna that he had hired another car as the other one had been found to have faulty brakes. The small matter of the car sliding down the slope would then have a rational explanation; not that Anna was likely to forget the hair-raising experience, but it cleared Harry of any complicity. When he suggested that they made a trip to see Mont Pele the next day, Anna was horrified. Harry explained that they could walk round the rim of the still active volcano without any danger. He assured her that there was no smoke or fumes and it had not erupted for many years. The views from the top were magnificent and many tourists visited it. Anna refused to go. She had had enough of Harry's views. Harry was disappointed. He had considered a small push into the crater for his next attempt to kill her, as long as they were alone.

'I'm never going along that coastal road again, Harry. I don't care how beautiful that part of the island might be, I don't want to see it. You can take me as far as Fort-de-France but that's all.'

To calm her fears he suggested they visited Les Trois Ilets which was not too far from the hotel. They could return by Les Anses~d'Arlet where they could swim from the beautiful beaches nearby. This would be a gentle drive which she would enjoy. Having more faith in the new car Anna agreed to what seemed to be a pleasant day out. She loved the pretty village of Trois Ilets where Napoleon's wife, the Empress Josephine had been born and visited the museum which used to be her home. They looked inside the church where Josephine's parents had been married and where she had been baptised. Anna was fascinated. It was all so romantic even if the story ended sadly. Harry was always by her side, behaving like an ever attentive new husband, especially when there were other people about. He wanted them to be seen together as a loving couple. They made a handsome pair and were often remarked upon as people wondered who they were. They swam and sunbathed on the beautiful beach at Grande Anse and then returned to their hotel for dinner. All around them French was spoken which Anna could not understand, but fortunately Harry was fluent in the language, having spent part of his life in France. As they sat looking across to the Diamant rock, Anna was thinking back to their perfect day together.

'There were some people water skiing at Les Anse d'Arlot this afternoon. Did you see them, Harry? It was when we were looking for the best beach to swim from.'

'M,m,' Harry took little interest in the sport. It was too energetic for him. 'I'd love to do some water skiing while we're here. Do you think I could?' Harry suddenly took an interest in the conversation.

'I'm sure you could, darling. I'll ask at reception which is the best centre to go to. We shall need to hire a motor cruiser and equipment, and you will need a wet suit.' On the way to their room that evening Harry stopped at the reception desk to make enquiries and was told to go to St Anne, which was a centre for water sports. That night he promised Anna they would go there the next day. Once they were in bed he took her in his arms and made love to her. It was the first time since their wedding and Anna felt it was high time he had felt like it. The plan forming in his mind to kill her had excited him – and made the act more thrilling. As he reached a climax Harry felt an overwhelming sense of power. She was in his clutches and would never escape. He had made her fall in love with him without her ever realising he had no love for her. He had manipulated her like a puppet for his own ends and tomorrow he would kill her. There must be no mistakes this time. When Anna had fallen asleep he gradually eased himself away to the other side of the bed, so he was no longer touching her body. She had outlived her usefulness and he wanted nothing more of her. In the morning they were both in a good mood as they set off for St Anne, Anna, because she expected to spend another day in Harry's company, and Harry, because this day was to see the culmination of all his plans. Once at St Anne, Harry hired a motor cruiser equipped for water skiing and Anna went to find a wet suit to fit her. While she had gone Harry bought a sharp knife which would serve his purpose. On her way back Anna collected a lunch basket and cans of drink, so they could spend the whole day on the boat. The sea was a clear aquamarine blue as they set off, glittering enticingly beneath a cloudless sky. It was perfect for water-skiing Anna thought, as they sped away from the beach. Harry drove the boat hard and they cut through the water at a rate of knots, soon leaving the coastline behind. Anna loved the speed. It was exhilarating and she stood in the bows with her long blonde hair streaming behind her.

'Don't be too adventurous, Harry. We don't want to get lost out here.'

Harry smiled to himself. Only one of them would be getting lost and it wouldn't be him. 'There's a coastal map and a compass in the wheelhouse, sweetheart. I think we've gone far enough anyway. I'll drop anchor here and we can swim from the boat.' They slid over the side and swam for a while in the warm sea, climbing back to sunbathe. As the sun rose in the heavens they repaired to the cockpit and ate their lunch in the shade. Afterwards Anna renewed her sun oil, rubbing it over her brown limbs, and then over Harry. She would have a marvellous tan by the time they returned home. They sat for a while, feeling sleepy in the heat. Harry had nothing to say to her and closed his eyes to avoid conversation. He wanted to get it all over with but needed to wait until any other craft had headed back to the shore. It was such a beautiful day to be out on the water. There was hardly a ripple on the surface of the sea and the boat rocked lazily as tiny wavelets nudged the sides.

'You'll need to go back closer to the shore before I can ski, darling,' said Anna, waking from a long sleep. This had not been Harry's intention, but as he wanted no trouble from her, he pulled up the anchor and they cruised slowly forward until the shoreline came into view in the far distance.

'Will this do?' asked Harry, as the engine idled.

'It looks as if it will have to,' replied Anna, who would have preferred to ski closer to the beach.

As she was busy pulling on the wet suit, Harry leant over the stern of the boat and took the knife from the pocket in his shorts. He had changed into his shorts while she had been dozing after lunch, and had slipped the knife into his pocket. Carefully he shredded the tow rope attached to the stern so only the top of the rope was left visible.

'I'm just checking everything is ready, sweetheart,' he called out to her.

Anna slid into the water, took hold of the tow bar and placed the skis in position. As Harry put the boat in motion she stood up expertly on the skis and he roared off at speed towards the horizon. He swung the boat round in wider and wider arcs, and was amazed to see she had not fallen off. She laughed and raised her hand to him in greeting. Harry waved briefly back. 'My God, she's better than I thought,' he muttered to himself, wondering how long it would take for the rope to break.

He increased the speed of the boat, heading further and further out until the shoreline disappeared. Anna shouted to him but he didn't hear her words over the roar of the engine. Would the rope never break? Perhaps he hadn't cut it through sufficiently.

At last he felt a jolt as the rope snapped and Anna was left floundering in the water. Harry looked straight ahead as if nothing had happened. After he had gone some distance he stopped the engine and looked over the stern of the boat. Anna could only just see him and waved frantically. Harry pretended to look into the distance to find her and then started up the engine again. The boat moved round in ever widening circles as if he was searching for her but he carefully kept far away from where he had left her. After some time Anna faintly heard the engine roar into life. The boat sped away at high speed and was soon lost to view. At first she thought he must have gone to seek help in looking for her, but no help came. It was no good staying where she was as Harry appeared to have lost her position, and would never be able to pinpoint the place where he had last seen her to the people searching for her. She remembered vaguely the direction in which to swim and knew she must try to reach land. She had waited long enough. The tow bar was still in her hand and she pulled the rope towards her only to discover that it appeared to have been almost cut through where it had joined the boat.

Why hadn't Harry noticed something was wrong? In future she would check everything herself; first the brakes on the car, and now this. She began to feel angry. He was hopeless and not at all practical. It was a terrible long way to swim and she wondered if she was capable of it. There was only one way to find out and that was to strike out for the shore and hope for the best. As she swam the fast flowing water swept her further and further away from the beach. To conserve her strength she floated on her back and let the tide take her with it. As darkness fell she felt her strength ebbing away and came close to giving up the unequal struggle. Her arms and legs felt like lead and she was getting cold -so very cold. The light swinging from the prow of a small fishing boat shone across something black, fl oating in the sea, close to the boat. One of the fishermen leant over the side to see what it was. 'Bon sang de merde!' he exclaimed.

'Qu'est-ce que c'est?' asked his brother, unhooking the light and bringing it with him. Had they come across a dead body? Together they hauled Anna into the boat and laid her down on a pile of ropes. They pulled the hood of her wet suit back and her long sun bleached hair fell round her face like a halo. The men crossed themselves. She was too young and beautiful to have lost her life in the sea. One of the brothers shook his head sorrowfully, 'Elle est mort,' he said, sadly. But his brother felt they should not give up hope. In the past he had had some experience of rescuing swimmers in difficulties, and he moved her into the recovery position. They abandoned their fishing for the night and turned back in haste to the village of St Luce from whence they had come.

Harry, meanwhile, had returned to St Anne after a time wasting cruise around the coast, to report Anna's disappearance. By the time a search was made for her she had been in the sea for some hours and it was getting dark. He directed the boat away from the area where she had been skiing and when she wasn't found the area was widened. But there was no sign of Anna. Harry collected their belongings from the motor boat and after leaving his name and the name of the hotel, he left, leaving instructions to be contacted the moment his poor wife was found. The owner of the boat noticed that the tow rope was missing apart from a few frayed ends. He found that strange as he had attached the rope himself, but he decided to say nothing. Hiring out his boat to holiday makers was his livelihood so the less said the better.

At St Luce the villagers were aroused by the unexpected arrival of the fishermen. They gathered round as Anna was lifted gently out of the boat and placed on the sand. The local doctor arrived after an urgent summons. He found a faint pulse and sent for blankets to cover her and rubbed her hands and feet to restore her circulation. After a while she began to cough and breathe normally. Her eyes opened and she saw the villagers gathered around her. Many of the women were praying and giving thanks for her recovery, and tears were running down the wrinkled cheeks of the old men. She wished she could thank them for their concern but she was too exhausted to speak. Nobody knew who she was until a man from the village, who worked in St Anne, and had returned home late, told them of the missing woman whose husband was awaiting news of her, at La Diamant. Harry was sent for, expressing great relief on hearing that his wife had been rescued.

On his way to St Luce to bring her back to the hotel he felt frustrated. All his plans had been foiled. It would seem that Anna was indestructible. He made his way through the crowd to where she lay on the sand. The men patted him on the back to show their support for him. His beautiful wife had been saved and they rejoiced with him. The two brothers who had rescued her stood apart from the others. Harry thanked them both and told them they would be rewarded in due course, after which he spoke to the doctor. The doctor assured him she would recover well but needed a few days rest before returning home. Anna was lifted into the car and made comfortable, as Harry paid the doctor for his services. They drove back to the hotel in silence, where Anna was received with open arms by the assembled staff and treated with great kindness. She was too tired to worry about Harry's silence during the journey back or the reason for it, and had kept her eyes closed for most of the time. Once in bed she slept soundly. Harry had taken another room for himself, ostensibly so she could sleep for as long as she liked and not be disturbed. He never intended to sleep with her again. He would leave her once they had returned to The Old Priory and fly to France, where he hoped some other plan might suggest itself to him. Leonie would treat it as a huge joke when he described his attempts to kill his wife, and would then rage at him for his incompetence. With Anna slowly recovering from her ordeal he had time on his hands. He drove into Fort-de-France and bought some brushes and watercolours to paint the dramatic scenery around La Diamant. The results were colourful landscapes; quite different from anything else he had painted. The guests at the hotel were impressed and he found a ready market for his work.

The teenage daughter of a wealthy French family staying at the hotel took more than a passing interest in Harry and his painting. She followed him round and sat with him as he worked. Harry could see he had made a conquest and encouraged her company. From the window of her suite Anna watched the holiday romance develop. The girl was a fool to get involved with him, just as she had been. He was unfaithful by nature, arrogant and egotistical, and seemed to have lost interest in her.

Anna began to wonder if he had ever loved her as she watched him kissing the French girl as if she was made of porcelain. He could be so charming when he liked, but it was all play acting. Her marriage had been one of convenience. She could see that now it was too late. He had made no effort to visit her or ask her how she felt. A cursory greeting each morning as he passed her door was all she could expect. Her marriage was over before it had begun. Anna was wretched. Something was wrong with Harry, she felt sure. There were two sides to his character, both so different it frightened her. He had a Jekyll and Hyde personality, and she no longer trusted him.

In the evenings Harry visited the Casino and took his young, adoring companion with him. Her parents raised no objections to their friendship. He was a wealthy English m'lord, and if he set up their daughter as his mistress it would give her a certain status in society. Harry's luck at the tables fluctuated. It mattered little to him if he lost large amounts of money as Anna had millions to spare.

He bought presents for his young companion whose tastes ranged from Creole jewellery and local dolls, to expensive clothes, and in return she gave him her nubile, passionate body to enjoy. For Harry his honeymoon had ended on a most satisfactory note. Once Anna felt strong enough to face the journey home, she made arrangements for the two brothers who had rescued her to receive the equivalent of a thousand pounds each, in euros. To their joy the nights fishing had brought them a fortune. Anna and Harry returned to Hewanorra airport and transferred to their flight to Heathrow. Anna had intended to collect the film of her wedding she had left to be developed. It was waiting for her to pick up at the airport but she left it behind. She wanted to forget her wedding to Harry and to start a new life without him.

On the flight home Harry mentioned that he would be flying to Paris the next day, on business. Anna simply nodded. She did not ask what business he had in Paris. She was just grateful he was leaving and she hoped he would be away for a very long time to come. In the meantime she had business to attend to herself, making sure that Harry could never inherit her wealth or spend her money to which she had so foolishly given him the right.

They were sitting in the first class section of the plane, keeping their distance from each other, as much as it was possible. Harry had taken a magazine from the pocket in front of him and was giving it his full attention. 'You never loved me, did you, Harry,' she said, in a low hard voice which she scarcely recognised as her own. 'It was all play acting, wasn't it—even the nights when you made love to me—I could have been anybody.' Tears welled up and she tried to control them.

'So why the marriage, which you wanted so badly?'

Harry took his time to answer. 'Work it out for yourself,' he said, grimly, as he got up and moved into an empty seat, three seats in front of her. The stewardess gave out the trays of food. Anna had no appetite. It looked like doll's house food in plastic containers. She picked up the small bottle of wine she had been given and threw it at Harry as he settled into his seat. She wished she could pour the contents of the tray over his head—hot coffee preferably. The bottle missed and bounced off the back of his seat and into the lap of an elderly man who awoke in some confusion, thinking it must have fallen from the luggage container above him. The stewardess apologised profusely and gave him an extra half bottle of wine to placate him and pretended to shut the already closed container. 'Are you feeling all right, Madam?' she asked Anna, knowing who had thrown the bottle, and wondering if this was another case of too much to drink in a rarefied atmosphere. 'Can I get you a sedative?'

'No, thank you,' said Anna, regretting her impulsive action once she saw that the recipient of her wrath was an elderly inoffensive gentleman. 'It was meant for my husband—but I would be most obliged if you could put a dose of poison in his coffee.'

The stewardess looked nonplussed and handed her a blanket and a pillow. 'Maybe a sleep would help,' she suggested. Anna stared out of the window at the blanket of clouds and made no reply.

Later, she saw her talking to Harry who was being his most charming self. They seemed to be getting on well together—

almost too well, she thought. Harry flirted outrageously with any pretty woman who crossed his path; no one was safe from his attentions.

Once on the connecting flight to Stanstead they were obliged to sit together as the plane was full.

'I want a divorce, Harry and the sooner the better. I don't expect you have any objections?'

Harry smiled. 'None at all my sweet, especially as violence appears to be one of your faults. You could have killed me with that bottle.'

'I'll see that you get as little as possible out of me now I know you're just a fortune hunter.'

Harry's eyes glittered, menacingly. The marriage had been consummated, willingly on her part, and a divorce would take time to arrange. He had plans for Anna while she was still his wife, which he hoped to put into effect as soon as possible. At Stanstead there was nobody waiting to collect them and they made the remainder of the journey by taxi, with Harry grumbling about Josh. 'He deserves to be sacked,' he complained, 'letting us down like that. I suppose you told him which flight we would be on?' Anna gave no answer. She had telephoned from Heathrow but nobody had taken the call so she had left a message. She had wondered herself what could have happened to Josh. He was always so reliable and she felt a pang of misery when he was missing. Something must have happened; he would never let her down. Everything had gone most horribly wrong and she longed to see his cheerful smiling face again. She had been such a fool—a stupid, blind fool—and she would never forgive herself for as long as she lived.

CHAPTER 15

The Old Priory seemed a lonely place after Harry had left—not that Anna had wanted him to stay. She heard the car drive away while she was still in bed, and rested back against the pillows with relief. He had slept the night in the old dressing room and had made no attempt to see her before he took his leave, making it clear that she meant nothing to him.

There was a gentle tap at the door and Mrs Hardy put her head round to see if she was awake.

'I've brought you your breakfast, madam,' she said. 'I thought you might want to stay in bed for a while after your flight.'

'Dear, Mrs Hardy, how thoughtful of you. Yes, the flight took some time as we had to change planes, but it's wonderful to be back.'

'It's been a lot quieter with nobody living in The Old Priory for a while, and Josh gone too.'

'Josh, gone—I don't understand. I wondered why he wasn't at the airport to meet us.'

'He left a letter for you, madam, hoping you would understand. I've put it on the tray. He has never taken a holiday in all the years he has worked here, the gardens meant so much to him. He used to say he would never be happy anywhere else. Of late Joe and I have found him really depressed. He needed a change.'

Anna looked intently at Mrs Hardy. Her words worried her. What if she had lost Josh too? She had been such a fool to believe Harry loved her. 'He is coming back isn't he, Mrs Hardy?'

'Well, we hope he will, but I can't say when. He's sure to come back one of these days. The Old Priory was his whole life.'

'One of these days?' Anna was alarmed. 'I don't understand. You make it sound as if he has gone for good. Where has he gone?'

'To New Zealand, madam. My sister and her husband emigrated some years ago, but Josh didn't want to go with them then. His late lordship offered him a position here when he left agricultural college, and he decided to stay here with us.'

'Josh told me something about that.'

'It was a pleasure to have Josh live here with us, as like my sister and her husband, we had no children of our own.'

'But I thought, Josh was—'

'My sister's child? We thought of him as that, but he was adopted when he was a few weeks old. He's always lived here since they emigrated.—Now don't forget your breakfast, madam. Your tea will get cold.'

Anna handed back the tray. She didn't feel like breakfast now. 'Just leave the tea, Mrs Hardy. It was so kind of you to think of me but since the flight I don't feel like food. They give you too much on the 'plane.'

'Well, I'll leave you to read your letter. I've arranged a light lunch for one o'clock, and I'm happy to bring it up on a tray if you wish to rest.'

'Oh, no; there's no need for that, really. I'll join you both in the kitchen now I'm on my own.'

Mrs Hardy hesitated in the doorway. 'Are you sure, madam? It hardly seems right now—'

'Now I'm Lady Charlesworth?' finished Anna. 'That makes no difference at all. Lord Harry has returned to France for an indefinite period and I'm not used to eating alone, so if that's all right with you ….'

Mrs Hardy beamed. It was good to have her back home, but strange for her husband to leave her alone so soon. Still, that was their business. Anna opened the letter and read it. He had addressed her as Anna and not Lady Charlesworth, stating simply that since her marriage he felt unable to take orders from her husband. Her marriage had placed him in an impossible situation and he hoped she would understand his leaving without notice. He wished her every happiness in her marriage and signed his full name. The letter was a formal resignation and nothing more. He made no mention of his future plans or if he ever intended to return to The Old Priory. Anna felt as if her heart had turned to stone. She had never felt so alone in her life before. She had thought of Josh as a friend on whom she could always rely, but after reading his letter she realised he had meant more to her than a good friend, and her relationship with Harry had wounded him deeply. She could only hope that the Hardys would keep in touch with him and that through them he would hear of her divorce, but by then it might be too late. Josh might find a wife in New Zealand. As she folded up the letter, tears spilled down her cheeks, and she wiped them away angrily. She had no one to blame but herself. She had been flattered by Harry's attentions and tricked into marriage, when Josh had truly cared for her. She showered and dressed in her old blue jeans and a simple shirt. She would never need all the grand clothes she had bought in Paris, and was unlikely to wear them again. From now on she would dress to suit herself. She unpacked the cases and put aside the items which needed washing and hung up her clothes. The expensive pink shift she had worn for her wedding she would take to a charity shop in Chelmsford. She hated the sight of it and would never wear it again. Perhaps someone, somewhere, would wear it for a happier occasion.

Having finished her task she took a walk through the gardens she had come to love, noticing the leaves which were beginning to fall from the horse chestnut trees which bordered the woodland area. The roses were over in the walled garden and she sat for a while on the stone seat and thought of the time she had cut some to take to the hospital for Amanda, her poor sister who was by then beyond smelling their heady scent. Her eyes filled with tears thinking of her, and she was reminded of her parents and their suffering. She must telephone them and tell them she was home, but she dreaded her mother's questions about her marriage and the honeymoon. The truth would be hard to explain—a marriage that had finished after a few weeks. They would never understand and would think she had not tried to make it work. She saw Joe Hardy raking up the leaves and walked across to speak to him.

'Morning madam. How was your holiday? Warmer than here I would imagine.'

'Much warmer, thank you, Joe. The Caribbean islands are beautiful .You would love all the exotic plants and their bright colours.'

Joe nodded. 'No doubt, madam. But I prefer the seasons here. They each have their own special beauty.'

Anna nodded in agreement, and decided to bring up the subject of staff. 'Now Josh has left, Joe, you will need more help. Can I leave it to you to make enquiries about employing two more gardeners? You will have to work with them so it would be best if you found some suitable candidates for me to consider. Josh knew so much about the estate he can hardly be replaced, I am aware of that, and I hope he will return one of these days, but until then—.'

Joe leaned on his rake. 'Josh will never be replaced here, madam. He put his heart and soul into this garden. He will be sorely missed.'

'I realise that, Joe, but until he decides whether or not to come back you will need help.' Joe nodded in agreement and returned to his raking as Anna walked on towards the lake. The tall bullrushes stood amongst the withered leaves of the long dead irises, like sentries, keeping watch over the placid water. A few mallard ducks were still in residence and some moorhens ran back amongst the rushes on their spindly legs as she approached. Anna stood there for some time thinking about Josh. His presence was everywhere in this garden making it into a veritable paradise for her.

When she had first come to The Old Priory she had taken little interest in the grounds, wanting only to discover all the treasures she had acquired with the house. The house had nothing to do with Josh; it had been Harry's old home and at the time that had made it more special for her, but things had changed and she would have been happy living in a gardener's cottage in the grounds, if Josh had been there. She longed to hide within the safety of his arms and feel the closeness of his body as he held her, and wondered if he missed her too, or if he had cut her completely out of his thoughts once she had married Harry.

She heard the dinner gong and made her way into the kitchen, where she was made welcome by the Hardys, who seemed pleased to have her with them. During the meal she told them about the islands she had visited and the beautiful flowers which grew wild there, especially on Martinique, called the Island of Flowers, where the sea was so clear the fish could be seen swimming amongst the coral. At no time did she mention her marriage or Lord Harry apart from telling them he had returned to France and she had no idea when he was returning. Mary Hardy noticed that she had removed her expensive engagement ring and there was no evidence of a wedding ring either. Perhaps, there had been a parting of the ways after the marriage. For Anna's sake she hoped that had been the case.

After lunch there were small gifts for each of them. They were surprised and touched that she had thought of them as she had been on her honeymoon—or so they had supposed. After lunch Joe took her to see the old groom's rooms above the stables which he felt might be used by an estate manager if a suitable candidate could be found. Anna looked around her. She had no idea that these rooms had once been used. From the outside the dusty, cobwebbed windows gave the appearance of store rooms, used to store tack and feed for the horses. Perhaps if she could have them made more habitable and furnish them comfortably Josh might be tempted to return. 'Maybe we should employ two people locally to help you, in the first instance, just in case Josh comes back. His position here should be kept open for him for a while, don't you agree? But in the meantime I'll have the rooms renovated in case we need to offer accommodation.'

'Just as you say, madam.'

Anna drove the Alfa out of the garage and set off to see her parents. It was a visit she was dreading, but they had to be told about Harry. 'It's marvellous. I love it.' Anna was enthusiastic when she saw the difference to the old Rows. 'But what a muddle. You're always welcome to come back to The Old Priory, Mum, until it's finished.'

'No thank you, dear. Your Dad enjoys helping the builders whenever he can. He couldn't be happier—it's given him something to do and made him feel useful—in fact there might be a possibility of him putting money in the firm later.'

Anna looked out of the kitchen window of the last house, where the family were now living, and could see her father busy laying the slabs for the patio. He gave her a cheery wave and a thumbs up sign.

'I can see he's in his element, Mum. I won't disturb him.'

'Come and sit down, love, while I put the kettle on. I want to hear all about the wedding and the honeymoon. You've brought the photos with you, I hope.'

Anna sighed. She hated to disappoint her mother or spoil this first visit since her arrival home.

'There are no photos, Mum. I left them behind. I just didn't want to look at them. Harry and I are separated. I'm on my own again and he's gone to France.'

Mollie sat down suddenly. 'What! Say that again. You must be joking.'

'No, Mum. It's not a joke. He never loved me; I know that now—he only wanted my money. I'm on my way right now to see the solicitor about making a will, so he can't inherit anything.'

Mollie was speechless for a moment. 'Your Dad always said he was wrong for you and for once he was right. He changed his mind towards the end, but he'll be sorry about that now.'

She opened the back door and shouted to her husband. 'Reg! Come and listen to this. Now, Reg! Not in half an hour's time.' Reg came in and washed his hands before sitting down gingerly on the edge of a chair. He was covered in cement dust, but for once his wife didn't seem to notice.

'Come and give your old Dad a kiss, Lady Charlesworth.' Anna pecked his dusty cheek dutifully, but frowned at the title.

'I hope I won't have that name much longer, Dad. Harry is a monster. You were right first time. He only wanted me for my money.'

Reg was shocked. 'Good thing you found that out before you married him, then.'

'Oh, but I did marry him. We had a wedding on the beach at St Lucia—all very romantic, but before the honeymoon was over he was already making up to a young French girl at the hotel and going off with her in the evenings. He soon lost interest in me and I hardly saw him at the end of the honeymoon. We came back together but he was off the next day, so that's that. The sooner we are divorced the better.' She had carefully avoided any mention of the attempts Harry had made to kill her. That would have been too much for her parents to take.

'Oh, Anna—that's terrible.' Her parents were full of sympathy for her. 'Drink your tea, dear, and then you get off to see the solicitor and sort things out. Finding that lottery ticket was a mixed blessing—your happiness has flown out of the window and here we are back where we came from, with Josie back at the comprehensive.'

'Oh, come on, Mum. There are a few compensations. It's not all bad.'

'Anna's right, Mollie,' said Reg. 'We're very happy to be back here, and the finished house will be wonderful, and as for Josie, she loves the comprehensive school and she has her beloved Pally, her horse, into the bargain.'

'There were some advantages, then,' said Anna, smiling at her mother, 'including a world tour, if I remember rightly.'

'Take no notice of your mother, dear. She loves a good grumble—you know her—makes her feel better.' Anna kissed them both fondly, leaving her presents for them all and left to see her solicitor and the Bank Manager.

'She looks troubled,' remarked Mollie. 'You'd have thought she would be feeling relieved having rid herself of that fortune seeking husband of hers.' Reg shook his head. He had never understood women despite having a house full of them, and he never would, however long he lived.

Anna explained her present situation to her solicitor who would need to contact Harry's solicitor before a divorce could be arranged. Anna hoped he would soon get in touch with her so the divorce could go ahead quickly. There was no reason why he should contest it once there was no hope of him inheriting her fortune, although she expected him to make difficulties so she would have to pay him off. The Bank Manager was glad to see her having discovered that all the money in her current account had been removed and that many of her cheques had bounced. It was no more than she had expected and she hastily had her account altered into her name only, and injected with money from her deposit account. Harry had spent a great deal of her money in a very short time. The solicitor was drawing up a will to exclude Harry, but she would need to divorce him quickly or he could contest it as her legal husband. Anna was a worried woman as she made her way home. It was early evening as she entered the house, and to her amazement Harry was waiting for her in the long sitting room smoking one of his reefers and drinking a glass of whisky as if he owned the place. 'Harry!' Anna was horrified to see him so soon. She had hoped he had gone for good, and here he was, back after a few hours.

'What a greeting to get from my dear wife!' said Harry, sarcastically. 'I'm not staying long, my dear, so there's nothing for you to get worried about. Just a bit of business we need to discuss.'

'I have nothing to discuss Harry, apart from a divorce. I've just come back from speaking to my Bank Manager to be told that you've bled my account dry. There'll be nothing left for you now. The account is in my name only.'

Harry laughed. 'What did you expect my darling? Took you long enough to discover that. And as for a divorce, that's exactly what I'm here to talk about. I've just had lunch in Paris with the sweetest little girl who has accepted my offer of marriage, so a divorce is on the cards, as fast as possible. I took your engagement ring with me by the way, so don't think you've lost it. It fits her finger perfectly.'

Anna was furious. 'How dare you, Harry! That ring was my property. All you've done is stolen it.'

'I doubt you wanted it, my dear, and actually I bought that with my own money for a change. I had thought of asking for a million pounds in exchange for a divorce, but taking into account the price of the ring, I'll let you off with a half.'

'A half of what?'

'A million, my sweet. You can easily spare half a million to get rid of me, and I've got a feeling you would be glad to be single again, now you have someone else in mind.'

'What do you mean? There's no-one else in my life or likely to be right now.'

'Not Josh?— Always had an eye for you, Anna, didn't he,' sneered Harry.

'Get out, Harry, get out!' Anna screamed, red in the face, thrusting a piece of paper at him.

'Here's my solicitor's name and address. He'll settle everything with you, but just get out of my life.'

Harry got up, stubbed out his cigarette on the table and straightened his tie. He smiled at her fury. It was obvious he had hit the nail on the head as far as Josh was concerned. 'I'm selling the motor cruiser by the way—that will give me a bit of pocket money now you've stopped my account. Thank you, my dear. No need to see me out.'

Anna picked up the nearest thing to hand which happened to be a Sevres vase and threw it at him. It missed and smashed against the door. Harry looked at the pieces and smiled. 'Tut,tut,' he said, mockingly, stepping over the pieces carefully. 'You don't know the value of fine pieces of china it would seem.' He let himself out and drove away. When Anna looked out of the window she saw he had taken the Alfa. He must have taken a taxi from Stanstead and no doubt intended to leave the car there to be collected.

Trembling with emotion Anna began to make her way upstairs to her room. Shocked by the raised voices and the few words she had overheard Mary Hardy put her head round the kitchen door. 'Is everything all right, madam? I couldn't help hearing all the noise.'

'You'll have to know sometime Mrs Hardy, so I might as well tell you now. Lord Harry wants a divorce so he won't be coming back here again. It's the only solution under the circumstances, but please keep it to yourself.'

'Oh, madam! What a tragedy. I'm so sorry '

'Please don't be. It's better this way.'

Having known Lord Harry for many years Mary Hardy had never trusted him and it had caused her much unease seeing Anna so infatuated with him. It was a relief to find she had seen through him and only wished it had happened sooner. 'Josh was in such a state while you were away, madam. He just couldn't stay, once you were married. Seeing you with Lord Harry was too much to bear. They never got on you know -there was animosity between them since childhood when Josh was expected to play with him during his school holidays.'

'So I believe— poor Josh— I'm truly sorry,' was all she managed to say.

CHAPTER 16

The relief of Harry's final departure was great, yet Anna was still trembling with anger as she went into her bedroom. She would never sleep there again in the bed where Harry had made love to her, and where she had believed all his lies and given him her body so willingly and passionately. She flung open the doors of her wardrobe and threw all her clothes onto the bed, and swept everything off the dressing table to add to the pile. She emptied all the drawers and then began on the bathroom. Anything that Harry had left behind she threw into the bin and then carried her own toiletries into the bathroom which had once belonged to the former Lady Charlesworth. This pretty, airy, room was on the other side of the house and overlooked the rose garden. Harry's late mother's room would be hers from now on, and the master bedroom could become a guest room. Gradually, Anna transferred all her things into drawers and cabinets and cupboards until she was satisfied with the result. Last of all she arranged her silver backed brushes and scent sprays onto the dressing table. The antique bow fronted table contained many tiny drawers in which to keep little knick knacks. They were too small for Anna's use but she opened them just the same. In one she found a hat pin and in another a button. She tried the long centre drawer but it appeared to be a false one with no means of opening it until she noticed a tiny wooden knob on either side amongst the delicate carving. First she pushed one knob and then the other but nothing happened until she pushed them both in together. Then the centre drawer opened to reveal a packet of letters. Anna took them out and turned them over in her hand. Each letter was in its original envelope and was addressed in the same hand to Lady Letitia Charlesworth, except for the last one, which was addressed and stuck down ready for posting. Anna pondered about reading someone else's correspondence, but curiosity got the better of her. Letitia Charlesworth was dead so no harm would be done by reading them and afterwards she would destroy them. Perhaps, they would throw some light on Harry's strange behaviour. It was getting late but she would never sleep until she had read them. She settled herself in an easy chair and switched on the table light. She began by reading the earliest letters first. These had been written twenty-seven years ago and had been sent to a clinic in Switzerland. The writer had signed himself with the letter J. and no address was written on the top of the letter. As she read them Anna realised they had been written by Letitia's lover and had been kept tucked away in the dressing table drawer for years.

Dearest Letty,
Thank God you have arrived safely and are in good health. My thoughts are with you day and night and I pray that your confinement will be swift and as painless as possible.
Once the child is born you must leave it with the good Sisters of Mercy to be adopted. It will be difficult for you, my darling, but it is the only way. You must be brave and not weaken in your resolve. Charlie would be devastated if he knew the truth and little Harry would be left motherless for the second time in his short life. On his return from South Africa, Charlie only need know you have visited the clinic for your health and feel much better for the mountain air. Keep me informed of events. I will visit you as soon as you return to The Old Priory. With all my love, my brave darling,
J.

The next letter which was a short note had an element of urgency about it.

Dearest Letty.
We must close this chapter in our lives but you will be my only love to the end of time.
J.

Anna's heart went out to poor Letitia Charlesworth. She had so obviously loved her baby and then to be left with Harry in his place. There had been another child later, Fleur, Harry's half sister, who according to Josh was an easy going girl with a love of horses. Her birth must have been a comfort after losing her son. To her surprise there were further letters, written presumably after Letitia had informed him of the birth of a son.

Dearest Letty,
I was delighted to hear you are recovering well after the birth of our son, but concerned about your growing attachment to the child. You cannot return home with him unless he is to be adopted. Under no circumstances can you bring him to The Old Priory, or leave him with me as you suggest. How would I explain his presence to my family and friends? It is an impossible idea. The sooner you return home without him the sooner you will recover from this trauma. Find him good loving parents before you leave. The nuns are used to such adoptions. Give your love to little Harry on your return. He may not be your child but he will need you more than ever since your absence. I will see you soon, my darling,
J.

The following letter was addressed to The Old Priory.

Dearest Letty,
I am coming next week so I can see you before Charlie returns from his hunting safari. You must be more cheerful when he arrives. I have heard of post-natal depression, but on no account must he know about the

child. You have little Harry to love and must think of him as your own, and later you may have another child. Bringing the child back to England with a nurse was foolhardy and dangerous, and against my wishes. Your heart has ruled your head, Letty. I would be in grave difficulties if it was ever known that I had given you a child. Charlie would throw you out without a penny to your name, and as the wife of my adjutant you would be ostracised by the women of the regiment. They are a formidable bunch and you would be made to suffer. Divorce is out of the question. I would lose my post and it would only make matters worse. I beg of you not to visit the orphanage where the child has been placed. It will be too obvious. The nurse has been well paid for her services. For both our sakes and our continuing love the child must be placed elsewhere and forgotten——

Anna wondered if the affair with J. had continued, but she decided to read no more. She had read enough. Suddenly she felt exhausted both mentally and physically and longed for her bed but sleep was a long time coming. She tossed and turned, thinking that Lady Letitia must have spent many an unhappy night in that bed thinking of her little son, but eventually sleep overcame her, troubled by strange dreams. She called out during the night and woke to find she was bathed in perspiration, before falling into an uneasy sleep which lasted until the morning. 'Poor woman -- poor woman,' muttered Anna, in her sleep.

'Wake up, madam. Are you unwell?' Anna opened her eyes to see the curtains had been drawn and Mrs Hardy was standing by her bed with a breakfast tray. 'I wondered where you were, madam. I thought for a minute you had gone away when I went into your room to see all your things had gone, and then I heard your voice.'

Anna yawned. She had to think for a minute to get her bearings. 'Sorry—I overslept. It took me some time to move all my things into here so I didn't get to bed until the early hours, and then I had a bad night.'

'If only you'd told me you felt like a change I would've been only too pleased to have helped you move your things. That's what I'm here for, madam.'

'You're too kind, Mrs Hardy—really you are—but I'm used to doing things for myself. Thanks for the breakfast, anyway. Time I got up.'

Mary Hardy smiled to herself as she made her way back to the kitchen. It was no wonder Anna wanted to move into Lady Letitia's pretty room. Time to make a change now Lord Harry had gone and she wished her well.

Anna set off to collect her mother for a days shopping in Chelmsford . Today she would change her Will while she was in Chelmsford so Harry would inherit nothing—that would be her first priority—then she could relax. A day in her mother's company choosing furniture for The Rows, and listening to her ceaseless chatter was what she needed right now. She would talk to her about her strange discovery of the letters. They were just another mystery connected to The Old Priory to intrigue her, but without any knowledge of the writer of the letters that would be an end to the matter. That evening, having left the warmth of her family circle to return to the empty Priory, Anna felt uneasy for no apparent reason. Much as she loved The Old Priory it needed people to bring the beautiful rooms to life. When her family had lived there with her it was perfect, but Harry had changed all that. He had spoilt everything for her and she hated him for it. She felt very alone and would have to do something about it. Moving was out of the question. The estate and the gardens that Josh had helped to create meant too much to her to leave. It was all she had left of Josh. She switched on the television and poured herself a drink, but it was hopeless. She just couldn't concentrate. She needed a plan for the future and somewhere more suitable to live. She had mentioned the stables to Joe as a flat for the new estate manager, but why not convert them into a house for herself. The Old Priory could be made into a home for retired people living in separate flats. Then she would never feel alone yet keep her independence. With this thought in mind she returned to Letitia's room and went to bed to read. As time passed she was aware of a soft click along the corridor but she took little notice of it as everything was quiet afterwards. Old houses had their own sounds which their owners got used to—they meant nothing, and were usually an expansion in the wooden joists, or the hot water system. Some old houses were known to be haunted but she had heard of nothing like that here. She read another page but still was unable to settle. A couple of sleeping pills should do the trick, she decided, and she got out of bed and went to fetch a glass of water. In the corridor outside her bedroom door there was a large pool of liquid leading to the front stairs. Anna recognised the smell immediately—petrol! She ran down the stairs in a panic and through the front door just as the flames flickered into the hallway. Another second and she would never have escaped down the front stairs. Terrified by now Anna ran across the lawn as a sheet of flame filled the house, burning the curtains at the front windows and cracking the glass. A car engine started up and a cream van drove quickly away down the drive. Anna could see a man at the wheel but no name on the side of the van. He was stooped over the wheel as if urging the vehicle to pick up speed, and his face was bent too low for her to take in his features. Terror gripped her. What if she had still been in bed, or had already taken the sleeping pills. She would be dead by now. An inferno was raging inside the stone walls.

The Old Priory was like a beacon against the night sky as she stumbled up the drive towards The Lodge. Joe and Mary Hardy ran towards her and led her the rest of the way to the safety of The Lodge. Anna was shaking with terror and her legs seemed to have turned into water.

'Come now, dear,' comforted Mary, as she sat Anna in a comfortable chair by the still warm range. 'Joe telephoned for the fire brigade as soon as we saw a glow from the back of The Priory. We were about to go to bed and I was pulling the curtains when I noticed that something was amiss, but we didn't expect this.' Mary Hardy was preparing a pot of tea as she spoke but Joe had already found the brandy and had poured a large amount into a mug and given it to Anna.

'Now, you drink this down. Better than tea at a time like this.' Anna took the mug in her shaking hands and gulped it down. She coughed as it stung her throat but it raised her spirits. 'What a fire!' exclaimed Joe, as he watched from the door, 'however could it have started?'

'Arson,' said Anna, bitterly. 'It was started deliberately. I've no doubt about it. I could smell the petrol when I went out onto the landing, and then I saw it on the floor, just before it was set alight.'

Joe was appalled. 'But whoever would do such a thing?'

'I've got a pretty good idea, haven't you?'

'Oh, surely not! We've never trusted Lord Harry, or the dirty games he got up to, but I can't imagine he would stoop so low as to burn you alive. Never! It must have been a matter of insurance, or vandalism.'

'Strange things happened while we were on honeymoon, but I could never prove that he was responsible. He's too clever by half.'

'And you such a lovely, sweet person.' Joe found it hard to believe that anyone would hurt Anna deliberately.

'She has a fortune. Don't you forget that.'

Joe was stunned. His wife could be right, but it wasn't their place to discuss the reason for the fire in front of Anna. It was a police matter and the sooner they were told about it the better. 'A cream van came tearing out of the drive just as I went to shut the gates. I'd never seen it before and I wondered what it was doing here. Could have been poachers, frightened off when the fire started and making a run for it, or a burglar, who thought the house was unoccupied.' At last the fire engines arrived but it was too late to save anything. The Old Priory was a mass of smouldering timbers and only the stone walls were left standing. Joe went to speak to the firemen and to look at the devastation. He could see the burnt and twisted remains of a petrol can and walked across the yard to the barn where he kept the large motor mower. The barn had escaped the fire and as he thought the can of petrol was nowhere to be seen. 'Got in with his own key, I suppose, the bugger,' thought Joe, grimly. 'He knew what he was doing, all right. I'm speaking to the police about this. Shooting's too good for him.'

Anna used the Hardy's telephone and spoke to her shocked family, and Mollie promised to bring some of her clothes for her to wear. While they were waiting for her parents to arrive, Mary Hardy prepared breakfast. It was still very early but it was strange to find how hungry they all felt. Anna found she couldn't stop talking there was so much to sort out. She wondered if it was the brandy affecting her. 'I must get in touch with the insurance company too. Some of the furniture was very valuable. Mind you if it's arson, I'm not sure what my position will be. I never want to live there again, anyway. The Old Priory brought me nothing but sadness, and without my family there I was very lonely. I had been thinking about having the stables converted into a house for myself and turning The Old Priory into flats for retired people, but I will never have it rebuilt now—never!'

'Don't you bother your head about such things right now, my dear. You're in a state of shock I should imagine,' said Mary, kindly.

'The stables weren't affected by the fire,' said Joe. '1 had a look when I walked across the yard, so you still might be able to have them converted.'

Anna looked up and smiled. 'That's good to hear. I didn't want to lose the estate. I've grown to love the gardens. They mean so much to me. I think that's just what I'll do.' And her heart lifted considerably at the thought.

Joe looked at his wife. All they needed now was for Josh to return, and perhaps once he had been told about the fire and the danger Anna had been in he would come back. As soon as Anna had left with her parents to return to the Rows, Joe suggested to his wife that she should lose no time in writing to her sister in New Zealand .

As the blaze flared up into the night sky Harry drove the van into a lay-by and got out to have a better look at the fire in the distance. The Old Priory had burnt far better than he had expected, lighting up the sky for miles around. There wasn't any hope of Anna surviving it. He had made sure of that by locking the door of the master bedroom where she would be sleeping. He had heard no sound as he had opened her door to remove the key and insert it into the outside lock, to lock her in. There was a sheer drop from the window to the ground and nobody could have got there fast enough to save her. Once he had heard of her death he would contact her solicitor at the address she had given him and have what was his by right. He had no interest in The Old Priory, or what was left of it, just the money the site would fetch. He had never liked living there: it reminded him too much or his hated dictatorial father. In the meantime he must leave this van outside the garage from where he had rented it; telephone for a taxi on his mobile and be driven to Folkestone to catch the train through to Paris in the morning. He had parked the Alfa in the long stay car park at Stanstead airport, and thrown the keys into a waste bin before catching a coach into London where he rented the van. When the Alfa was found it would look as if he had caught the last flight to Paris. Nobody would suspect him. It had all been so easy. He still had his keys to The Old Priory and he knew where Joe kept the petrol for the mower. Joe would be off duty by the time he returned late that night, and Anna would probably be in bed. If the lights were out downstairs and she was in her bedroom he only needed to lock her in and set fire to the place. Watching the blaze die down Harry congratulated himself as he started up the van and drove away. Once back in Paris his marriage to Chantelle could take place without the need for a divorce because his wife would be dead. It was most satisfactory—especially as he was in love for the first time in his life with the adored and only daughter of the richest industrialist in France and she loved him in return.

Leonie might be a problem once she realised after Anna's death he did not intend to make her into the next Lady Charlesworth. As his mistress she had had her day. He would let her keep the drugs that she still had in her possession, to use or to sell. That should suffice to keep her out of his life. He had never loved Leonie. He had only used her for his sexual fantasies and the animal passion for one another they had shared. She was hooked on heroin and her days as a top model were numbered.

He had introduced her to heroin before he had been forced by his father to seek help at the clinic. Now he was more careful and only supplied the hard stuff to his friends for payment. It gave him their dependence on him and the power he held over them. Sex with Chantelle was the only thing he needed now to turn him on, and she wanted him as much as he wanted her. His old way of life would have to come to an end.

Harry arrived at the garage where he had rented the car and left it outside. They would find it in the morning. He stood on the pavement and rang on his mobile for a taxi to take him to Folkestone, telling the driver in a phoney French accent that he was a French tourist who had been hitch hiking in England and needed to get to the Chunnel on time. The driver, hearing his accent, decided he was a bona fide passenger, despite the lateness of the hour, and took him to Folkestone, to be rewarded with a large tip. Harry boarded the next train and was soon on his way back to Paris with no one being any the wiser as to his absence.

CHAPTER 17

When Harry arrived back in Paris he put up at the Ritz for one night only. It was very expensive but he needed to make an impression on Chantelle's father, whom he had to ask formally for her hand in marriage, despite the ring having already been accepted. Monsieur Le Brun met him as arranged in the opulent surroundings of his office in the Rue Royale, having sent his own car and his chauffeur to collect him. There was no problem over Harry's acceptance into the family, once he had explained about his wife's recent death under such tragic circumstances. Chantelle's Papa would give his spoilt little daughter anything her heart desired and on this occasion it was to be Lord Harry Charlesworth. Harry came away from the interview with an invitation to stay as long as he liked at the Chateau in the Loire Valley, or to use the family apartment in the elegant residential region, north of the River Seine. The chauffeur took Harry back to the Ritz after a lengthy lunch with his future father-in-law, where he telephoned Chantelle with the good news, collected his overnight bag and took a taxi across Paris to Leonie's apartment.

Leonie was overjoyed to see him and made a great fuss, throwing her arms around him and almost devouring him with kisses. Harry eased himself away from her clutches and sat down on one of her uncomfortable antique chairs. He had a difficult task to accomplish: Leonie was not a reasonable woman—she had too passionate a nature for that.

'Get me a drink, darling, please, and get one for yourself.' Harry had intended to approach his forthcoming marriage immediately and then to make his escape, but Leonie made that impossible. He would have to wait for the right moment or, knowing her, she might let fly at him in anger.

'Is she dead, 'Arry? You've done what we planned, eh? Now you are rich—yes?'

'Yes, yes," said Harry, crossly. 'I have no wife now. She's dead.'

"Ow you do it, 'Arry? Tell me—tell me! I want to know it all.' Leonie stood behind his chair and stroked his hair. 'Clever, clever, 'Arry.'

Harry brushed her hand away and began to walk around the room in an agitated state. 'I don't want to discuss it, Leonie. What does it matter how it happened.'

'Ah—you loved her a little—yes?'

'No, I never loved her.'

'You did it for me—so we could live as we pleased—c'est vrais?'

'I did it for the money; just for the money—you know that.' Leonie sighed. Once she got him into bed he would soon forget whatever it was that was worrying him.

'When you telephone me, I arrange a party for you—lots of fun, lots of girls- you like that 'Arry? To-night—to cheer you up.'

Harry had not intended to stay but it would ease his news if it came after she had taken drugs and was drinking too much. Leonie could be lethal, and the thought of those long nails scratching his eyes out was something he would rather not think about. With the other party guests around he would have protection. Harry was a coward and never faced up to a situation alone if he could help it. 'O.K., O.K., pussycat. We'll have a party to cheer me up.'

Her smile was that of a satisfied feline who had just caught its prey. She had a perfect set of white teeth and thick sensuous lips and was aptly named the black panther on the cat walks of the fashion houses. 'We go to bed—yes?' asked Leonie, walking towards the bedroom door, and slipping off her wrap as she went. She stood stark naked with her statuesque black body leaning seductively towards him. Harry felt an uncontrollable desire for her. What did it matter, this last time.

'We go to bed,' he said, removing his clothes with some urgency. There was a dark and dangerous force within Leonie which he had never been able to resist. They were two of a kind and bad for each other. In future he must leave her alone or she would find some way to damage his relationship with Chantelle.

That evening, once the party had reached a degree of intimacy, but before the guests had coupled off, Leonie raised her glass of champagne. 'Silence,' she demanded, taking Harry's hand in hers. "Arry is back with us.' Some of the guests clapped. Harry felt uncomfortable. He knew he was popular because he supplied them with the drugs they craved but there was no need for Leonie to make such an obvious statement. 'I am to be his wife -the new Lady Charlesworth.'

Harry knocked the glass out of her hand. 'I never promised you that, Leonie -never.'

Leonie was taken aback. 'You promise me everything, 'Arry. Everything - once your wife is dead.'

'Not marriage, Leonie. My title goes with marriage, and I'm not marrying you.' The guests shifted uneasily—they were aware of Leonie's volatile temper, and the look of fury on her face made them step back. There was going to be a row and they would be better out of it.

'You lie! You lie,' she screamed, as she grabbed hold of him and began to tear at his hair.

'Get her off, for God's sake,' Harry entreated, as he struggled to extricate himself. Some of the men pulled her away, getting scratched in the process, as Harry made for the door and rushed into the street. He hailed a passing taxi and was dropped off at the Ritz. He had sufficient money to pay off the driver, and fortunately he had his mobile in his pocket. The doorman looked at him suspiciously as he looked as if he had been in a fight. Harry was afraid he might prevent him from entering so gave his name and said he was a resident. Nothing was said as Harry walked through the revolving doors and into the foyer. Once inside he telephoned Chantelle and told her he had been attacked at a party. He was waiting at the Ritz without money or bank cards. Then he had a sudden brainwave. 'I had no idea, my little darling, but it turned out to be a drugs party I had been taken to. The owner of the apartment is the supermodel, Leonie. Apparently she keeps drugs there and supplies them to her friends. I have met her casually at fashion shows in the past, but I can't say I know her well.'

There was a childish shriek of dismay from the other end of the line. 'Mon pauvre cheri. C'est terrible.'

'Yes, it is terrible. When she offered me drugs I refused to buy them and it was then that I was attacked. I think the Police should be told about her. Such people contaminate society.'

'I will tell Papa. He will report it. This woman should be arrested.'

'I beg of you, Chantelle, make sure my name is not mentioned. The press are only too glad to take a person's good name in vain, especially if one has a title. I was an innocent bystander at this party. Drugs are not my scene.'

'Of course not, cheri. I understand—we want no trouble, you and I. I will ask our chauffeur to come and take you to our apartment for to-night, and then to bring you to the chateau to-morrow.'

'Merci bien,Chantelle. I will be with you soon. Je t'adore.'

'I love you too, my Harry. See you soon, cheri.'

At the Le Brun's chateau, Harry found himself enjoying every luxury life could offer, plus the delights of his little fiancée's love. The family insisted that he considered it as his home now, and after his marriage to their precious child. The family apartment in Paris was his to use whenever he wanted, although Chantelle's father intended giving them an apartment of their own when they were married with, of course, the necessary staff to run it for her. As she would rarely be there was of no consequence—her life would revolve around skiing in Austria, racing in the season, holidaying on the family yacht and travelling round the world wherever and whenever she wished. Harry's future was assured; or so he thought. There was only one thing worrying him and that was the lack of news in the English papers of the tragic death of his wife. He scoured the newspapers every morning without success. It concerned him greatly as Chantelle was already making wedding plans and had placed a formal announcement of their engagement in the society columns of the Paris newspapers.

If Anna had survived the fire, which he very much doubted, he would have to arrange a quickie divorce through her solicitor. He could hardly marry Chantelle bigamously, but how could he explain his mistake in telling her family he had lost his wife in a tragic fire, if he still had a wife. Harry disliked difficulties and this was one of his own making. He contacted a French lawyer to see if he could discover from Anna's solicitor whether she was alive or dead, and if the former, to make arrangements for a rapid divorce. Despite living as he was, in paradise, he felt sometimes as if it would all disappear, like a dream. His lawyer eventually discovered that Anna was still alive and well. The news did nothing to restore Harry's peace of mind. He would not be inheriting a fortune as her husband and would only have his empty title to give to his new wife. Although his future father-in-law was a multi-millionaire he would not expect his son-in-law to live off him. Harry was a troubled man.

Meanwhile, Leonie had read about Harry's engagement to Chantelle Antoinette Le Brun in the Paris society columns of the papers. No wonder he no longer wanted to keep his promise to her. Chantelle Le Brun was the daughter of the richest man in France. Leonie had torn the paper into shreds and wished she had done the same to him when she had her hands on him. She was no longer considered the top model in the fashion world. She was often late arriving for fashion shoots, and when she appeared on the catwalks she hardly knew where she was going, and glided along in a daze. More and more fashion houses were dropping her as the word went round of her heroin addiction. Then one day, the police arrived at her apartment with a search warrant. They were looking for drugs, they told her, after a reliable tip-off. Leonie objected to the search of her property and needed to be restrained forcibly while the search took place. The drugs were soon found under the floorboards; a large haul of heroin and cocaine. This would be sufficient to keep her in prison for many years. Leonie screamed her innocence as she was taken away for questioning. "Arry Charlesworth hid them there,' she kept shouting. 'I was his mistress and he used me. Lord Charlesworth, you know, the man who is going to marry Chantelle Le Brun. He must have tipped you off.'

'It's no good you shouting, Mademoiselle. It will get you nowhere. That English lord might have been your lover, like many other eminent people no doubt, but that means nothing here. It could have been anyone of your lovers who told us about the drugs, but we know nothing about this Lord Charlesworth. He is an innocent party in this affair which you most certainly are not. You supplied drugs from this apartment, did you not? We have witnesses to prove it.'

'But only to my friends. 'Arry was the one who brought them here for me to keep.' Leonie might have been telling her accusers the truth but they preferred not to listen.

She possessed a large cache of drugs, wherever she had obtained them, and would doubtless receive a prison sentence. Because of the serious nature of her situation, Leonie was remanded in custody, awaiting trial. She knew that in some parts of the world the possession of over one hundred grammes of heroin meant the death sentence, and she had far more than that. She would be shown no mercy and expected to receive a long sentence in a bleak women's prison, unless perhaps she could do a deal with the police. She knew something terrible about Harry Charlesworth; something he had done years ago. He had confided in her when he was maudlin with drink and had needed to get it off his conscience. The police should be interested to know about this unsolved crime if only she could make them listen and take her seriously. If the opportunity came her way she would tell them all she knew and destroy him, as he had destroyed her.

CHAPTER 18

It had been a long time since Josh had seen his parents, and after six years he wondered if he would recognise his father when he walked out of the air terminal. The journey had seemed endless, sleeping and eating sitting in the same seat for hour after hour. He had thought of visiting New Zealand on many an occasion, but it would mean a long holiday to make the journey worthwhile and he never felt it would be fair to leave the estate for such a long time. Plants were like people and needed to be cared for by someone who knew them. It was too much for Joe to do on his own, but now he had left no doubt more staff would be employed. It had been a bitter disappointment to his parents when he had pulled out of their plan to emigrate to New Zealand when his father had accepted a position in the Parnell Rose Garden in Auckland being an authority on the growing of roses. It had been too good to turn down with a bungalow as part of the deal and an excellent salary. They had almost pulled out of the arrangement when Josh decided to stay behind and live with Joe and Mary at The Lodge, but Josh would have none of it. They had given him the best years of their lives and now must consider themselves. He was happiest working on The Old Priory estate he had known all his life, but he would keep in touch and come to see them. The promise had not been kept until now and he felt guilty about that. His arrival was sudden and unexpected. He had telephoned briefly to say he had obtained a single ticket on an otherwise full aircraft and would be arriving the next week. There was no reason for his visit, but it was time he came to see them. Perhaps he would stay and apply for permanent residence, he wasn't sure, but he had given in his resignation. His parents were puzzled, but overjoyed to know he was coming.

'Dad!' Josh picked up his case and walked across the tarmac to greet his father with an affectionate bear hug.

'How are you, son? Exhausted I reckon!'

Josh laughed. 'Never sat down for so long in my life before! How's Mum?'

'Oh, she's fine—busy cooking the fatted calf in your honour—can't wait to see you. Here's the car—hop in.'

'I could see the two harbours from the 'plane as we were coming in to land. What a sight!'

'Wait 'til I've shown you around, Josh. It's a wonderful place—plenty to do in Auckland and marvellous scenery everywhere. We love it—I'll take you up to Mount Eden on our way home. It's only a short distance from here and you can see the whole area.' They left the air terminal and set off through the city streets and were soon looking down from the heights of Mount Eden. Josh was amazed at the sight. The city below him spread out into a vast mass of coloured roofs, gardens and parks, spilling down to the small sandy bays of the sparkling Waitemata harbour. Cars, like dots were crossing over the Harbour Bridge as people came from the North Shore suburbs to work in the city, and boats bobbed on the blue waters of the harbour. 'We call it the City of Sails,' said Dick. 'It's an outdoor life here and a lot of people aim to own a boat, however small.'

'Do you have one, Dad? I can't see you as a sailor.'

Dick laughed. 'I'm a landlubber, son. Sick as a pig as soon as I step on a boat—I'm happiest when I'm with my roses -well, lets get home to see your mother, or she'll never forgive me if I keep you to myself.' On the way to the suburb where Dick and Eileen lived, Josh told his father his plans. He wanted to travel round the country to discover it for himself and not to look at it as if he was a tourist. He wanted to meet the people and get a feel of what New Zealand was all about. He could only stay for three months in the first instance but if he liked it well enough then he would apply to stay and look for a job.

'Look around you, Josh. Everywhere there are trees and gardens. We have warm summers and frostless winters so plants flourish. With your experience you would find a good job in next to no time.'

'I haven't made up my mind yet, Dad. It was a sudden decision to come and I need time to think.'

'Of course -we understand that. You do your own thing.' The car drew up outside a bright yellow bungalow with a garden full of colour. Eileen came running to the gate to welcome him, looking younger than when he had last seen her. She was overjoyed to see him again and Josh felt a lump forming in his throat. He hardly ever wrote to them, leaving his aunt to give them the news, and he felt as if he had let them down by not coming sooner. It must have been a terrible wrench for them to leave him behind. The times he had heard the story of how they had chosen him, a tiny baby in the orphanage in Chelmsford; the answer to all their prayers. Lady Letitia had been to court on their behalf to vouch for them as responsible people, and they had been allowed to keep him. He couldn't have had such good, loving parents if he had been their own flesh and blood. After the enormous meal Eileen had prepared in his honour they sat on the veranda and chatted. Eileen wanted to know why her handsome son had felt he wanted to leave The Old Priory estate but Josh was non-committal. Anna was in his every waking thought, and the distance they were apart made no difference to his love for her, but he could hardly tell that to his parents. 'Mary wrote to us about the deaths of Lord and Lady Charlesworth, and the sale of The Old Priory to pay off the death duties. A terrible accident apparently—we felt shocked. Lady Letitia was such a sweet person—it was a terrible way to die.'

Josh nodded, feeling sleepy after the large meal and the long flight. 'Didn't you get on with the new owner?' asked Dick, thinking that could have had something to do with Josh leaving.

'It was her husband I couldn't work for, not her.'

'Her husband! What did he have to do with it? She was the owner of The Old Priory wasn't she? Mary told us that Joe found her easy to get on with—not at all like his late lordship. He was forever interfering and complaining. Joe could never do anything right for him.'

'I know, Mum. I remember—he used to pick on everyone.'

'Old bastard, he was—an old bastard,' muttered Dick, puffing on his pipe. 'And that son of his was just as bad. Glad to see the back of him when The Old Priory was sold, I shouldn't wonder.'

Josh looked into the distance and listened to the drone of the bees amongst the flowers. His mother got up and went indoors to see to things, thinking that Josh needed time to rest and not to be bothered too much with a lot of conversation. Just having him home was enough for the present. If he wanted to tell them his reason for leaving he would, in his own time. 'The owner of The Old Priory married Harry—Lord Harry now he has inherited the title,' he said eventually. 'I couldn't stay and work for him - you can understand that Dad, can't you?'

Dick's mouth fell open with amazement. 'Well, that explains it—you two never got on, right from childhood—but I don't understand—'

'No, nor do I, Dad, so lets drop it shall we. I feel a bit odd to tell you the truth—jet lag I suppose.' Josh got up and stretched. 'A shower and my bed and I'll feel a different person tomorrow.'

Dick got up too and put an arm round his son's shoulders. 'You do that, my boy. If you feel up to it tomorrow I'll take you to see the Parnell Rose Gardens. It's a sight you'll never forget.' As promised Dick took Josh to see where he worked. It was an unforgettable experience; the sight and the heady scent from the mass of four thousand bushes. As they walked amongst the roses Dick pointed out hybrids which Josh had never seen before and showed him the new stock he had propagated after many years of experimenting. His father's knowledge amazed Josh and he listened to him with interest. Dick was in his element. After the hours spent in the gardens Dick showed him the restored Victorian houses in the nearby Parnell suburb, and then took him to the museum at the top of Domain hill to give him an introduction to the Maori culture before he set off on his travels. Josh was patient—Auckland was obviously an exciting city but he wanted to get away and lose himself in the wilderness, trekking through forests and climbing snow capped mountains, to release him from the heartache he was feeling. In time he hoped he could put his past behind him and start again. His welcome to Auckland had been warm and heartfelt and he had felt at home immediately. He had three months in which to make up his mind and he would stay if it turned out well.

At a downtown car rental office Josh found a car to suit his purposes and armed with maps and suggestions as to the best places to visit he set off the next day on his journey, promising to return before his three month stay had expired and spend some time with them both. He made for Rotorua where he could walk through the Whakarewarewa Forest along the walkways past pools of bubbling mud and geysers. The sulphurous smell and the steam rising from the cracks in the ground filled him with awe. This place was how the earth must have been at the beginning of time. It was a frightening place with its pools of bubbling mud and Josh was glad to move on to more pleasant pastures, where sheep grazed. Around the East Cape he drove along the rugged road and followed it into the mountains and narrow gorges where no tourists ventured. He walked along deserted beaches and was amazed at the beauty he found there. The deep blue of the sea, bordered by the pohutukawa trees which were just beginning to burst into red flowers. He never felt far from Anna although she was on the other side of the world. She was always in his thoughts and a part of the beauty surrounding him.

He travelled inland through the hills until he came to the Maori village of Te Reinga, beside a waterfall. Here he received a warm welcome and enjoyed a few days amongst friendly people who made no charge for his stay amongst them. Josh discovered it was the custom to offer a gift, but having only money, he left what he hoped was an appropriate amount and continued on his journey feeling refreshed after such hospitality. Eventually, he arrived at the tip of North Island and took the ferry across Cook Strait to South Island. Here, he hoped to find the peace of mind he was seeking amongst the isolation of the mountains and forests. The scenery was awe-inspiring. Josh had only once seen anything remotely like it when young, on a rare trip to Scotland with his parents, but this was even better. He drove from Christchurch to Mount Cook National Park and put up at the Youth Hostel. It was here that he met up with two girls who were trekking in the area. They were booked into a full day excursion in the park and Josh joined them. It was hard, tough hiking, past waterfalls and through forests to the glacier, and well worth it for the views. The girls were both strong and used to trekking, and took a liking to the strong, good looking Englishman with his ready smile and blue eyes. Gradually they discovered that his parents lived in Auckland and he had recently left his job on an estate in England. He was considering staying if the country suited him and he could get a suitable job. One of the girls had a father who worked in the famous Botanic Gardens in Christchurch.

'Did you see them while you were there?' she asked.

'I did—wonderful displays. I was very impressed.'

'Come and meet my Dad when we get back. He'd love to talk to you.'

A few more days in Mount Cook National Park and Josh set off for Queenstown. As the girls were hitch hiking he joined them. They were good company and he began to feel in holiday mood. They all booked for a seven hour expedition of white water rafting, which the girls had experienced before. The excitement as they shot over the rapids made Josh realise how much he was missing, and for a few hours he forgot his heartache. He left the two girls in Queenstown and made for Milford Sound to take a three day trek from Lake TeAnau, promising to collect them on the way back. Here, he passed towering mountains, waterfalls and forests, mirrored in the deep lakes, until he reached the road to Melford Sound, where the rock walls towered thousands of feet above him; the images of the snowy summits mirrored in the calm depths of the fiords. As he stood on one of the bridges and gazed up at Mount Tutoko, he felt very small and insignificant. If only he could show all this magnificence to Anna. With her beside him he would be the happiest man in the world, but right then that seemed an impossible dream. He made up his mind at that moment to find out how things were at The Old Priory from Joe and Mary, and if all was well with Anna he would stay here forever. He would pick up the two girls as promised and take them back to Christchurch, and meet Marti's father. She had made no secret of the fact that she fancied him, so there was a possibility that he might settle in Christchurch eventually. Marti was as unlike Anna as anyone could be. She was a good natured, stocky, muscular girl who thought of a man as a good mate rather than a lover. Josh was not adverse to female company, in fact he enjoyed it, but there would never be anyone but Anna in his heart. His trek over, he returned to Queenstown, picked up the two girls and drove them through sheep farming country and back to Mount Cook village. The next day they returned to Christchurch, where Marti insisted that he should spend a few days with her family. Josh declined at first but the welcome he received as a stranger from Marti's family made it impossible to refuse. He talked for hours to her father about the Botanic Gardens and his own work at The Old Priory estate and found they had a lot in common. The leafy parks and gardens and the easy pace of life in Christchurch appealed to Josh. Marti's father promised to look for a suitable position for him if he wanted to stay, but despite Marti's pleas to return Josh gave no promise to do so.

'Maybe—it depends on what news I have from England, but I'll keep in touch.' Marti's farewell hug and kiss left him in no doubt that he would be sadly missed. Josh sent a card to say when to expect him back in Auckland and took the long way back, ambling along the coast around Hawkes Bay and the Bay of Plenty before he arrived at Auckland. He felt refreshed and his old cheerful self again after his journey of discovery.

His mother met him at the door with a worried expression on her face. 'What's up, Mum? Dad's O.K. isn't he?'

'Nothing like that, son. It's a letter we had from my sister, Mary. There was a terrible fire one night and The Old Priory was burnt to the ground. Lord Harry's wife was in bed, but she got out just in time. Mary says they are worried for her—it was arson you see.'

Josh hid his face in his hands and groaned. 'Dear God; I shouldn't have left her. I was afraid she might be in danger—but what about Harry? Did he get out?'

'He wasn't there. She was alone. He had gone to France, where he has another woman, whom he intends to marry once they are divorced.'

'He never cared for her,' raged Josh. 'But she couldn't see it. He wormed his way into her affections for her money, and now this has happened -God knows what might.happen next.'

Eileen was saddened by his outburst. It was obvious now as to why he come to see them, and she knew that there was no hope of him staying, feeling as he did. 'You loved her, Josh—was that it?'

Josh nodded. 'Nothing I could do about it with Harry around—the swine.'

Eileen sighed. Her heart went out to him. 'Has she any feelings for you? Don't go and get hurt all over again, will you. There are plenty of fish in the sea on these shores. You'll soon get over it if you stop brooding.'

'I'm going back to her, Mum. I've got to find out how she feels about me. I can't make anything of my life until I know that—try to understand—I have to know.'

'Of course I understand.'

'I'd almost decided to stay as I had no job to go back to, but it will be different I feel sure now she's on her own. There was the possibility of a job in Christchurch but I can't do anything about that until I've seen Anna.'

Eileen was disappointed. 'Go and find out, Josh, and then come and see us again won't you, and don't leave it so long.'

Josh hugged her. 'It's a promise, Mum.' He picked up the 'phone and began the business of organising a reservation on the earliest flight back, as well as 'phoning Marti to say he would not be coming back to Christchurch for some time, if at all, due to unforeseen circumstances.

She wished him a good journey, said it had been fun knowing him and put down the 'phone.

'A woman, I suppose,' she said to herself. 'Some people have all the luck!'

CHAPTER 19

As the weeks passed and the rubble from The Old Priory was cleared away Anna put her mind to the alterations to be done to the stable block. The architect kept her interested with all his ideas for her future home, and work began almost immediately. The upstairs flat which had once been used for the groom was completely gutted to make three long beamed bedrooms of character, complete with en suite bathrooms. The end bedroom which overlooked the rose garden was to have a wide window, opening onto a balcony. It was the same view that Lady Letitia had enjoyed from her room in The Old Priory and Anna wanted to have this as the main bedroom. The stable block was a long building with stabling for twelve horses and a tack room at the end. With a bit of imagination the architect had planned a long low sitting room with a large outside patio, a study and a cloakroom. The tack room would be extended to make a modern kitchen, with a dining annex. Anna wanted her new home to be both practical and comfortable without the grandeur of The Old Priory. This would be her new home and have no association with Harry. There would be no memories here to keep her awake at night.

The stone front of The Old Priory, now a windowless ruin, would be left to be covered eventually with the ancient wisteria, parts of which had survived the worst of the fire. Joe had scraped away some of the bark to find life still there in the twisted branches, much to his satisfaction. It had been the pride of The Old Priory in the past when the pale purple clusters of flowers hung down in massive profusion in the early summer, softening the stone facade of the building. It might be some years before it returned to its former glory, but it was still alive. One day it would make a pleasing backdrop to the new water gardens Anna was planning with the help of a garden designer, to take the place of the area previously covered by The Old Priory. There would be waterfalls and fountains and a series of lakes for exotic fish, with small bridges linking up the lakes, and perhaps a Japanese garden. The whole idea intrigued her. She wanted to add some ideas of her own to the other gardens which had been created many years ago. When it was all finished she wanted to open it to the public, and possibly have a plant nursery. It was like a whole new beginning with the past left behind her. Sometimes, as she was busily working she thought she saw Josh in the distance, but it was never Josh, just one of the extra gardeners she had employed to help Joe, on a part time basis. It broke her heart to think that by her ill-fated marriage to Harry she had sent Josh away and she worked hard to try and forget her unhappiness.

Joe told her once that gardening was therapeutic and she believed him, but the pain in her heart never got any better. Her parents had been supportive and encouraged her to look to the future. The gardens and the estate gave her new hope. If only Josh would come back then everything would be perfect, but the weeks went by and Josh seemed to have settled down on the other side of the world. Autumn was coming to an end and it would soon be winter. There would be less to do in the garden and the extra help would no longer be needed.

One cold morning as Anna was pulling out dead clumps of leaves from the water iris round the lake, she saw what she thought was one of the gardeners speaking to Joe -a tall fair haired man whom she had often mistaken for Josh in the distance. Joe pointed her out to him, and the man walked towards her, and then, Anna realised that this time it really was Josh. She threw down her wet gloves and ran towards him to be folded in his open arms. 'Oh, Josh—I've missed you so much. I kept hoping you'd come back—I made a terrible mistake.' Josh kissed the top of her head and held her tight. He hadn't been sure what his welcome would be, but now there was no doubt. She loved him as he loved her.

'I couldn't tell you how much you meant to me, Anna—how could I? You were besotted with him—you wouldn't have listened. I was afraid for your safety, and rightly so it would seem.' Anna shivered and he led her to the lakeside seat where he could wrap his arms around her. They sat for a while, content in each other's company, with her head on his shoulder, as he kissed her.

'Please forgive me, Josh -I must have hurt you so much.'

'It's in the past, my love—time to think of the future. I'm here now. I thought of you so much – I couldn't get you out of my head. If Mary hadn't written to tell my mother about the fire I would never have come back.'

'Thank God you're here. Harry tried to kill me while we were away. I'm sure of it.'

Josh was horrified. 'Did you tell the police?'

'Not then I couldn't prove it—but I called the police after the arson attack. Harry had gone back to France the day before, so I don't know who set fire to The Old Priory—but he might have been behind it.'

'I'm never leaving you again, my darling—never.'

'Oh, Josh—I'm so sorry—I've treated you so badly—please forgive me.' Anna was becoming tearful. She had longed for this moment, and now he was here at last, holding her so close to him: her happiness was almost unbearable.

'Come on, sweetheart—it's so bloody cold here I'm turning into a block of ice—well, not quite every part of me, if you know what I mean.'

Anna began to laugh. 'I know exactly what you mean, you naughty boy!'

'Let's go to The Lodge—I want you all to myself.'

'But what about—?'

'Joe and Mary have gone to see a film—I heard the car driving off a while ago. Joe said they wouldn't be back until the evening, so we'll have The Lodge to ourselves.'

'Being diplomatic were they?'

'Something like that.—Come on, I've waited a long time for this.'

They ran across the lawn, hand in hand like children, longing to be together at last. Josh swept her into his arms and carried her into The Lodge and up the stairs to the spare room. The bed was unmade but neither of them noticed anything in the delight they found in each other's closeness.

Josh undressed her gently. He stroked the satin skin of her thighs and aroused her with the touch of his fingers between her legs until she parted them to receive him. As he lay on her she felt the strength in his muscular body and his desire to possess her. Suddenly, she reached a climax she had never known before, calling out in ecstasy, and wanting it to go on and on forever. As they lay together locked in each other's arms she fondled him until he was ready for her again. Anna had never known such happiness; with Harry lovemaking had been to suit him, and never for her pleasure. He had taught her different ways which often she had found objectionable, and in her ignorance she had complied with his wishes, thinking it was her fault not always to enjoy his love making. With Josh it was so different. He truly loved her and treated her with respect, waiting for her to come, so their pleasure was mutual. How she loved him. Her heart felt like bursting with joy as they made love over and over again until they were content just to lie in each others arms.

'Come back with me, Josh. We have a meal about seven and it's almost that now. We've been here for hours—do you realise that? It's time I tidied up the bed and we left.' They put on their clothes reluctantly, hugging and kissing as they did so, not wanting to lose physical contact with one another for a minute, but there was some urgency about leaving The Lodge before they were discovered upstairs.

Anna drove them back to the Rows where her family were gathered to welcome Josh back with a celebratory dinner. As soon as they walked through the door it was obvious they were deeply in love. Anna was smiling and found herself blushing as Josh put his arm round her; was it so obvious, she wondered, that they looked as if they had spent the afternoon making love? Mollie welcomed Josh, warmly. She was delighted to see them so happy together after all her daughter had gone through recently. Josh was well liked by everyone, with his happy, caring nature and his ready smile, bringing a twinkle into his merry blue eyes. He looked sunburned and fit after his trip to New

Zealand and his handsome features were wreathed in smiles as he looked into Anna's eyes.

'We knew you were back, Josh. Joe told us yesterday but as you were sleeping off the jet-lag we decided to let Anna find out for herself when she went to The Old Priory.'

Anna was furious. 'Dad! How could you!'

Mollie laughed. 'It was meant to be a big surprise.'

'And so it was,' said Josh, giving Anna a hug. After the meal, when Josh was entertaining them with stories of his holiday Anna asked her mother if Josh could stay with them. It would be an agony now to sleep without his arms around her.

'We haven't room, Anna, you know that. It wouldn't seem right with Josie here. He is always welcome here but not to sleep. It's best if he goes back to The Lodge until the stables are finished—then you can be together. As far as the village is concerned you are still married to Lord Harry, and the sooner that comes to an end the better. Try to see it my way, Anna. It could be difficult for us after what has happened.'

Anna sighed. She supposed she would have to wait until the stables were finished before they could live together, and hopefully that would be soon. That night Reg drove Josh back to The Lodge where the Hardys were sitting up waiting to hear all the news of their family abroad, and it was very late before they retired to bed. Once Reg and Josh had left, Mollie remembered to give Anna a letter that had arrived for her that morning. It was from Mr Appleby, her solicitor, requesting a meeting urgently. Thinking it would be about her divorce from Harry, she decided to go to his office first thing, before going to The Old Priory. Her divorce was all important now. She would leave a message for Josh in the morning to say she would be arriving later than usual. It would give him a chance to see what had been happening round the estate while he had been away. On arriving at Mr Appleby's office Anna was surprised to discover that Harry's lawyer had been making enquiries as to her well being, on Harry's instructions. 'How odd—why should Lord Harry care about my health?'

'The wording was to discover whether you were alive or dead, Lady Charlesworth, so the divorce, if necessary, could be completed quickly.'

Anna was instantly suspicious. 'Why should my husband ask such a question, Mr Appleby, unless he thought that I might be dead?'

'I considered that point myself.'

'The fire at The Old Priory was only mentioned in the local papers. It was of no interest to the general public as no lives were lost, so how could he possibly have known about it in France—unless of course—.'

Mr Appleby raised his bushy eyebrows. 'The thought had occurred to me and that's why I asked to see you rather urgently. I think perhaps you should take this letter to the police who investigated the cause of the fire. They might find it of interest.'

'I certainly will. I went to them before with my suspicions but of course they could prove nothing. Joe found the Alfa Lord Harry had parked in the long stay car park at Stanstead Airport and I drove it back with the spare keys. It looked as if it had been parked there before the fire, when he had travelled back to Paris. There was no evidence for the police to go on, and I don't think they were sufficiently interested to pursue the matter. They were looking for a cream coloured van and there must be hundreds of them about.'

Mr Appleby nodded. It was certainly very odd, but not a matter he felt he should remark on. It was a police matter. Anna took the letter to the police station and asked to see the detective inspector who had investigated the fire. He placed the letter in a file which Anna could see contained other papers.

'One moment, Lady Charlesworth.—if you would take a seat for a minute, perhaps you could tell me if you recognise these.' The inspector handed her a package. Inside were the photographs of her wedding. Anna looked through them in amazement—they really were very good. She looked so happy and carefree she could scarcely believe she had felt like that a short while ago. 'This is your wedding at St Lucia, I believe. And this is your husband, dressed in black with a black blazer?'

'Yes -but how did you come by them?'

'You left them behind I understand. The photographer who developed them for you left them at the airport for collection.'

Anna nodded. 'I didn't want to bring back any memories.'

The inspector coughed slightly. 'Forgive me for asking such a personal question, Lady Charlesworth, but was there any specific reason for that?'

'I thought my husband had tried to kill me while we were on honeymoon.'

'Ah. Maybe you would like to make a statement as to why you thought that. I will call my colleague, if you will excuse me. Perhaps you would like a cup of tea while you are waiting. This may take some time.' The inspector left and returned with his colleague and a police woman, carrying a cup of tea. He introduced them both and then prepared to take her statement.

'But I don't understand what my photos have to do with anything.'

'There is a murder enquiry on the island. The airport gave your photos to the police as everyone who was on the island that day is being interviewed, whatever their country of origin, to eliminate people from the enquiry. Tourists are of importance there and the authorities want this enquiry to be settled, as you can imagine, so I will begin by asking you about the day you were married before we go on to your suspicions regarding your husband. Firstly, do you recall a limbo dancer on the beach, the night of your wedding?'

'Yes I do. She was very good.'

'What did you do for the rest of the evening?'

'I danced to the music of the steel band with everyone else. Then I talked to another English couple who had been married the same day. Harry joined us; we had a drink with them and then went back to our room.'

'So Lord Charlesworth wasn't with you all the evening?'

'No. I suppose not. He doesn't care for that kind of dancing.'

'How long was he away?'

'I don't know that he was away. I just didn't see him. He could have been at the bar having a drink.'

'How long would you say, was it before he joined you and the other couple?'

'Perhaps about half an hour. I can't be sure exactly.'

'When you returned to your room was his behaviour towards you—normal?'

'I was asleep before he came to bed. I was very tired after all the dancing.'

'Thank you, Lady Charlesworth, for your co-operation. Now perhaps you can tell us why you thought your husband tried to kill you while you were on St Lucia'

Anna described her fright in the car, but the more she told them the more she wondered if it was true that the brakes had been faulty. Harry had returned the car and hired a better one. She only had his word for it that the brakes were faulty and she had believed him. But his behaviour on Martinique had made her wonder. She described her hours in the sea and being rescued by the fishermen and Harry's callous behaviour to her afterwards.

'What made you think it was deliberate?' asked the inspector.

'The tow rope had been almost cut through,' replied Anna. 'I pulled it towards me when I was left holding it.' Anna told them the name of the beach where they had rented the boat and then described the owner. He must have noticed that something was wrong when the boat was returned. Then she described Harry's sudden appearance after his lunch in Paris with his new girl friend, to demand a divorce, and the fire the next night.

'Had you refused to divorce him?' asked the inspector.

'Oh, no, just the opposite. I never wanted to see him again.'

'I understand that you won a considerable amount of money on the lottery?'

'Yes, I did—ten million pounds. Harry has been helping himself to a large amount of it since our wedding, but I've put a stop to that. His fiancée is from a rich French family. A girl he met while we were in Martinique.'

The inspectors looked at one another and the policewoman smiled. This Lord Harry Charlesworth was a fast worker, especially where money was concerned. 'As a matter of interest, how did Lord Charlesworth come into your life? I presume he has no money of his own, courting all these wealthy ladies.'

'His father disinherited him so I understand. All the property had to be sold to pay off debts and death duties. He had once lived at The Old Priory and he turned up one day to collect some of his easels. He was very charming and I'm afraid I was quite taken in by him. Unfortunately the divorce will take time, so legally I am still his wife.'

'And he can inherit your money as your husband. I think its time we looked at that letter your solicitor showed you.' Having read the contents the two detectives showed some concern and suggested to Anna that she had a plain clothes police escort until such time as her divorce was settled. Anna refused. She had Josh with her all day and at night she lived away from The Old Priory at the Rows, with her family. At last the interview was over and Anna left for home, wondering what Harry had to do with the death of a limbo dancer. It was highly unlikely that he had been anywhere else than on the beach with everyone else. He had seemed perfectly normal when he had come to talk to the other couple. She had no idea where he was now but no doubt the French police could find him. An English lord who has just become engaged to the daughter of the richest man in France would find it impossible to just disappear. He would soon be found and questioned as the police had just done to her. After Anna had left, the detective inspector in charge of the arson at The Old Priory, DI Johnson, felt considerable concern for her. He felt fairly sure after talking to Anna about her fears for her life, that Harry had caused the fire. The fact that the Alfa had been found at Stanstead airport meant nothing. It was time to check the passenger lists on the flights to Paris that day. He had certainly taken an early flight to have lunch with his new girlfriend and then returned later to surprise his wife, taking her car back to the airport, but had he boarded a plane at the same time? Somehow he doubted it.

'The clue to all of this is the cream coloured van seen at the place of the crime.' said the inspector, 'and we have to find it, and find it quickly. All the garages that hire out vehicles in the vicinity of Stanstead Airport must be visited and the staff questioned. If that doesn't yield any information we must ask the Crime Watch programme to assist us. In the meantime one of these photographs can be used to provide a good likeness of this man. Someone, somewhere must have seen him. The arson attack would appear to have been an attempt to murder his wife. This Lord Charlesworth is a dangerous man. He might have had nothing to do with the murder on St Lucia, but I'm inclined to believe his wife when she says he has tried to kill her before. We must see if there is anything known about Harry Charlesworth. Does he have a family we can approach to discover more about him? Perhaps Lady Charlesworth can tell us where to contact his relations, or his friends—that is if she stayed with him long enough to find out if he had any!'

'Someone could have told him about the fire, I suppose, although I doubt it after what we've just heard. It sounds as if we might be dealing with a psychopath. Lady Charlesworth is a fortunate woman, by the sound of it.' Finding someone who had seen Harry afterwards proved to be more difficult, until his likeness was shown on television, when the taxi driver who had driven him to Folkestone contacted the police. He remembered it had been early in the morning when he had picked up his fare, as he was on his way home at the time, and even better, he remembered where he had picked him up—outside a garage on the outskirts of Epping. The cream van was found at the same garage, but there were no fingerprints. It had been thoroughly cleaned before being hired out again. However, the garage attendant recognised the man in the photograph; or thought he did. When he looked into the book to see the name of the person who had rented it, he saw the name, HC Worth, and an address in Somerset which proved to be fictitious. The van had been paid for in cash, for one days hire, and left on the garage forecourt during the night. This was all the evidence the police needed to bring Harry in for questioning about the attempted murder of his wife. But Harry was somewhere in France and the co-operation of the French police would be required to find, and question him, so it was agreed to wait and see if there was any further feedback from the television programme while they looked into the murder on St Lucia -a decision they were later to regret. That evening the family at the Rows gathered round the television to watch the Crime Watch programme. Josh was with them, and decided afterwards that Anna was never to travel anywhere without him. She objected to this curtailing of her freedom, but Josh was adamant. In future he would collect her every morning and take her back to The Old Priory, or anywhere else she wanted to go, and every evening he would return her safely back home.

'You'll be sick of the sight of me before this is all over—but I'm not losing you ever again,' said Josh, putting his arm round her.

Anna looked up at him, fondly. 'Never?' she asked.

'Not in a million years,' said Josh, with feeling.

CHAPTER 20

A week after Harry's likeness had been shown on the television a woman rang the given number and asked to speak to the detective in charge of the case. DI Johnson took the call. The woman gave her name as Fleur Flambard, the wife of the MP Hugh Flambard, explaining that she was Harry's half-sister. The inspector wasted no time in going to see her, for Fleur would know him better than anyone. Fleur opened the door to him, holding her chubby daughter in her arms.

'Forgive me, inspector, but I'm usually in a muddle at this time in the morning. Babies have a life of their own and we revolve around them. Please go into the sitting room and I'll make you a cup of coffee when I've put Charlotte in her cot.' The inspector made himself comfortable and looked around him. It was a homely room with no pretensions of grandeur and Fleur appeared to be a sensible motherly young woman. Not at all the person he had expected to meet, brought up in a world of privilege, and she appeared to be looking after her baby herself.

'I expect you are wondering why I got in touch with you, inspector, as I can throw no light onto my brother's whereabouts. It was seeing his face on the television that made me feel that I ought to speak about something that has worried me for some time.'

'Carry on. I was hoping to find someone who knew him well.'

'Well—I understand that you wish to contact him about a fire at The Old Priory.'

'That's correct. By great good fortune, Lady Charlesworth got out in time, but we are afraid that it might have been a deliberate attempt to kill her.'

'That's what I wanted to talk to you about. You see I've always had my doubts about my parent's death. They died in a car accident, near our holiday home in Brittany. Nobody else was involved in the accident, or witnessed it. My father was a careful driver and never drank beforehand. He had been an army officer and did everything by the book. His car was kept in good condition—he would never have had it any other way. It had just been delivered back from the garage after a check up so the car should have been in perfect order. When it crashed into a tree at the bottom of a steep hill near to our house, it caught fire and was burnt out, so there was no evidence that could prove that the car had been tampered with, before my parents set out.'

'What did the French police have to say about the accident?'

'What could they say? They thought my father might have had a stroke and lost control of the wheel, but I don't think so. I had left them only a few hours before it happened to return to England, and my father was his usual self.'

'So you thought someone might have tampered with the car?'

'Yes.'

'Did you mention this at the time?'

'Of course, but it was impossible to prove.'

'So, what is different now? Nothing has changed, has it?'

'It was hearing about the fire at The Old Priory. It was the sort of terrible thing Harry might think of doing. He always had to have everything he wanted, and if he wasn't given it he made sure he got it, by fair means or foul—mostly the latter. He has no feelings for anyone but himself. I've always thought that Harry had our parents killed, and I want the case reopened. I owe it to my parents. They suffered from his behaviour all their lives and now they are dead they should be allowed to rest in peace.'

The inspector was thoughtful. Most families had their problems, often caused by greed or jealousy, yet Fleur Flambard was not acting out of such motives, she simply wanted justice for her parents. He could understand that. The baby was getting fretful and Fleur left the room to pick her up and comfort her, returning with the child over her shoulder.' Tell me about your brother and his relationship with your parents.'

'I find it difficult to talk about Harry. I learnt to keep my distance from an early age as he was spiteful towards me. My father's first wife died when Harry was born. I was the child of his second marriage, which was never a happy one. I suppose my father married my mother so Harry would have a step-mother. She did her best for Harry but he was a wilful, devious child and my father used to punish him cruelly. I don't think he ever forgave Harry for being the cause of her death in childbirth. He could never come to terms with losing her, and that was probably at the bottom of Harry's bad behaviour. He just never felt wanted—a scapegoat for his mother's death, but that's just my opinion of course, I could be completely wrong.'

'What was he like when he was a teenager? A problem, I expect.'

Fleur smiled. 'He was expelled from Eton for smoking cannabis, and his friends were undesirable people—young men from wealthy homes who were drug addicts and gamblers. As long as there was big money involved my brother was interested, and there was a lot of money to be made from drug running. He became ill and our father paid for him to go to a drug rehabilitation clinic, hut he left before his treatment was finished. He came back to the house in Brittany to ask my father to pay off his enormous debts to his Newmarket trainer, but he refused. It was just after that when they had their fatal crash. It's too much of a coincidence in my opinion.'

'And where was your brother when it happened?'

'He'd been away skiing for a week. I'm sure he paid someone to do it—it's a feeling I have. He did it for the money. I'm sure of it.'

'Feelings can be unreliable,' said the inspector, 'but I'll do what I can.'

'He's quite capable of earning his own living. He trained at the Slade, the school of art, and is a good portrait painter but prefers the easy way out. That's Harry for you.'

'He married a rich woman. Did you know?'

'Yes, so we heard. We were invited to their engagement party at The Old Priory, but we didn't go. Harry's friends were probably there so it would have turned into a high society rave up—I wonder if his wife shared his tastes?'

'She seemed a most charming young woman when I met her. As a matter of fact she is in the middle of divorcing your brother.'

'The best thing she could do, in my opinion.'

The baby was getting restless and it became obvious to the inspector that Fleur had no more of interest to tell him, so he took his leave. The French police would never reopen a case unless new evidence came to the fore, and where could that be found after all this time had elapsed. The matter of Harry obtaining and supplying large quantities of drugs interested him far more. His wife hadn't mentioned it and probably it was something he kept from her, as well as his murky past. On his return to the office there was a fax awaiting him. The French police had a woman in custody, awaiting trial for the possession of a large quantity of drugs. She had given evidence about a crime committed by a Lord Harry Charlesworth of The Old Priory near Saffron Walden. They would like to have a meeting concerning this man if someone from the police could meet them in Paris at a suggested commissariat.

DI Johnson set off for Paris the next day and Leonie was brought to meet him at the arranged rendezvous, under police guard. As she walked into the room, all eyes turned to watch her, admiring her dusky beauty and her perfect figure. She sat gracefully on the hard chair offered to her, and crossed her long elegant legs. She had lost none of her poise or her power to overawe an audience since she had been confined to a woman's prison, awaiting trial. Bail had not been granted to her due to the seriousness of her offence, but she hoped after this interview her position would be reviewed. 'I understand that you knew Lord Harry Charlesworth well,' began the inspector.

'Yes, very well. I was his mistress for the last four years.'

'He sold and supplied drugs, I believe.'

'Yes. He kept them at my apartment, under the floorboards. People were invited to his parties for that purpose. He sold drugs to them, sometimes in large quantities, and sometimes he gave them pills, to get the party going. I don't know where he got them from, perhaps from his friend Simon. He had a yacht and used it for drug running. I just kept them for him, and arranged the parties.'

'I see, and you used drugs yourself presumably?'

'Of course I did. 'Arry liked to see me join in the fun.' She smiled knowingly.

DI Johnson looked at her intently. Her glittering black eyes were sunk deep into their sockets. She must have been using heroin for some time, he thought. She was still a magnificent specimen of womanhood, but she would age quickly, and that would be worse than death to a person like her. 'No more Harry, and no more of his kind of fun,' remarked the inspector, quietly.

'No, no more' Arry,' repeated Leonie, bitterly. 'He promised to marry me when his wife was dead, but he not keep his promise.'

'His wife is still alive, Mademoiselle.'

'Alive! I don't believe it; he is going to marry someone else. I read it in the paper. She is the daughter of Jacques LeBrun.' Leonie's face was a mask of hatred.

'What made you think that his wife was dead, Mademoiselle?'

'Because 'Arry told me so, himself.'

'Then he was wrong. Perhaps he wanted her to die, but she is very much alive. Do you know anything about a fire at The Old Priory -Lord Charlesworth's home?'

Leonie laughed. 'I know of no fire, but I know he meant to kill her once they were married. We talked about it often.'

'What else did you talk about?'

Leonie shrugged. 'Oh, what we would do when he had all her money.'

'And what did you intend to do?'

'What does it matter now he has gone and left me here while he is still free to enjoy himself.'

'Not for much longer, perhaps, if you can tell me what you told the French police.

I need to know, Mademoiselle, so I can question him. If what you say is true, he will be brought to court.'

'Arry is a clever man. You will not catch him out however much you question him.'

'With your help, Mademoiselle, we will. Do you want him to stay free to marry his new girlfriend, and enjoy all that life has to offer, while you are locked up for years?'

Leonie's face grew ugly with rage and frustration. 'He told me he had arranged to have his parents killed, in an accident.' There was a long silence in the room, and all eyes were on Leonie.

'And yet you still remained his mistress—didn't you believe him?'

Leonie made no reply to that. 'He paid a man to cut the brakes of their car, so he could inherit the estate. He did not kill them himself. Someone else did it.'

'Who?'

'The mechanic who worked at the garage and looked after their car did it. 'Arry called him Bernard.'

'No other name?'

'I know of none. Afterwards this man blackmailed 'Arry. Every month he wanted more and more money to keep quiet, until 'Arry had a job to find so much. There was no money for 'Arry when his father died, so he had to find some other way.'

'I see—did you by any chance meet the present Lady Charlesworth?'

'I came to The Old Priory for a few hours to their engagement party. I wanted to see her for myself. 'Arry did not love her, so I did not mind after I had seen her.'

'Did not mind what?' asked the inspector.

''Arry marrying her, of course—she would not live long—'Arry promised me.'

Detective Inspector Johnson found it difficult to look this evil woman in the eye after this terrible admission. 'Thank you, Mademoiselle. You have been a great help to our enquiry.'

Leonie stood up to leave. 'I hope this will mean I will receive a shorter sentence.'

'That has nothing to do with me, Mademoiselle.' After Leonie had left, Detective Inspector Johnson and his French counterpart discussed the case. It would appear that Lord Charlesworth was guilty of being an accessory to murder, but proof was needed. 'There is no one more lethal than a woman scorned,' remarked the inspector, as they set off to find the garage in Brittany where the car had been serviced. After finding the holiday home which had originally belonged to the Charlesworth family, it did not take long, with the help of the local police, to track down the local garage, which was still owned by the same man. They asked to speak to a mechanic named Bernard, who had worked there at the time of the accident.

'Ah you mean Bernard Le Valet,' said the garage owner. 'He came into some money and bought his own garage in town.' Once Le Valet had been tracked down, he was taken into custody and interrogated about the Charlesworths' fatal accident. At first he denied doing anything to the car, but on hearing the name of Harry Charlesworth he broke down and told the truth. He thought that Harry must have already confessed to paying him a large sum of money to tamper with the brakes of his fathers' car, and had told the police that he had been blackmailing him ever since. As Le Valet was taken into custody, Detective Inspector Johnson spoke to the French detective on the case. 'I think we have all we need to know to pick up Lord Harry Charlesworth, and bring him back to England to face charges of attempting to murder his wife. Whether charged or not, he can be returned to France to face the other matter of his involvement in the death of his parents. I doubt he will be considered as a suitable husband for his new bride, after this'

The French police were sent to the chateau to arrest Harry, but they were a day too late. Harry had received his decree nisi but before it became absolute he had a little matter to attend to in England. Chantelle could go ahead with the final preparations for their grand wedding next month. He would be back long before that.

CHAPTER 21

Chantelle looked out of a high turret window in the chateau and watched as the workmen erected the arbour, under which she would be married to Harry. She wanted it to be placed exactly where she wanted it. She had decided to have it covered in silk flowers on the morning of the wedding—mostly lilies and roses, to match the flower arrangements in the grand salon of the chateau where the reception was to be held. As the weather might not be clement, a waterproof covering, swathed in pleated cream silk was being fixed above the arbour and a canopy, similarly decorated in silk, covered the gold chairs where the guests would sit for the ceremony. This canopy would extend the length of the red carpet leading up the steps to the front entrance of the chateau. Silk flowers would abound, both inside and out, turning the event into a fairyland. At heart Chantelle was still a child: a sexually promiscuous child, but a child nevertheless. It made her attractive to men of a certain persuasion, who were happy to spoil her in the same way as her Papa. Harry was different, and for the first time in her short life she had fallen in love.

The most famous chefs in Paris were preparing the food for the reception and crates of the most expensive champagne had already arrived. Chantelle sighed with pleasure. Her head had been in a whirl these last few weeks, with the fitting of her magnificent wedding dress, designed by Versace, and trying out the style of hair which would best suit the diamond family tiara. She intended to take everyone's breath away as she walked down the red carpet on her Papa's arm, to marry her beloved Harry. Her step-Mama, Marie, her Papa's third wife, had enjoyed all the preparations almost as much as she had done. Marie was only a few years older than Chantelle, and was quite jealous of all the fuss. She had been Jacque LeBrun's mistress and had him wound around her little finger at present. He had divorced his second wife in her favour, which had not pleased Chantelle, who felt that Marie had displaced her as Papa's little girl. Hopefully she would not last long as her Papa had a roving eye for the ladies. She had watched Marie flirting with Harry, and although she was given to flirting with unavailable men herself, Harry was very special and Marie would find herself in trouble if she upset their relationship. Papa had always put his little girl first, and no one would ever take her place in his affections. Chantelle's mother had run away with a Spanish waiter when she was a few months old and her Papa had coped with the humiliation he had felt at that time by spoiling his baby daughter. He would never go through that again and made sure there would never be any other children—she would be his one and only child.

Harry had taught her how to make love in ways she had not discovered, although she had been sexually active since her early teens. She found his love making exciting and satisfying and better than anything she had ever experienced before. She loved Harry and she was sure he loved her and she wanted it to last forever. Jacques LeBrun, realising that his daughter was a nymphomaniac like her mother, was only too pleased to see her married to a man who could satisfy her physically, and whom she obviously loved. Nothing could be better, and he welcomed Harry wholeheartedly. His yacht was placed at their disposal for the honeymoon, and they could travel wherever the fancy took them.

When an official looking letter arrived for Harry a few days ago, he had insisted on leaving for England immediately, and despite all Chantelle's pleas for him to stay, he had left. All he would tell her was that he had urgent business to attend to before they were married, and that the business concerned his estate. Chantelle knew nothing of his estate in England, but presumed, being an English lord he must either own a castle or a very large country house where one day she would preside as the lady of the manor. The day after he had left, two respectful French policemen arrived, who had business with Harry. Chantelle was unworried, thinking that their visit must be connected to the attack on Harry at the drugs party he had been taken to, without realising the reason for the party. Her Papa had dealt with the matter, and the woman who had supplied the drugs, the famous model Leonie, had been taken into custody. She had asked the policemen the reason for their visit, but they had explained it was a private matter, and nothing for her to be concerned about. She told them he had left for England the day beforehand, on personal business, but he would be back shortly as they were to be married in a few weeks time. The policemen thanked her politely and took their leave, but not before noticing the workmen busy in front of the chateau, setting up an ornamental arbour with an elaborate canopy. It looked as if Lord Charlesworth might be back in time for his marriage to his wealthy little fiancée, and if so, then they would be back too—possibly masquerading as wedding guests, so there was no chance of him taking flight.

Detective Inspector Johnson however, on hearing that Harry had already left for England returned back to base in haste and alerted the police force to be on the look out for him. A watch was to be kept at all the airports and the ferry terminals, and the police were to be very vigilant in the Chelmsford area. He knew only too well what Harry's personal business would mean. Before Anna's decree absolute was granted she was still his wife and Harry's only hope of inheriting a fortune. It was vital to apprehend him immediately. His wedding to Chantelle LeBrun was in three weeks time and that did not leave them much time to prevent yet another murder.

Before the watch on all the ports and ferry terminals had been organised, Harry had slipped into England under an assumed name and was already in London, staying in a cheap boarding house where nobody took any notice of him. Normally, he would have stayed at a comfortable hotel and spent his time in fashionable bars and taking the opportunity to buy some new clothes, but this stay would be somewhat different. His room was the size of a cupboard, the bed was uncomfortable and the bathroom was shared. Harry had never experienced such a way of life before, and as soon as possible he intended to leave.

Tourists of all nationalities came and went, staying for short periods, and Harry avoided conversations with any of them if they passed on the stairs. He bought his meals at pavement cafes and kiosks, and ate them sitting on benches, with an assortment of companions. He disliked the greasy food after the carefully prepared French cuisine which he had recently enjoyed, but it would all be worth it in the end. Soon he would be surrounded by luxury for the rest of his life, so he must endure a few weeks of deprivation to achieve his goal.

At night he lay on the uncomfortable mattress in his miserable room and thought of a plan to abduct Anna. His idea was to demand an enormous ransom for her return, and then to slip back to Paris, but if this didn't work he must kill her while she was still his wife, and leave clues as to her whereabouts, so she was found before the decree absolute was granted. His divorce, although a vital necessity before his marriage, would bring him no money, and Harry desperately needed money. In fact, he could remember no time in his life when he wasn't desperate for cash, but this was different. Without a large income he could never afford to keep Chantelle in the way to which she had been accustomed, so one way or another, Anna must provide it. He still had some of the money he had milked from her account during the honeymoon, but it wouldn't keep him going for long.

After some deliberation on the matter he decided to make another attempt on her life, and if unsuccessful, like the others, he would abduct her. The abduction might be foiled by the police, as often happened in such cases when the ransom was left for the kidnapper, and he could possibly be apprehended. That would mean an end to everything. Harry, as usual, was nervous about having to face up to the consequences of his actions. He needed a disguise and that must be his first priority, and then he must buy an inconspicuous car. He had hired the van, and had anyone seen it at The Old Priory before the fire, it might have been traced back to him, although he very much doubted it. He would have had the police on his trail before now, but as the fire did not put an end to his wife, it was just a case of arson and not murder. This time he would be more careful.

During his daily walks around the back streets of Soho, he had come across a joke shop. He rummaged amongst the piles of masks and found a soft rubber mask of an old man. That would do nicely. Harry tried it on and was surprised at the natural appearance of the horrible thing. Then he found a grey wig. Together they completely transformed him. Harry bought them, wondering if this shop provided disguises for criminals. It was certainly seedy enough. Then he found an Oxfam shop. The very idea of buying clothes to wear from such a place amused him, and he enjoyed looking along the racks of coats and trying them on. Eventually he found a well-worn grey mac, and on a shelf, a green cap. His own mother would never have recognised him, he thought, grimly. Back in his room he tried them all on and was pleased with the result. Now he must get used to wearing them, but not the mask. That was for wearing when he approached Anna. Now he was ready to find a car. Wearing his wig, coat and cap, he packed up his few belongings, paid his bill and took the underground from Bakers Street to Kilburn. After walking for a while he found a small garage offering second hand cars for sale and decided upon a fawn coloured Ford. He stooped slightly while speaking to the man on the forecourt, and lowered his voice, hoping to sound more like a man in his late fifties, than one of twenty-nine. He offered the asking price, without a trial drive which surprised the garage employee who was used to people haggling after careful examination of the vehicle. Harry wanted to make as little contact as possible. He filled the car with petrol and set off on his way out of London towards Saffron Walden.

He by-passed the town and drove, in a round about way to The Old Priory, where he parked some distance up the road. He got out of the car and walked slowly, stooping slightly as if he had a limp, and walked up to The Old Priory gates. As he passed the entrance he could see the gaunt remains of the house, and wondered how Anna had survived the fire. He stopped further along the old stone wall to watch a car coming out of the entrance. It was his Alfa, with Josh driving. Anna sat beside him as they sped up the road towards the outskirts of Chelmsford.

Harry wondered where they were going. It was late afternoon and time for people to be returning home from work. Obviously, Anna no longer lived here; perhaps, she now lived with Josh, which would make it more difficult to catch her unawares. He would never be able to go fast enough in the old Ford to see where they were heading. It would have to wait until tomorrow. Harry collected something to eat from a take away, bought a few cans of drink and went back to the car. Tonight he would spend in the car and tomorrow he would watch her movements from a distance, and make plans to run her down.

Sitting in a lay-by, eating his take away, Harry suddenly saw the Alfa flash past, with only Josh in the driving seat. So he had dropped Anna off somewhere. Harry hastily drove the car onto the road and followed the route the Alfa was taking. Josh was returning to The Old Priory. Harry drove past, as Josh parked the Alfa outside The Lodge and went inside. After an hour or two Harry drove back past The Lodge. The Alfa was still there. It looked as if Josh had returned to live at The Lodge with his aunt and uncle. But where was Anna? Harry drove back to the lay-by. He would stay the night there in the car and follow the Alfa in the morning. After falling asleep eventually on the back seat, Harry was disturbed by an insistent tapping on the window, and woke to see a police officer peering into the car. 'Everything all right, sir?' asked the officer. Harry put his hand up to adjust his wig which was slightly askew, and put the window down slightly.

'Just taking a nap, officer. Tired, that's all.'

'Been drinking, have you?'

'No, not at all, officer.'

'Better to breathalyse you to be sure, sir. We don't want you to start driving off if you're not fit, do we - would you get out of the car, please.' Harry got out carefully, holding his old raincoat together. His expensive shirt and trousers did not go with the rest of his disguise and would be a give away. After blowing into the breathalyser which showed a negative result the officer apologised for waking him. 'Better to take a rest than have an accident, sir.' The police car drove off. The officer felt sure that

Harry had been wearing a wig and smiled to himself. The vanity of some men, he thought. He'd have looked better if he was bald rather than cover up a patch with a terrible old wig like that. All the local police had been told to keep a look out for Lord Charlesworth, and he had a blown up photograph of that gentleman in his pocket. He had asked Harry to get out of the car so he could see him more carefully, but it was obvious, wig or no wig, that the scruffy looking individual in the equally battered old Ford did not fit the description. But, had he asked to see his driving licence he might have been very surprised, for it was in Harry's name and the search would have been called off. Harry, now totally awake, felt as if he'd had a narrow escape. There was no reason for the police to be looking for him as far as he knew, but the encounter had given him a nasty shock. This road to The Old Priory was well used and in future he must hide the car away on a side road, where it would not be seen by police patrol cars. About eight o'clock, Harry watched all the cars passing the lay by in the direction of Chelmsford, with the ignition switched on. When Josh passed him, he was ready to follow behind at a discreet distance. As Josh turned into the Rows, Harry parked a little further on and waited until the Alfa reappeared with Anna sitting in the passenger seat. He waited until the car was out of sight and then walked up to the entrance. This interesting long house must be the Rows, where Anna had lived originally with her parents. He remembered them discussing the possibility of turning the terrace into one house, when they had bought the property. The result was very pleasing. A high brick wall surrounded the front area with a paved parking place, and garages, at the side. The cul-de-sac which had been formed by the building of the bypass had given the Rows privacy, where before a busy road into Chelmsford had passed close to the front windows of the houses, giving them a grimy appearance. This was a vast improvement.

As he watched a builders van drove through the gates and men unloaded tiles and a ladder. So they were still working here. With so many people about this was not a good place to make an attempt on Anna's life. He would have to look elsewhere. On the way back to the little village where The Old Priory was situated, Harry stopped off at a Little Chef for breakfast. His throat was parched and he was glad of the coffee. A young, tired looking girl took his order and brought it over to the table where he was sitting. She would never remember the scruffy grey haired man, he decided; she looked too gormless to remember anything. Sitting drinking his coffee he wondered if Anna ever drove the Alfa on her own. He would have to wait outside The Old Priory all day to find that out. He already felt bored and longed for his pretty little Chantelle, but he dared not telephone her. He needed complete anonymity if he was to get away with his plan to kill Anna. Chantelle would be wondering about him, but there was no way to get in touch with her without somebody hearing about it. He hoped she would be patient, and amuse herself with the wedding preparations. Perhaps he would be back before too much longer.

Harry paid his bill, bought a newspaper and continued on his journey back to The Old Priory. Unknown to him, Josh never left Anna alone in the car since receiving a call from DI Johnson, to the effect that Harry had returned to England and might be heading in their direction. Josh knew that it would only be a few weeks before Anna would be free of her marriage, but she was inclined to treat the matter as if it was a fuss about nothing. The police were on the look out for Harry and Josh would never let anything happen to her. The work on the old stables was almost completed and she longed to move into her own home with Josh. Making love on the spare bed back at The Lodge, when the Hardys were out was almost as fraught as going back to the Rows for a few stolen hours together. Their longing for one another was becoming a daily torture, and finding somewhere to be alone together was often difficult. 'A few more weeks,' was all the builders would say when she tried to hurry them along, but like builders everywhere they worked at their own pace and she had to be patient.

This was one of those days when Anna felt frustrated and threw caution to the winds. Joe and Mary were out shopping. She had no idea when they would be back, so she went to find

Josh who was working in one of the greenhouses. 'Come inside, sweetheart—they're out at the moment, but I don't know how long for.' She began to kiss him passionately, aching for him to make love to her.

'It's too risky, Anna. I need time to make love to you properly, so we enjoy every precious moment.'

Anna looked at him pleadingly and his heart melted. The urge to take her was unbearable, and the waiting to be together was getting him down too. Taking her hand in his they hurried across the lawn to The Lodge and up the stairs to the spare room, stripping off their clothes as they went, but before they had fallen onto the bed they heard the Hardy's car pull up at the door. Josh pulled on his trousers and ran back down the stairs, cursing under his breath. It had been a risky thing to try and make love without knowing how long they had together. Anna arrived in the kitchen just as the Hardy's came through the back door, breathless and flushed. 'I thought I'd make some coffee,' she said, cheerfully, as if that was the only thing on her mind. 'Would you like some?'

'Lovely—thank you, dear—oh, we forgot the milk while we were out, Joe.'

'I'll just go across the road and get a couple of pints. I won't be a moment.' Anna ran through the gates without a thought of any danger and crossed the road to the village shop. At that moment Harry was driving round the corner and saw her. With his foot down hard on the accelerator he drove towards her, but she had just reached the other side of the road. The Ford mounted the pavement at speed, hitting some wooden gateposts before it slid back onto the road. Anna saw it coming and screamed, grabbing hold of the gate as it came towards her. The car swerved as it hit the gateposts sideways on, forcing the gate to open. Anna fell through onto a gravel path. Hearing the sound of screeching tyres people ran out of the shop and on seeing the splintered wood, ran towards Anna and helped her onto her feet.

'It's Lady Charlesworth, isn't it? Poor thing. Are you all right?' Anna was too shaken to answer and just nodded her head in reply. 'He must have been a madman, or lost control of the car. Did anyone see him?' A little group gathered round her, full of concern. She gladly accepted their help in taking her back across the road, and into The Lodge. Perhaps, it had been a fault in the car's steering, or the driver had been taken ill. Whatever the reason, the car had driven away as suddenly as it had appeared. Anna had only glimpsed the driver and noticed he had worn dark glasses and a cap, but that was all. It was odd that he hadn't stopped afterwards. He must have realised that he had nearly killed her. As she stumbled back to The Lodge all she could think about was Josh. In the heat of the moment she had forgotten his warning. Suddenly she found herself weeping. Their future happiness had almost been destroyed in a few seconds and all because of her thoughtlessness and a hit and run driver.

'Shock—that's what it is,' remarked one of the women, helping Anna along. 'One of us ought to warn them about the accident at The Lodge.'

Joe came to help Anna indoors while Mary Hardy ran to find Josh. Josh was horrified; what had she been thinking about! He gathered the weeping Anna into his arms and comforted her, kissing her and stroking her hair. 'It's all right now, sweetheart. It's all over.' Anna clung to him, loath to let him go, as he sat her down in his aunt's old rocking chair, and stood beside her holding her hand tightly in his own. The group of village women moved quietly towards the door, exchanging glances. Whatever next!

Mary watched their faces and put on the kettle to make a cup of tea, forgetting she had no milk. There would have to be some explanations or the wrong story would be all round the village in no time. 'Come into the front room ladies, please. I would like to speak to you, and I'm sure Josh would like to know what you can remember.'

'And the police will want to know, too,' said Josh. 'I'm just going to 'phone them. I hope you can wait for a few minutes.' The group of village women moved into the tiny front room to wait. Wild horses would not have stopped them. Such excitement was rare in the village and they wouldn't have missed it for anything.

'There isn't any milk - sorry,' said Anna, with a wan smile, feeling a bit more in control of her shaking limbs. She must pull herself together so she could give an accurate report to the police, in case it was of some importance.

'Don't you worry about the milk, my dear,' said Mary, filling the teapot. 'Joe can get some. I expect the shop is a-buzz with what has just happened, but Joe is good at keeping his mouth shut, when it suits him.'

Detective Inspector Johnson got very little information from the group of ladies in the front room, when he arrived. The car had gone by the time they had run out of the village shop. As he moved into the kitchen to speak to Anna and Josh, Mary shut the door and had a word with them as they sipped their tea. She explained Anna's forthcoming divorce and Lord Charlesworth's new marriage. It was by mutual consent, and Anna and Josh were soon to be married themselves. Anna was a lovely girl and they were both very fond of her. 'We all make mistakes at some time or another,' said Mary, eyeing them all like a schoolteacher, 'and I hope you all understand, so no tittle-tattle goes round the village. The marriage ended before they came back from the honeymoon. They had both made a great mistake, that's all.' The women shook their heads in sympathy, but did not understand how Anna could prefer Mary Hardy's nephew to the very rich and handsome Lord Charlesworth. It defied belief, but then the young were strange these days in their choice of partners and marriages lasting did not seem to be their priority. Just living together and going off with someone else as soon as something went wrong. Their daughters were just the same, in some cases, but to part while on honeymoon—they had never heard of such a thing. There was much to chat about and shake their heads as the little group made their way back home. It would be the main subject of conversation in the village for a long time to come.

It had all happened so quickly that when DI Johnson came to question Anna, she could tell him very little. The car had been a dirty fawn colour she thought, but she had no idea of the make. The driver had worn dark glasses and a cap and had an unshaven appearance, but she could remember nothing else. The car had been driven at speed as if the driver had intended to run her down; but of course that might not have been the case. 'Was it anyone you recognised?' the inspector had asked.

'No. It happened so quickly. He swerved to avoid the lamp-post and hit the gate posts sideways on—he would have hit me otherwise.' As Detective Inspector Johnson left he begged her to be vigilant at all times. Anna had been so shaken by the experience that she assured him there was no doubt that she would be in future. When a message came through to all police cars in the area to look out for a fawn coloured car, make unknown at present, involved in a hit and run accident, with possible scratches and dents on the off- side, and driven by an unshaven man wearing a cap and dark glasses, it jogged the memory of one of the patrolmen. It could be the man he had breathalysed the night before, who had worn an ill fitting grey wig, and was driving a fawn coloured Ford, about ten years old. DI Johnson, on hearing the message, felt sure it was the same car and the same driver. It was very possibly the man they were looking for, Harry Charlesworth, and the hunt was stepped up.

CHAPTER 22

Harry hurried along the back roads towards Colchester and stopped to review the damage to the car. He was furious to think he had missed Anna by a hair's breadth and damaged the car so badly that it could easily be recognised. He took off his cap and the wig and put them into the boot of the car with the raincoat. He saw no point in wearing them again, as Anna might have glimpsed them and he would dump them somewhere with the car. The mask he kept, pushing it to the bottom of his overnight bag. It still might come in useful. He took his own jacket out of the boot, ready to make a quick get away once he had left the car in an inconspicuous place. Driving into the town by way of the barracks he saw a side street where people without garages parked in an area near their houses. He left the car there and walked into town. In the High Street he found a travel agents which advertised a day trip to Calais on the ferry, leaving from the Bus Station. As it was leaving the next day it suited him well, and he waited until the shop was empty and booked a ticket. He would be almost invisible travelling on a coach with a lot of other people, and he could spend a few days with Chantelle, while the police looked for the hit and run driver. Once the search had calmed down he would return to make his abduction attempt. Anna must have been born under a lucky star to have survived all his efforts to kill her.

Having booked his ticket, Harry whiled away the hours, sitting or walking in the castle park, keeping away from people. When the evening approached and the gates were shut, he wandered across to the Bus Station, and ate some fish and chips and drank a few cans of Cola, in one of the shelters. After the local shops shut and the small back streets emptied of people he walked round to pass the time. A prostitute approached him to his annoyance and he returned to the Bus Station to read his newspapers and to doze until the passengers for the coach began to arrive in the early hours. Harry kept apart, keeping his back to them, and once on the coach he found a seat to himself and caught up with his lost sleep. At Dover there was a definite police presence, but they appeared to be looking into cars as they lined up for the ferry. They had probably had a tip off about something or somebody. Harry slid down on his seat and bent over his newspaper and the coach passed through with only a brief glance from a customs official standing on the step into the coach. Coach parties were not known to harbour police suspects, and as far as Harry knew, his only crime known to the police, was as a hit and run driver. That did not warrant a police presence at a ferry port, surely. Still it was best to keep a low profile. The party got off the coach on the ferry and Harry enjoyed a decent meal. It was a pleasant crossing and he sat on the upper deck and enjoyed the sea breeze. Anna could have been a thousand miles away. He would have to return to England in a few days time to complete his plan of abduction, but in the mean time he needed to allay any fears that Chantelle might have about him coming back in time for their wedding.

Once back on the coach they travelled into Calais where the driver left them to look around the town and shop in a multi-superstore. Harry bought some rope and thick tape, and then hired a Renault and drove off in the direction of the chateau. It was a long drive but one he could enjoy, as he was now on what he considered as his home territory with Chantelle waiting for him at the end of it. The coach driver hung around and waited for him to appear as long as possible, and then drove off without him. He could not be responsible for passengers who did not meet the departure time. There was a ferry to catch. It took some hours of driving to reach the chateau and Harry found the place empty apart from Marie, who was in the indoor pool.

'Harry, mon cher.' Marie was overjoyed to see him. 'Come and join me.' Harry looked at the enticing blue water, and the even more enticing Marie, who was swimming in the nude. He felt so filthy after sleeping in a car and on a bench in the Bus

Station in crumpled clothes, which he had longed to change. He showered in the poolside cubicle and joined her. The water was wonderful and so was Marie. Her breasts were more shapely than her step-daughters', and her hips wider. She was made for love as Harry could see, and she wanted him.

'Where is everybody?' asked Harry, who was anxious to behave correctly, although it was becoming clear that Marie had no such intention, as she started to kiss him.

'Chantelle is in Paris, buying more clothes for her honeymoon, and Jacques is in Munich, on business, and I am here, all on my own.' She rubbed her body erotically against his nakedness as she spoke and wrapped her legs around him. Harry's need to have sex with her was physically apparent, and Marie pulled him towards the steps and climbed out of the pool. Harry followed her, running up the stairs behind her and into a bedroom. Making love to Marie was an experience he savoured. She had fancied him from the moment she had first seen him, and had hoped there would be an opportunity to show her appreciation of his sexy good looks. The opportunity had come unexpectedly, and the experience had been amazing. She envied Chantelle having such a man in her bed every night. Afterwards, Harry tried to explain to her that he truly loved Chantelle, and Marie belonged to her father, so there was no possibility of him having an affair with her. If she needed lovers she must find them elsewhere. Marie thought otherwise. Chantelle and her father need never know, she had argued, but Harry would have none of it. This must not happen again. She must promise. Marie was disappointed and pouted seductively. She looked so like Chantelle when she put on her spoilt little girl act, that Harry weakened. 'But we are here, and they are not, so what does it matter,' implored, Marie. Harry found her deliciously attractive and threw his good intentions to the winds. He made love to her again and again until they were both exhausted. He could see that Marie was going to be a problem when he married Chantelle. They were sitting in the conservatory enjoying a glass of Jacque LeBrun's best champagne when Chantelle arrived home at the end of the day. Harry greeted her less enthusiastically than she had expected. She was so relieved to see him again, and not at all pleased to hear that he had to return to England to finish his business.

'I came back just to see you, ma petite cherie. I could not keep away from you a minute longer.'

Chantelle kissed him tenderly, as Marie looked on from a distance, a smile lingering on her lips. For all his good intentions she would find Harry so easy to seduce. 'The police came to speak to you, Harry, but you had just left.'

'Really. What did they want?'

Chantelle shrugged her shoulders. 'How do I know? I think it must have been about that party you went to, in Paris. The one you told me about.'

'Oh, that! Did they tell you that?'

'No, but what else could it be?'

'I've no idea. Are they coming back—did they say?'

'When you came back; but they were not worried, so it could not have been very important.' The police might not have seemed worried, as far as Chantelle was concerned, but Harry certainly was on hearing the news. There were things in his past that verged on the criminal, and not even a wealthy father-in-law would be able to use his influence to keep him out of court. Once they were married perhaps they could make their home in a country where neither French nor English justice could touch him. He was tired of his past life, painting flattering portraits of society women to earn enough to buy the drugs he sold to his wealthy friends at an exorbitant profit, at the parties Leonie organised. It was a way of life he no longer wanted now he had found his dear little Chantelle. He had cut down his appetite for drugs considerably, but still could not kick the habit completely, and continued to smoke cannabis. When he had made love to Marie he had the feeling that she was high on something, but with Chantelle it was pure unadulterated love.

Harry went through his clothes and repacked his bag. Denim trousers, check shirts, an Italian jacket, trainers and a baseball cap, would complete his new look. His stubble was starting to look like the beginning of a beard, with a dark area growing across his top lip. Chantelle did not like it. She preferred him clean shaven. It scratched when he kissed her and he no longer looked so handsome, but Harry refused to shave it off.

'Give it a few weeks,' was all he would say when she asked. 'I promise you, cherie, I will shave it off for the wedding.' And with that she had to be content. That night, as he held her in his arms he explained how necessary it was for him to return to England to complete his business before the wedding. He wanted to sort out a financial matter so they could live well in the future—that was all. He would be back before she had missed him. Chantelle clung to him and wept as if she would never see him again. Harry tried to comfort her but she was inconsolable, and once she had cried herself to sleep he slipped away, taking his things with him. In the early hours of the morning he drove off for the ferry port. By the time he had arrived the ticket office was open and he booked a place on the ferry and joined the queue of cars waiting for the boat to dock. There were fewer tourists about now as the holiday season was over. Just as the ferry arrived the heavens opened and the rain poured down. There would be no sitting on the upper deck this time, he would have to sit inside with everyone else. He parked the car on the car deck and climbed up the stairs to the lounge. There was a tap on his shoulder and he turned round to see the coach driver whom he had kept waiting.

'Sorry, mate,' said the driver. 'I thought you were someone else—a chap I left behind on my last journey—but I can see I've made a mistake.'

'Ce ne fait rien,' said Harry, smiling, hoping the driver would consider him French and not English. Hopefully, his new image would fool anyone else looking for him. When the ferry docked at Dover there was nobody checking cars. The police were concentrating on the queue of cars about to board the boat. So, they were still looking for someone, thought Harry, who had no idea they were looking for him. Once on the road he drove towards Cambridge. A city of students would suit him well. Now he would have to find a flat, posing as a mature student. A flat where there was a back entrance, close to where he could park the car. Harry was in good spirits as he drove along. It was a crisp bright day now the rain had ceased and the city was sharply defined as he drove down the hill towards the outskirts. He passed many tall Victorian looking houses close to the colleges, and decided they must have been made into flats for students. Perhaps, he could rent a basement flat in which to imprison Anna until her ransom was paid. Harry found it more difficult than he had bargained for to acquire a flat. The new term had begun and students who were not fortunate enough to find a place in a hall of residence had taken every flat in the city, apart from one, and that was not fit for occupation. Harry went to see it and rented it immediately. He did not have to stay in it; only Anna. He could book into a hotel close by so he could visit her from time to time, to see she survived until the ransom money was paid. He needed her to write plaintive letters to prove she was still alive. There was no point in him killing her once he had abducted her as her death might one day be traced back to him.

A fatal hit-and-run accident could be the fault of anyone and a drowning while on honeymoon, or the fact that the brakes were not engaged properly, could all be put down to accidental death, but this was different. He would be in France, and might even be away on Jacques LeBrun's yacht by the time Anna was found—in which case the abduction could have nothing to do with him. Harry had to be above suspicion whatever the circumstances. It had been a part of his character since his childhood, and had caused him to be thoroughly disliked by his peers. His father had tried to make him face up to his wrong doings without any success, turning his son against him as a result. Harry felt no regret at having been the instigator of his father's death. It had been a pity that his stepmother had to die too. She just happened to have been there at the same time. He had no quarrel with his stepmother who had always been kind to him, but he had to admit that his life was much easier once they had gone, and he felt no guilt at their passing. Harry looked round the flat before leaving. No wonder no one rented the place. A smell of decay was apparent as soon as he had opened the door. Mould grew on the paintwork and damp brown patches covered the walls. Rusty water dripped from the tap in the tiny kitchen and the toilet did not flush. The poorest student would have turned up his nose at it. A sagging mattress covered the bedspring, and a chair which looked too flimsy to sit on was propped against the rickety table. The flat was the basement of a four floor building, with an outside wall with room to park the car away from prying eyes. The first floor flat was occupied so Harry intended to use the back door and not to go down the front steps into the basement. The occupants would have no idea that anyone was there. It suited his purposes perfectly. Now he had the most difficult part of his plan to carry out -to abduct his wife. After bolting the front door he went out of the back, locking the door behind him. He had seen a hotel near the river, where punts were for hire, and booked a room there for a week. It would be inadvisable to stay longer in one place. With a backpack he could be taken for a student, and once he had Anna safely tucked away he would hire a bicycle, to look the part.

Harry was pleased with himself and the preparations he had made. Tomorrow he would drive to The Old Priory and then to the Rows to see if he could find her.

CHAPTER 23

Josh had been using the chainsaw to cut the long hedge which enclosed the orchard. It was an everlasting task to keep it neatly trimmed and this was to be the last trim of the year. He had completed the sides to his satisfaction and was now working on the end, standing on a ladder to reach the top of a high hedge. The Hardys had recently acquired a springer spaniel which was proving a handful to control. He was an excellent gun dog when Joe helped with the pheasant shoot at a neighbouring farm, but he had an exuberant nature and needed to be kept in a run, or in the house when work was being done on the estate. He had begun to chase the tractor when Joe was using it, and got under everyone's feet. Joe would have returned him to the kennels but for Mary, who had grown fond of the animal. Seeing Josh at the top of the ladder the dog began to climb up the rungs towards him, thinking it was a new kind of game. Josh felt the ladder move slightly and looked round briefly.

'Get down, boy,' he shouted.The dog wagged his tail, thumping it against the sides of the ladder. 'Go on! Get down!' In a second the chainsaw had slipped and had cut the tip of his thumb. Josh cried out with the pain and threw the chainsaw to the ground, as far from the ladder as possible. The dog yelped with fear as the ladder fell down and Josh landed beside him on a huge pile of brushwood.

'My God! Whatever's happened!' Joe, who had been raking up the cuttings, was soon on the scene. 'Bloody dog,' swore Josh, wrapping an old cloth tightly round the base of his thumb to act as a tourniquet. 'The top of my thumb is nearly sliced off.'

'Dangerous those things,' said Joe. 'I'd never use them, even if they do take a fraction of the time.' He pulled Josh onto his feet. 'Frightened the poor dog. Got his tail between his legs right enough—good job you broke your fall, Josh, or you'd be in even more trouble.'

'For heavens sake, Joe. I need medical help. What the hell do you think you're doing at a time like this. Forget about the dog. I need medical help to stitch my thumb together.'

'I will get Mary to wrap it in a bandage with some ice, then I'll get you to the A and E department at hospital. The quicker the better. You don't want to get an infection in it.' Josh felt sick. 'Just get me to the car. Anna can drive us there.' Joe helped him back to The Lodge, calling to Anna who was busy in one of the greenhouses. She rushed to fetch the old family car when she heard what had happened, and left Mary to put a clean bandage on his thumb. As they made their preparations Joe told Mary about the dog and his part in the accident. Mary felt guilty. She had stopped Joe from taking the dog back to the kennels and now look what he had done. She had opened the door just for a moment and he had slipped out. There was no keeping him in—he loved the outdoors.

'I'll stay, my dears, and find the poor animal. I can't leave him to wander about. He might run off. He knows he's done wrong.'

'Mary's got a soft heart,' said Joe, as they set off, 'but that dog's going back if I have anything to do with it.' Anna drove quickly to Broomfield hospital, and Josh was taken straight into the Outpatients. The top of his thumb was sewn back during a delicate operation, and Anna and Joe were told that he would have to stay in hospital overnight, but if the surgeon felt he was well enough he could go home the next day. Josh was still recovering from the operation when Anna and Joe left. She hated leaving him there but there was no point in staying. All being well they would be sending him home the next day. Joe drove Anna back to The Rows. By now it was too late to return to The Old Priory. Joe knew why Josh never let her drive alone these days and promised to come and collect her in the morning. They could go together to see if Josh was well enough to come home. It was much earlier than Anna usually went home and the house was empty. Her father was always there when she arrived with Josh, and her mother was usually busying herself with something. Once Josie got back from school the house was full of noise -usually the sounds of the latest pop group, or the TV which Mollie switched on as soon as she got home. They were a family who only felt alive when surrounded by noise. Anna found the silence eerie. She had never been in the house when it was empty and quiet. She looked at her watch. It would be another hour at least before anyone got back by her reckoning, if her father had gone to the club and dropped her mother off to shop in town. They made a point of being home in time for her arrival so she was never alone. Josh insisted on it. He was very protective of her since the fire and the hit and run incident.

Anna filled the kettle and made herself a cup of tea. Her family would be surprised to find her home before them. She began to wish she had thought of staying the night at The Lodge - she could have slept the night in the little room Josh used. The thought of him lying on the hard mattress making love to her would have been a comfort to her. In a few hours she would telephone the hospital to find out if he was recovering well from the operation. That thought cheered her up. They might even let her speak to him. It was then that the bell rang. Anna put down her cup and looked through the peephole in the front door. A man in a baseball cap stood with his back to her. It might be something important, so she ought to ask him his business. She could see he had backed his car almost up to the front door and had opened the boot. Her mother was forever having things delivered to her new house, so perhaps this was another piece of furniture. Anna opened the door keeping the chain on.

'Yes?' she asked.

The man bent down as if he was lifting up a heavy object so she could not see his face. 'A parcel for you,' he said, in a low voice. 'You'll need to sign for it.'

Anna opened the door to receive the parcel and found herself face to face with a man in a hideous mask. She gasped with terror and tried to slam the door but he was too quick for her, putting his foot inside so she was unable to close it. He knocked her to the floor with a heavy blow to the side of her head, and while she was still dazed, he quickly tied her hands together and then her feet, so she was unable to move. As she began to scream he gagged her mouth with tape and then blindfolded her. Picking her up clumsily he bundled her into the boot of his car and drove off at speed. As the car bumped over the indentations in the road, Anna felt bruised all over. She knew that nobody would have heard or seen anything. The Rows were now set back off the road and stood on their own behind a high brick wall. From the road the car would have looked as if it was parked in the short driveway. Nobody walked in front of the house any more as the footpath had been taken away. The Rows stood in splendid isolation, quite apart from any other houses. As her head cleared, Anna wondered what was to be her fate. He could have murdered her in the hallway, as nobody was in the house, but that did not appear to be his intention. The hit and run man had wanted her dead, but this man wanted to keep her alive. What had they in common? The answer came to her as she was flung from side to side with the movement of the car. It was money—it must be her money. When the blindfold came off, as it would do if he wanted her to write a ransom note, she would look at his hands. Harry had long artistic fingers, and she could tell from that if it was him, although he had probably got someone else to do his dirty work for him if he was behind her abduction. A lot of people knew she was very rich so it could be anyone, but Harry had tried to kill her before, which she never allowed herself to forget. After what seemed a very long journey the car stopped. The driver got out but did not come to fetch her. She heard his footsteps move away and the sound of other cars being parked close by. A short while passed and he got back in the car and they set off again. Her hands and feet hurt from being tied and the gag felt as if it was splitting the sides of her mouth. She prayed that he would release her bonds once they had arrived at their destination.

At last the car slowed down and turned into a parking space and stopped. The boot was opened and she was lifted out none too carefully. She was propped up while he unlocked a door and pulled her inside and laid her on what seemed to be a bed, which creaked under her slight weight. The smell of the place was putrid and she hoped she would not be kept there for long. She heard the door being locked and was aware that he was bending over her. He untied her hands and loosened the rope around her ankles and took off the blindfold. She looked around her as she rubbed her wrists to ease the pain. The place was a slum; a stinking slum. She could see a wall outside the window which blocked out most of the light. She must be in the basement of a building. The man loosened the ties on her ankles, and now she could see his hideous mask more dearly. It was that of an old man but from his movements she knew her abductor was not old.

Anna pointed to her mouth hoping he would remove the tape.

'Not yet,' growled the voice. 'When you have done what you are told, then you can eat. First of all move over to the table and pick up the pen.' Anna was thankful that was all he had in mind; for a terrible moment she had wondered just what he had wanted of her. She shuffled over to the table where paper and envelopes were spread out. 'Copy what I have written in your own handwriting and sign it. Make two copies and then write on the envelopes—one to your parents and one to your boy friend. Then copy the next letter to your bank and mark it urgent.' His hands were covered by rubber gloves as he pushed the writing paper towards her so she had no opportunity to see his hands, and his prints would not be found on the letters. The copy was badly written in block capitals which Anna copied in her own handwriting, placing each letter into the envelopes and sticking them down. The food the man had stopped to pick up and cans of drink were put in front of her and the gag taken out of her mouth. 'Nobody can hear you here, however much you shout,' he warned her. 'I'll be back in the morning, so don't run away.' He laughed in a sinister fashion at his sick joke. 'If they come up with the money I'll tell them where to find you, and if they don't then you will rot here.' He picked up the letters, unlocked the back door, walked out and locked her in again. Anna could scarcely see her surroundings now it was getting dark. She tried to undo the rope round her ankles without success, but she was able to shuffle with some difficulty. The light switch did not work and then she realised there was no bulb in the socket. She sat on the edge of the wretched mattress with her head in her hands, in a state of utter despair.

***

Mollie was amazed to find their front door slightly ajar when she and Reg returned home and thought that perhaps Josie was back early from school. 'You closed the front door when we went out, didn't you Reg?' Reg nodded. 'Perhaps Josie is in. After all I've told that child about being extra careful these days,' grumbled Mollie. Once inside she called to Josie but there was no answer. 'She's not here, Reg, and it wouldn't have been Anna at this time of the day. So who left the door open? Could we have had burglars?'

'One way to find out,' said Reg, walking through all the rooms and finding no one there. 'Nothing seems to have been taken.' Mollie was worried. Something was wrong she felt sure. In the kitchen there was an almost untouched mug of tea which had not been there when they had left the house that afternoon. 'Could Anna have come home early, do you think?'

Reg looked puzzled. 'I'll 'phone The Lodge,' he said, 'they'll know.'

The 'phone call alarmed everybody; Josh was in hospital after an accident and Joe had left Anna at The Rows on his way home. So where was Anna now? She had no car with her and would never have walked along the road on her own since the hit and run driver had almost killed her. Reg decided to call the police despite Mollie's pleas to the contrary. She felt sure there must be a reasonable explanation. Perhaps, Anna had taken a taxi back to the hospital after they had rung to say he was not so well, but a call to the hospital proved that was not the case, and the police were informed that she had disappeared. Detective Inspector Johnson sent a team of officers to The Rows to search for clues, without success. Anna had disappeared into thin air.

She had refused a police escort despite his warnings and now they had a difficult case on their hands. The Ford Harry had left in a back street in Colchester had been reported by the person to whom the parking lot belonged. The car had been towed away by the police who recognised the description as being the one they were looking for. In the boot they found the mackintosh, cap and wig Harry had used, and on the boot a set of fingerprints. Harry had wiped the steering wheel and the off side door, but he had forgotten his fingerprints would be on the boot. Finding the Ford had been a good lead at the time, but then the trail had gone cold. The police had nothing to go on.

When Joe went to Broomfield hospital the next day, Josh was much better and ready to leave. Joe was very nervous. He felt as if it was his fault, leaving Anna alone at the Rows, although he had no idea at the time that the family were out. He doubted that Anna knew that either when he had left her. He waited nervously outside the ward until Josh appeared with his hand heavily bandaged and his arm in a sling. 'Thanks for coming, Joe—I don't like hospitals—but where's Anna? I thought she would be coming to collect me.'

Joe swallowed hard. He wished someone else had come to break the awful news- anyone but himself. 'We don't know where she is, Josh. I'm sorry—I really am.'

Josh took a few minutes to take it in. 'Whatever do you mean?' he said, angrily. 'You left her at the Rows, I presume? Was she there alone?'

'I left her there in all good faith, Josh. I had no idea she would be there on her own, and nor did she. I would have stayed otherwise. You know I would.' Joe's voice began to falter.

Josh turned to him. It wasn't Joe's fault and it was wrong to take it out on him. 'Tell me what happened—do the police know? Do they think she was abducted?'

Joe filled him in with as much as he knew, which was very little. 'Nobody knows what happened, you see. The front door wasn't shut, so the police think she could have been abducted, but it wasn't like Anna to open the door to a stranger. The police think he must have been watching the house and saw her parents leave, and then saw me bring her back and drive away. He must have taken a chance on her being alone.'

'If it was Harry, he's up to every trick in the book,' said Josh, grimly. 'I hope I get my hands on him once the police have found Anna. He'll get no mercy from me. He's obsessed with her money and there's no telling what he'll do next. My poor darling—if only there was something I could do. I'd move heaven and earth to get her back.'

'The police say his next move will be the ransom note and it's important not to take things into your own hands. They have experience in dealing with these things.'

'Do they indeed! We'll see about that!' said Josh, with feeling. 'I'll see what her parents think about it, but I have my own ideas on that score.'

CHAPTER 24

The next day two similar letters in Anna's handwriting were delivered to Josh at The Lodge, and to her parents at The Rows.

> *In two days time bring a million pounds to Magdalene Bridge in the city of Cambridge, packed in a suitcase, at 3a.m. Leave the suitcase at the bottom of the steps leading to the riverside footpath, under the undergrowth, at Jesus Lock. Do not inform the police or you will not be told where to find Anna Charlesworth. You will be told once the money has been delivered.*

The ransom note had been posted in Cambridge. Josh immediately telephoned Anna's parents and discovered that they had also received an identical note written in Anna's handwriting and signed by her. There was no doubt that it was genuine. Reg was all for telephoning Detective Inspector Johnson immediately, but Josh was firmly against it. The ominous warning about never seeing his beloved Anna again, struck home. He dare not risk it. 'We have to find her, if he doesn't telephone after the deadline then that's the time to inform the police. We know she's somewhere in Cambridge. She must be. The letters were posted there yesterday. I'll take the money to the place he says, but I'll look around there beforehand if I have time, in case I can see him lurking around anywhere. If I can I'll follow him and hope he will lead me to Anna.' Reg doubted it would be so easy but said nothing. Josh was grasping at straws in his anxiety over Anna. 'I'm going to her bank in Chelmsford now to see if they have heard anything,' continued Josh. 'If they won't release the money then we'll have to ask the police to intervene.'

Reg was in a quandary. He knew he should tell the police, but he might lose his daughter unless he followed the instructions in the ransom note. It was a terrible situation, and he decided, reluctantly, to go along with Josh. 'But, what about your injury, Josh? You can't go alone. Let me come too—I'll do the driving. Two heads are better than one. I might see something that you would miss, and I can help you look for her.' Josh agreed. His bandaged hand made things difficult for him, and someone to drive the car was essential.

Reg set off for The Lodge and collected Josh and they drove to Chelmsford to Anna's bank. Josh was concerned that if the Bank Manager had not received any instructions they would need to seek the help of the police, but fortunately Anna's urgent note had arrived and everything was in hand. It would take at least twenty-four hours to release so much money, they were told. Josh was horrified. They only had two days to find that amount of cash and he stressed the importance of speed. He was promised it would be there in time and had to be content with that. The Bank Manager was curious as to why so much money was needed in notes, and why Lady Charlesworth was not there in person to receive it, but his professionalism prevented him from asking. Perhaps it had something to do with a loan, but cash, that was very strange, as well as requesting her estate manager to collect it. Reg and Josh sat in the car and discussed the situation. They could just manage to leave the money on time with a bit of luck. In the meantime they would travel to Cambridge and find the place where the money was to be left.

As they drove away from the bank they were tailed by a black unmarked police car, driven by a plain clothes detective. DI Johnson knew there would be a ransom note eventually and feared that the contents would prevent the family from contacting him. They kept watch on the bank until Reg and Josh arrived, and once they were inside, the driver asked for two more detectives to join him. Reg had been carrying a large case as he went into the bank, and for all they knew he might already have the ransom money with him when he came out. Reg drove to Cambridge along the Huntingdon road as Josh followed the route on the map. It seemed the best way to find Magdelene Bridge, away from the city centre. When they arrived Reg parked for a few moments while Josh got out and looked around. The black police car watched from a discreet distance. A traffic warden appeared from nowhere and one of the detectives got out of their car and had a few words with him, explaining that they were watching a suspect. The traffic warden, on seeing the detective's identity card moved swiftly away, leaving Reg amazed at his good luck. He had expected a fine and was about to move off. Now, hopefully, he could stay until Josh had finished looking around.

Josh walked down the steps leading to the footpath beside the river. It was fairly open with nowhere for anyone to conceal themselves, and he thought it a strange place to leave a million pounds in a suitcase. The person collecting it would have to come down the steps or along the footpath in full view of the road. Under the bridge, beside the river Cam, there was a large area of nettles where nobody would have walked. Josh decided to leave the case there. It would be well camouflaged, and only someone who was actively searching for it would find it. At Jesus Lock there were some pleasure boats moored beside the bank; their covers tied down ready for the winter. Nobody would be using them at this time of the year. The place looked deserted, and at that time in the morning nobody would be walking beside the river. Josh decided that he would wait on the opposite side of the bridge after leaving the money at the appointed place a few hours early. Once Harry appeared—presuming it was Harry—he would get Reg to follow him in the car, having left the car in a side road close by. His thumb might be useless but his legs could still run, and he hoped he could make as fast a get away as Harry, unless he ran along the footpath, and if so Reg could cut him off at the other end, using the car. They would have to see where the path ended.

As he came back up the steps and got back into the car, he suggested that they found a car park. They could trudge round the streets for a while before returning home in the faint hope of seeing Harry, and then, on the way back see if they could find out where the footpath ended. The detectives in the black car followed them to the car park and then got in touch with their inspector. Josh had left the case in the car boot when he had gone down the steps so the money had not yet been handed over, but they felt that Magdalene Bridge was to be the drop off point.

'Keep him under close surveillance,' said the inspector. 'You might be right about the place but we don't know when. It could be anytime. In the meantime leave an officer there to watch the bridge at all times, and to note the people who use the steps in the next few days. And get the Cambridge police to begin a search for the girl, especially in any old property, although it's quite possible that she isn't in Cambridge at all.' Detective Inspector Johnson knew that looking for Anna amongst the warren of student flats and bed sitting rooms was like looking for a needle in a haystack. Visiting every house in the city would be a mammoth task but it would have to be done, even if they failed to find her alive and extra police would have to be drafted in to help with the search. He was soon on the 'phone to the Chief Constable to see what could be done. Notices were hastily printed of Anna's description and placed on the college notice boards and in public places, asking for information. All the letting agencies were asked for details of vacancies, in case there was an empty flat somewhere, but there were none. If Josh and Reg bungled the drop, the girl might never be found. Abductors rarely left instructions as to where their victim was to be found. Once they had the money their only thought was to make a clean get away. Detective Inspector Johnson's one ambition in life right now was to apprehend Lord Harry Charlesworth and bring him to book for his crimes. It filled his waking thoughts and denied him his sleep. How he had got away with so much in his life never ceased to amaze him. He was a right slippery character, but they would catch him in the end. Josh and Reg returned to the car park having mingled with the crowds of students and shoppers without a sign of Harry.

'We probably wouldn't know him if we saw him,' said Josh, feeling dejected. 'I expect he's changed his appearance. How we're going to find Anna without any leads I have no idea.'

'You'll have to ask the police for help, Josh. We can't do this alone—it's hopeless. I'm as worried about her as you are. She is my daughter, don't forget.'

'I want to get my hands on him, Reg, and you can't blame me for that.' Reg could see his point, but he was still deeply concerned. 'Wait until after I've left the money. If we don't catch him then or he doesn't leave a message, as to where we can find Anna, then I promise I'll get in touch with them.' Reg felt this was not the way to go about things. The police might not be very co-operative when they were told after the ransom money had been handed over. He became more and more worried about the situation once they had been to look at the route of the footpath and found a bridge a little way along the footpath which linked up with a road. Josh suggested that Reg parked his Jaguar on this road, to block off access from the footpath, while he chased Harry on foot.

'But what if he has left a get away car on the other side of Magdalene Bridge?' asked Reg. 'You couldn't do much about that, and I couldn't see what was going on.'

Josh thought about it. 'I'll have to take the Alfa and park it out of sight, in a side road. Then we'll have him covered whatever he does. It's unfortunate that he knows the Alfa but it's a much faster car than mine, and you can come behind me if we pass you. I expect I can manage to drive if I take this sling off.'

Reg said nothing. It sounded like a crazy idea to him—a bit like cops and robbers but he'd better go along with it. One of the detectives had watched as they got out of the Jaguar and walked across the small bridge to the footpath. There had been a long conversation between the two men before they got back in the Jaguar and drove away. It was fairly obvious what their plan was to be to the watching detective. The police car followed them back home and saw Reg drop Josh off at The Lodge, after which they reported back to the station. 'Once we know that they have the money with them' said DI Johnson, speaking to the crime squad, 'then it's all systems go. I want this man caught at all costs. He's a drug dealer and a murderer, and I don't want him slipping out of our grasp—so see to it. These two amateurs will probably mess things up, so make sure they are never out of your sight. This could be a delicate operation.' He then proceeded to outline a plan for them to follow, once the money had been released by the bank.

***

On the second day of her imprisonment Anna's captor visited her briefly for the last time, and left some filled rolls and cans of drink. She felt too sick from the stench in the basement to eat, but she was grateful for something to drink. The tap dripped ceaselessly with rusty water which was undrinkable. She had tried to loosen it so the water ran cleanly but it was solid with lack of use. When her captor came close enough she had tried to pull off his mask to see if it was Harry, but he had avoided her grasping fingers.

'Try that again, and I'll tie up your hands,' he warned. 'You're on your own now until they find you, so you'd better start praying.' Anna shuddered. Now she had to rely on this man telling Josh where to find her or she would die here. Tears rolled down her face and he stopped at the door for a moment and looked back, feeling no pity for the anguish he had put her through. He hoped she would be found alive just for his own sake. Her death would complicate matters if it was ever discovered that he was behind her abduction. How simple it would have been if she had died as the result of an unknown hit and run driver, who could not be traced. He would have inherited part of her wealth as her husband. Now he had to rely on getting a ransom for her so he could marry Chantelle. It was nearly all over, and hopefully he would be back in France by this time tomorrow, as long as the ransom was delivered on time. It would be an enormous relief not to have to think of Anna any more. He locked the door to the basement for the last time and Anna heard him drive away. Her thoughts were all of Josh. She knew he would never give up until he had found her. Josh could not rest. He telephoned the bank every hour to see if the money had arrived. At last, just before the twenty-four hours had elapsed, he heard the good news. They could get it to the appointed place in time. He rang Reg who came to The Lodge, to follow behind Josh, in the Alfa. Josh had dispensed with the sling and was managing to hold the wheel with his left fingers while driving using his right hand. Fortunately, the Alfa was an automatic which helped considerably. They collected the money, putting it into a large suitcase and set off for Cambridge. Their movements were closely monitored by the police who were following at a discreet distance. Reg had told his wife of the plan to leave the money in case something went wrong, in which case she was to get in touch with the Hardys and the police if they did not return by the next day, with Anna. But nothing would go wrong he assured her. Mollie certainly hoped not. The last few days had been terrible for her, and brought back memories of losing her eldest daughter. Reg had promised faithfully to enlist the help of the police if necessary, and Mollie had to be content with that. She wouldn't sleep a wink for worry.

Reg and Josh arrived at Cambridge as it was getting dark and parked near Magdalene Bridge. Josh took the case and hid it amongst the nettles at the bottom of the steps. Then he drove the Alfa into a side street and sat and waited, while Reg parked his car on the road by the second bridge. At midnight he intended to block the access to the footpath. A green Renault with a French number plate passed him, driven by a bearded man wearing a baseball cap. Reg took no notice apart from the direction the car was travelling. He didn't recognise either the car or the driver. Although it was getting very dark the driver of the Renault recognised him and the Jaguar and decided to make his escape by a different route once he had the money. He knew where Reg was, but where was Josh? There were no police cars to be seen so they had kept to his instructions in the ransom notes. It was possible that the money had already been left for him, as Reg appeared to be a look out. Rather than leave it until the time he had suggested, he would collect it now and catch them off their guard, and then be on his way.

CHAPTER 25

Harry had made his plans carefully. He had driven round the roads off Bridge Street and had decided that if he parked the Renault at the corner of Thompsons Lane he ought to be able to reach the river as the Cam flowed close by at this point. He did not want to be seen going down the steps or across the bridge. He had bought himself a black wet suit with a hood and intended to float towards the bridge in what he hoped would be dark water, keeping close to the bank, and using the moored boats to hide him from anyone on the footpath. Passing Reg guarding the footbridge had been a shock, as he hadn't expected Reg to have anything to do with leaving the money. Josh was such an independent person he would have wanted to do everything his own way. Perhaps, Reg had insisted on taking part as Anna was his daughter. However, his plan did not include driving in that direction so he could discount Reg. He would probably sit there all night waiting for something to happen. The idea had amused him. It had been so easy to fool Reg into thinking he deplored drug dealers, when he was one himself. He was too clever for Reg, but Josh was a different matter. He was a strong, upright, thoroughly decent man—the kind of man his father had tried to turn him into, and he hated him for it. Harry feared Josh and hoped he was nowhere around as yet. The pick up was much earlier than he had intended, and with the sky so overcast the conditions were perfect. He took off his baseball cap and the leather jacket and left them in the car. His other clothes were in the overnight case and he would change into them when he stopped at a service station on the way to Dover.

He locked the car, hanging the keys round his neck, and zipping them inside his wet suit. It only took a few moments to reach the river, and he slid silently down the bank and into the water. For a while he hung onto the chain mooring one of the boats and took stock of the situation. He was too far away from the bridge to see it properly in the darkness and would have to hope that Josh was nowhere around to see him pick up the case. As he floated silently closer he could see the steps down to the footpath. He thanked his lucky stars that there was nobody there and nobody looking over the parapet. Harry swam under the bridge and found the case in the nettle patch. So they had left it there a few hours early as he had hoped. He swam back to the boats, pushing the case in front of him. It was only a short distance and the case stayed afloat until he reached the bank. As he climbed out of the river, a police diver slid into the water on the other side of the bridge to await Harry's arrival, but Harry was already streaking across the grass and back to his car. Once inside he put on his leather jacket over his wetsuit so he would not attract attention if seen and started up the car. Josh was waiting on the opposite side of the river, having parked the Alfa where he had a good view of the riverside footpath, but it was too dark to distinguish anything. He had just decided to walk across the bridge and wait at the bottom of the steps when he saw the lights of a car on the other side of the river opposite him being switched on. If this was Harry he could drive round the western side of the city on the ring road and cut him off as he made for the M1. Josh sped round Queens Road and into the Fen Causeway, passing three stationary police cars without lights, on his way. As he turned into Trumpington Road a green Renault sped in front of him. Josh recognised Harry in his headlights by his dark curly hair. He had grown a beard, but it was definitely Harry. The Alfa was capable of high speeds and kept up with the Renault, driving alongside it. Harry glanced out of the side window to see who this lunatic was and saw Josh, in the Alfa he had given Anna. Behind them came the three police cars with their sirens blaring. Josh was forced into the side of the road and had to stop, but Harry sped on. Just ahead was the turning into the M1 where a police cordon had been set up. Harry found he was unable to slow down and smashed through the barrier. The car turned over twice and slid to a stop with smoke pouring from the engine. Harry crawled out of the wreckage and staggered to the side of the road as the car burst into flames, preventing anyone from reaching him. Josh could see the inferno in the distance and was thankful he had not been caught up in it.

A police officer from the car which had forced him off the road, opened the off side door. 'We're taking you in for speeding and dangerous driving,' he told Josh. 'You're lucky you're not a part of that bonfire.'

'It's the most expensive bonfire you'll ever see,' said Josh, shakily. 'That's a million pounds going up in smoke in front there.'

'Whew! You don't say!'

'It's the ransom he wanted before he told us where to find my fiancée.'

The police officer looked amazed. 'A wealthy lady, is she?' he asked.

'A very wealthy lady, more's the pity. It's brought her a lot of trouble—including that gentleman in the car up front. That's why I've been chasing him. I want to know where to find Anna. He's put her somewhere, but God knows where.'

The police officer felt sympathy for Josh. 'They'll just put you on a charge for dangerous driving and then you'll be able to leave until you get called to court. I can only wish you the best of luck in finding her.' At the police station Josh was told that if he hadn't taken things into his own hands the police might have caught Harry, in which case they would have questioned him about Anna's whereabouts until they found her. Now they had nothing to go on, as Harry needed to be found, either alive or dead. Josh was desperate. Where did he go from here? The police were looking for her and if they couldn't find her then how was he expected to. If only he had taken the ransom note to the police in the first place. If only he could turn the clock back—but such thoughts served no useful purpose. He must find Harry, if Harry was still alive.

Harry heard a fire engine wailing in the distance as it came to put out the flames stretching across the road. It was a miracle he hadn't been burnt to a cinder in that inferno. They would soon be coming to look for him once the police realised the car didn't contain a charred body. It was a pity about the money, but it was all the fault of that fool, Josh. He hadn't intended to tell him where he had hidden Anna, so the car chase was a waste of time. Let the police find her, if they could, before it was too late. He wasn't going to help anybody—he was the one who needed help right now. There was a ditch by the side of the road and Harry rolled into it before the sheet of flame was extinguished. The fire burnt so furiously that the police officers needed to stand well back on the other side of the road until they were dampened down. Harry knew they would soon be looking for him in the burnt out wreck of the car, and then the search would widen. Josh would soon tell them about the ransom and the reason for it. He pulled himself along the dirty ditch on his stomach until he came to an elder bush blocking off the rest of the ditch. Above the bush was a field; the elder was a part of the hedge. There was nothing for it—he would have to struggle through into the field. The police would be poking along the ditch to find him in next to no time. Harry was scratched, and his coat torn before he got through the tangle of undergrowth and into the field. There was an odd sound which at first he was unable to place until he realised it was the deep breathing of cows, munching and chewing the cud. Every so often he heard a cough which was almost human. It was a strange experience finding himself amongst a herd of cows in the darkness. He decided to stay close to the hedge until it was beginning to get light. He didn't want to bump into a cow in the dark, or a bull if there was one amongst the herd, or slip in a cowpat for that matter. He found the sounds around him unnerving and hoped the herd would move off once it got light.

Reg sat in his Jaguar until morning. Nothing had happened and he hadn't seen Josh. He had known all along that he ought to have gone to the police with the ransom note, and he wouldn't put it off any longer. He drove around the city streets as people were beginning to go to work until he found the city police station and went inside to ask for help. He was given a cup of tea in an interview room and poured out all his worries to an understanding detective. Reg was told that a search was already underway but his daughter might not be in Cambridge although the ransom notes had been sent from there.

'How did you know about the ransom notes?' asked Reg, in great surprise. 'Josh thought if best to keep it to ourselves or we would never know where to find our Anna.'

'We kept a watch at the bank. We expected you to be asked for a ransom, and you were followed when you collected the money.' The detective paused for a moment. 'I'm afraid there has been a car accident. We don't know yet if Lord Charlesworth survived. If not we shall have to find your daughter without his assistance.'

'Was Josh involved?' asked Reg, feeling alarmed. 'He's all right, isn't he?'

'He's fine, but he's in deep trouble. He caused the accident.'

Reg covered his face with his hands and groaned. He should never have gone along with Josh and his ideas. The detective put a hand on his shoulder. 'I suggest you go home,' he said. 'We have no reason to keep you here. We'll tell you as soon as we have any news of your daughter.'

'Do you mind if I 'phone my wife? She'll be ringing the police if we don't get home soon.'

The detective handed him a 'phone. He had a daughter himself and felt sorry for Reg.

Reg made his way home with a heavy heart. The police were questioning Josh and he wasn't allowed to see him. If only they had done things his way they might have found Anna by now.

Reg didn't know if Harry was alive or dead and for that matter neither did the police. He must have crawled away from the scene of the crash but he could have been so badly burned that he might not have survived. Nobody had seen him leave the car as it had caught light once it had righted itself, and his body was not inside the burnt out remains. In the light of the morning a search of the surrounding area would be carried out and hopefully the elusive Harry Charlesworth would be found. On leaving the police station Josh overheard a telephone conversation. Apparently, Harry had not been found after the crash and a police search was being organised. Josh set out to find him for himself. He was convinced that there was no way of finding Anna without him. Going back to the scene of the crash might not be such a good idea. It would soon be crawling with police. Josh examined his map. There was a road running parallel to the road along which he had been travelling, and a small road meandered across country to join up with it. Josh decided to drive slowly along this route to see if he could see Harry anywhere. There was a herd of Friesian cows in one of the fields wandering towards an open gate in a long line, as if they were making their way to some distant buildings. A man with a stick was walking behind them. Josh thought they were being taken to be milked at first, until he saw the man was wearing tight leather trousers, like the bottom of a wet suit. He stopped at the gate as the cows came into the lane and surrounded the car. Harry saw the Alfa before Josh realised it was him, and took off up the lane to the farm buildings. Unable to move with the cows rubbing up against the car, Josh got out and followed Harry on foot. He could see him disappearing into a barn and sprinted after him. Bales of straw were stacked up against one side of the barn with a ladder propped up against them. The early morning light filtered in through the gaps in the door and chickens were beginning to scratch about on the dusty floor. The cockerel had been disturbed by this early activity and left his harem to greet the dawn in the stockyard outside. It was very quiet and still in the barn but Josh knew that Harry was in there somewhere.

'I'm coming to get you, you bastard!' shouted Josh. 'You won't get away this time.' Harry kept very quiet, hardly daring to breathe. He was terrified of a confrontation with Josh. He knew he didn't stand a chance if things got nasty. There was a pitchfork leaning against the wall. Josh picked it up and began to poke it into the straw bales. Harry must be amongst them somewhere. There was nowhere else for him to hide. Josh was very thorough, taking one section of the bales at a time, and Harry knew he would find him eventually. He shifted his position slightly and the ladder clattered to the floor. 'If you don't want me to spear you with this, Lord bloody Charlesworth, then you'd better show yourself. I'm getting—closer—and closer—and closer—.' Josh dug the fork into the bales as he spoke, more and more ferociously. Realising that he would soon reach him Harry parted the bales and jumped down to the floor. Josh was getting too close for comfort. Josh took hold of him and used him like a punch bag.

'Tell me where she is,' he screamed. 'Come on, where is she?'

Harry's nose was streaming with blood and his mouth was cut. He grovelled on the floor and begged for mercy. Josh was so angry he found it hard to stop hitting him but he had to give him a chance to speak. 'Well!' roared Josh, pulling him to his feet.

'In a basement -in the last of the tall houses—flats I think—opposite a playing field. There are some horses in the field.'

'That tells me nothing,' said Josh, shaking him violently. 'What's the name of the road?'

Harry felt sick. 'Chapel Street. You turn into it at the city junction. It leads down to The Backs eventually.'

Josh threw him onto the dusty floor, disturbing the chickens which ran squawking out of the barn. 'You'd better be right or next time I'll kill you. Make no mistake about that.'

Hearing the noise outside the farmer stopped eating his breakfast and picked up his gun.

'If that fox has got in the barn again --.' he muttered to himself, as he strode outside. To his surprise the cows were waiting patiently outside the milking shed. He looked down the lane and saw a red Alfa being turned in the gateway to the cow's pasture, and wondered just what was going on. In the barn he found Harry leaning up against the straw bales, trying to staunch the blood pouring out of his nose. 'What's all this about?' asked the bemused farmer, but before Harry could answer a police car drove into the stockyard.

'There's one of them here but the other one has just gone,' said the farmer. 'He drove off in a red sports car.'

'We just passed him,' said the police officer. 'This is the one we want.' Harry was taken away by the police, leaving the farmer to puzzle about his unwelcome visitors.

CHAPTER 26

How long would it be before someone found her, thought Anna, as she shuffled round the tiny room. The cans of drink were empty now and the food unpalatable. Josh would be looking for her everywhere. Holding on to the thought of him kept her sane in this terrible place. She had tried and tried to undo the knot that held her ankles together but without success. Slipping off her shoes and twisting her feet round to get through the knot had not helped either and only made her ankles more sore from the chafing. She could just get her fingers between the rope and her skin and rubbed her ankles to keep the circulation going from time to time. The smell of her prison seemed to have become an integral part of her being and she was becoming immune to it. It had been some days since she had smelled fresh air. The rain outside as it pattered against the window made her think of the fresh sweet smell of grass after a shower and she longed to be outside and feel the rain on her face and the water running down her parched throat. She pushed the rickety table in front of her as she moved about. It helped her to balance. She was afraid of falling and not being able to get back onto her bound feet. Nothing could be worse than that. Having a little exercise, however limited, was vital under the circumstances. Leaning on the table had made it even more unsteady and one of the legs had begun to wobble, giving Anna an idea. Perhaps, she could ease the leg out of the socket. She sat on the bed and pushed the table onto its side with the legs towards her and tugged and twisted the loose leg until it slipped out. Anna felt a huge surge of relief. Now she had a tool with which to bang on the windows and the doors. She had shouted until she was hoarse, and if anyone in the flats above had heard her they probably thought the sound was coming from the street outside.

Her abductor had said she would never see him again so she had to do something to help herself. Even his frightening presence had helped to break up the day, much as she loathed the man. Now she felt completely alone, like a prisoner in solitary confinement. She began to bang on the doors and windows with the table leg and then remembered that it was the middle of the morning, and the students living there were probably out or at lectures. The rain was coming down harder now and she could hear thunder in the distance. She banged the window over the sink with sheer frustration until the glass began to crack. Little by little the glass shattered and fell outside on the pathway. Anna pushed her hands through the splintered window and collected some raindrops. At first she smoothed the raindrops over her face to refresh herself, and then placed the empty cans on the windowsill to catch a few drops of the welcome water. The sweet smell of the fresh rain was like a breath of freedom and she stood by the broken window, drinking it in.

Both the doors had small panes of glass inserted into the top panels and she joyfully smashed these to pieces. The window facing the basement wall was larger and took longer, but eventually there was a gaping hole where the glass had been. When she had finished demolishing the glass she suddenly thought of the rope which bound her ankles. The glass had all fallen outside. She was dismayed when she realised she could have used the glass to cut her bonds. There were still a few jagged pieces left in the window frames and these she removed with care, using her skirt to wrap round her hands to protect them. Even so her hands were cut and bleeding by the time she had finished. It was a painfully slow business and she needed many slivers of glass before her patience was rewarded and the rope began to shred. After many hours and cuts to her hands and ankles she had freed herself. Anna sat on the lumpy mattress and wept with relief. Her ankles were red and painful and when she got back on her feet she found she could still only shuffle. She began to rub them vigorously to encourage some feeling in them, and sat and moved her feet round, this way and that, to get the blood circulating. The windows were nailed down and had been made with small panes so there was no hope of climbing through them, but she hoped someone would hear her now. A wind drove the rain inside and it was very cold, but she welcomed it, blowing away the smell which had built up over the years when the basement had been left unoccupied. Someone hurried up the steps to the front door of the flats and rang the bell. Anna banged with the table leg and shouted frantically for help. A black face appeared over the wall of the basement area.

'Help me, please help me!' croaked Anna, as loudly as she could. 'I can't get out of here.' The face disappeared and spoke to the person who had opened the door. Anna shouted again. Then two people came down the steps of the basement and looked through the broken pane in the door. 'Help me to get out—please,' begged Anna.' 'I'm locked in'

'Gee man, what a state to get in,' said a West Indian voice. 'We'll do our best. The owner won't mind if we damage his door, will he? We can't exactly pay for a new one.'

'I'll pay for it,' said Anna. 'And I'll pay you for getting me out of here.'

'You'll what!' laughed the men, who found that hard to believe. 'We'll take the building to pieces, brick by brick in that case. How about a thousand pounds each?'

'Whatever you say' said Anna, wearily, 'but just get me out.' Two large pairs of rugby boots took turns to crash into the door until it gave way, and two hefty West Indian students walked through the door. There was no more good-humoured repartee once they saw the state of the place.

'How did ya get in here, gal?'

'I was locked in—on purpose. I think I've been here for three days.'

The two men looked at her with pity. Her face was streaked with weeping and her hands and ankles were cut and bleeding. Something terrible had happened to her. 'Can you walk?'

'I don't think so. My ankles have been tied for days.' The men picked her up between them and carried her up the stairs and into the hallway of the flats above.

'Lulu!' called one of the men. A girl came out of one of the downstairs flats. 'Look after her, Lulu. We found her locked in the basement. Get her a coffee and keep her warm. She needs help. We can't stay—we shall be late for lectures. Talk to her, and find out what you can.'

The girl helped Anna into a chair. 'Are you the woman the police are looking for?' she asked.

'Yes -I expect so. Josh would have alerted the police. How did you know?'

'There's a poster on the notice board in my college. You just rest—you look terrible. I'll get you some coffee and call the police.' Anna was grateful for her kindness and had begun to doze off in the warmth of the gas fire by the time the coffee arrived. 'We heard some knocking from the basement one night,' said Lulu. 'I suppose that was you.'

'If only you had come,' said Anna. 'I was in there for days.'

Lulu laughed. 'My boyfriend, who helped you to get out, is superstitious. He thought it was a spirit knocking. I couldn't persuade him to go and look.'

Anna smiled. 'A huge man like him—afraid!'

'A student hanged himself down there a few years ago, so it's always empty. No one will live there. They'd rather sleep on the street.' Anna shuddered. She was glad she hadn't known about that when she had been in the basement.

'I'm not surprised,' she said. 'It's a terrible place—enough to make anyone feel suicidal.' There was a ring at the doorbell and two policemen and a policewoman stood there.

Lulu showed them in.

'Glad we've found you,' said one of the policemen. 'We understand you were held in the basement here. We've been searching for you for days, and have only just started looking in this area. Cambridge is a large city for a full scale search.'

'Who put me here?' asked Anna. 'I never saw his face. Was it Harry?'

'Lord Charlesworth? Can't say, ma'am, but that gentleman is in custody now. He was picked up early this morning.'

'Who's this Lord Charlesworth?' asked Lulu, as they helped Anna onto her feet.

'He's my husband -but not for much longer, I hope.'

'Jeez!' exclaimed Lulu, under her breath.

As Anna was helped towards the door her cut and bruised ankles became apparent, and the policewoman radioed for help, to take her to hospital. An ambulance soon arrived and Anna was taken to Addenbrookes Hospital for some badly needed attention. It passed Josh going in the opposite direction, who had just discovered where Anna had been held captive. Running down the basement steps he found the front door had been kicked in and the windows smashed. Inside the place was filthy with stained paper hanging from the walls, a dirty mattress was spread on the bed and there was broken furniture strewn around. He swore under his breath and wished he had killed Harry when he had found him. 'I'd lock you up in here, mate, and see how you'd like it,' he muttered, under his breath. 'It would be worse than a prison cell to you—starvation and no creature comforts. I hope to heaven that my Anna got out of here safely.' He walked across the broken glass and got into the Alfa, hoping the police had found her before he got there. His next stop would be the city police station. Perhaps they had some news of her whereabouts.

CHAPTER 27

The bed in the police cell was not made for comfort. Harry sat on it with his back against the wall and his hands behind his head. He looked a mess. Josh had turned his face into a bloody pulp and he was bruised all over. He had punched him with his right fist, keeping hold of his head in an arm lock. His left hand was wrapped in an enormous bandage which had begun to unravel during their fight and which had obviously given Josh some pain by the look on his face as he had struggled to hold him. Harry wondered how Josh had come by his injury, but whatever it was he had still got the best of him. Harry had never been one for pugilistic sports—his good looks could have been marred for life – and now look at him. He was bruised and battered beyond belief and his handsome features all but destroyed. He was lucky that idiot Josh hadn't killed him. If he hadn't told him where to find Anna the beating would never have stopped. The police surgeon had been to see him and had patched him up but he still ached in every bone in his body. He had been handed a revolting meal on a tin tray which he had not deigned to eat. If this was a sample of prison fare he would fade away to nothing by the time he was released, if they convicted him. He had been told that they were waiting for a Detective Inspector Johnson who was coming to interview him, as he was dealing with his case. What case, Harry had asked himself. He might be accused of abducting his wife and demanding money for her release, but they had nothing else on him. He had always covered his tracks. They knew nothing about his past. Nobody had seen him abduct Anna and he had never shown Anna his face. He had no money, unfortunately, but that meant they had to prove it was him who had sent the ransom notes, and he had left no fingerprints. Nobody saw him take the money from under the bridge and he could have got away with it if only Josh hadn't recognised him in the car. The police barrier had surprised him. Perhaps, it had been set up to stop someone else. He found it hard to believe that they knew it was him who had abducted his wife at that time. Telling Josh where to find her was a mistake, but he had no option at the time. She would have been found by now, safe and well, so they couldn't pin her death on him.

Harry twisted and turned things round in his mind to get himself out of this trouble. They couldn't hold him if he didn't admit to anything. He knew enough about the law to know that. He had asked to see a solicitor and he would be here soon. Harry hoped the solicitor was a man with plenty of experience who would argue his case well. There were the drugs of course. He had been a drug dealer for years but they would find nothing in this country. Leonie kept the hard drugs in her apartment in Paris and if she was caught he would deny knowing that she had any.

Chantelle's father would give him a good character reference, he felt sure, but he hoped they would never find out about Anna. He had told them she had perished in a fire, as he had thought at the time. The thought of his darling, sexy little fiancée saddened him deeply. The wedding would have to be postponed—perhaps indefinitely. It would break her heart, but he had done it all for her. What would she think of his bruised and battered body now; and the delicious Marie. Harry sighed at the thought of the afternoon he had spent with her. No more fun with Marie. He had lost so much in his quest for a fortune. If he had to spend years in prison he might as well be dead—no sex, nothing. He seemed to remember hearing somewhere that they put something in the prisoner's tea to control their sexual urge. They would have to give him a double dose to control his! The solicitor was shown into his cell. Harry was not impressed. He looked as if he was newly qualified and unlikely to have had much experience, but he hoped he could guide him through the forthcoming interview. They discussed the abduction of his wife. Harry was vague about the details and said little until he heard that Anna had been found and had been taken to hospital for treatment.

'Who found her?' he asked. He was curious to know if Josh had found her but the solicitor had no information to give him. At least she had been found alive and he wouldn't be held responsible for her death. 'I didn't benefit from any money. It was all destroyed when the car caught fire,' complained Harry, as if that fact might be a point in his favour.

'The abduction of your wife and demanding money for her release is a very serious offence, as you must know,' said the solicitor. 'And giving information as to her whereabouts places the blame for her abduction firmly with you. There is no way I can help you on that point. The case will be brought to court and it will be up to the judge to decide your sentence. I will help as much as I can, as long you co-operate.'

Once Detective Inspector Johnson arrived, Harry was taken into an interview room to be questioned. A large file of papers was placed on the table between them. Harry looked at them curiously. Surely all these papers were not necessary. It was nothing but red tape these days. The inspector took a folder of photographs out of the file and handed them to Harry.

'Do you recognise any of these, sir?'

Harry looked at them with mounting annoyance. 'What is all this about?' he asked angrily. 'These are just wedding photographs.'

'Your wedding, I believe, sir—on St Lucia. Did you wear the same clothes in the evening?'

'I think so, but not the coat. It was very warm.—Do you mind telling me what this has to do with abducting my wife?'

The inspector ignored the remark. 'Your wife says that you left her for part of the evening.'

'I may have done.'

'To go off with a limbo dancer—is that correct?'

'I really don't remember.'

The inspector handed him another photograph—this time of the girl lying with a broken neck beside the boat. 'Do you remember now, sir?'

Harry looked at the photograph with distaste. He would not be accused of her murder. It was unfair, dragging this up, and he would say so. His solicitor, seeing Harry was about to launch into an explanation tried to intervene, but Harry would have none of it. He would not stand accused of something he had not intended, and he would say so. 'It was an accident that was all. I meant her no harm. I just pushed her away. She wanted more money and I hadn't any. She was pestering me. I didn't kill her, I tell you. She fell against the boat, and that's the truth.'

'Thank you, sir. I'm glad we've cleared that up. Now we can go onto another matter. I should mention that this interview is being recorded, but I'm sure you are aware of that.'

'I thought this was about my wife,' complained Harry.

'We are coming to that, sir, but first of all I want to discuss another matter. The French police are interested in the model, Leonie.'

Harry looked up with interest. So they had taken her in after he had informed on her. She would never bother him again. 'Well. What has that to do with me?'

'She was your mistress I believe, for some years?' Harry laughed, derisively. 'Since when has that been a crime, inspector?'

'Storing drugs is a crime, sir, and she is now in custody for that offence. You were a drug dealer, Lord Harry, and you used her as a front for your activities. She admits to arranging parties for you so you could sell drugs to your socialite friends.'

'She would say that, wouldn't she. I had nothing to do with it.'

'That seems strange as your friend Simon Beacham, who is at present serving a long sentence for drug running, has informed us that you sailed to Holland with him for that purpose.'

Harry was silent. He could think of nothing to say in his own defence this time. 'There is another matter, sir, which we must discuss. I havc to tell you that the French police have a Bernard Le Valet in custody, who has admitted to tampering with your fathers' car on your instructions, with the intention of killing your parents.'

'What rubbish!' shouted Harry, standing up. 'My parents' death was an accident.'

'The case has been reopened, sir. Monsieur Le Valet admits to blackmailing you for a period of some months. The French police have checked your payments into his account; payments which increased every month.'

Harry was astounded, and sat down heavily in his chair. He had refused to pay Le Valets' increased demands recently, being out of funds himself, but he had never expected the man to admit to being a blackmailer to the police. He wondered how they could have found this out. It was uncanny. His past was being unfolded before his eyes and there was nothing he could do about it.

'As to the abduction of your wife, Lord Charlesworth, and the large ransom you demanded for her release—have you anything to say?'

'Nothing.'

'And the attempts to kill your wife while on honeymoon, and later by setting fire to her home, The Old Priory, and in a hit and run accident outside the gates.'

'I am innocent of such charges—innocent, I tell you!' Harry shouted, rising to his feet. He was restrained by an officer in the room and sat down again, reluctantly.

'We have a set of your fingerprints, Lord Charlesworth, which you gave us on your arrival at this station. They match with a set on the boot of an abandoned Ford car, and the clothes in the boot, which you used as a disguise when trying to run down your wife. Fingerprints can be used as evidence. I am therefore charging you with this offence.' The charge was read out to Harry, who refused to speak. He had said too much already, but he had only admitted to causing accidental death and perhaps that had been unwise, when he heard, to his horror that he was to be transferred to a remand prison to await the court case. The solicitor had a few words with him before he left. He had requested bail but this was denied to him due to the seriousness of the charges. Back in his cell Harry banged his fists on the wall in total frustration. He had just discovered that being Lord Harry Charlesworth counted for nothing here. It was all Anna's fault; if only he had never sought her out when he had read of her unexpected fortune in the newspapers. At the time it had seemed such a wonderful opportunity to get his hands on her money, and look where it had got him. None of his past would have been discovered, and the death of his father and stepmother would have remained unsolved. Now all of that would be raked up again. How on earth had the police got new evidence about that? LeValet would never have gone to the police of his own accord to find himself incriminated in a case of murder. Someone must have tipped the police off—someone with a grudge against him. The realisation hit him like a blow. Leonie! It must have been Leonie—nobody else knew. He had been within an ace of getting everything he had ever wanted, with the richest prize of all – his dear little Chantelle. It was all gone—all of it. Life was so unfair.

Josh had been told by the police where to find Anna and set off to the hospital immediately. He wasted little time, only stopping to buy the largest basket of flowers he could find on the way. His fight with Harry had dislodged the top of his thumb, but losing it was worth the beating he had given him. The bandage was bloody and fast becoming unravelled but he would get it attended to and tidied himself up before he saw her. By the time he arrived at the door to her room he looked more respectable, but he felt embarrassed carrying the flower basket with the huge bow on top, and gave it to the police-woman sitting outside the door to give to her before making his presence known. Through the half open door he could see the pleasure on her face as she received them and was told who had sent them.

'The flowers are lovely, but why isn't he here?' asked Anna, with concern. 'Nothing has happened to him, has it?'

'Just a few bruises,' said Josh, smiling, as he walked into the room and took her in his arms. He held her close not wanting to let her go. The agony of not knowing where she was for the last few days, or what she was suffering, had made him realise the intensity of his love for her. Anna sighed with joy. The feel of his strong arms holding her and his heart beating against her breast as he kissed her tenderly, filled her with such desire for him she could hardly breathe. She loved him so much, and wanted him to pick her up in his strong arms and keep her safe forever.

'I knew you would come, Josh,' she whispered. 'I knew you would find me in the end. Take me home, please. I just want to be home again with you.'

'You can't just walk out of here, sweetheart. You've had a bad time. I'll need to see the doctor first, but I'm not leaving you whatever happens. We'll have to go back to The Rows first for a few weeks while we get the old stables furnished. But it won't be for long I promise you. I want us to be together in our own place as much as you do, and I want you there as my wife.'

Anna burst out laughing. 'But you've never asked me, Josh. I might refuse!'

'Haven't I?' Josh sounded surprised. 'Well I can soon put that right.' He went down on his knee in front of her chair and took her hand in his. 'Will you marry me, Anna? Please, my darling. I can't imagine life without you.' He was so serious in his request that Anna had tears in her eyes when she accepted his proposal. He would always love and care for her. She had known him long enough to be sure of that, and this time she would be happy; the happiest person in the world.

There was a knock, and the doctor came into the room feeling as if perhaps he should go out and then come in again. Josh got to his feet.

'So sorry; I didn't time my visit very well; my apologies.'

Anna smiled at him. She looked radiant. 'No need to apologise, doctor. I've just accepted a proposal of marriage.'

'My congratulations to you both; nothing like a proposal of marriage to get you feeling well again—better than all the medicine in the world.'

Anna wanted to leave immediately but the doctor decided she should stay until the next day. She had been through a terrible experience and a few more hours of complete rest would be beneficial. Josh persuaded her to do as the doctor suggested. He would stay in a hospital guest room over night, and the police presence would remain outside her door until she left the hospital, so she had nothing more to fear. Once they were left alone together Anna wanted to know how the police had found Harry. Josh told her about hiding the money under the bridge and keeping watch, while the police were watching him and her father; and the police chase once Harry had taken the money.

'Did he tell you where to find me? I wondered if he would.'

'No. He didn't intend to. He was just going to take the money and run.' Josh told her about the police barrier and the accident with the car.

'So he didn't have the money after all,' said Anna. 'I'm glad. That was all he ever wanted; it took me long enough to realise that.'

'It is all over now, sweetheart. He'll never worry you again. You can forget him. He'll be locked away for years. Prison is too good for him after what he did to you. I looked for him after he left the scene of the accident and by great good fortune I found him before the police did—driving a herd of cows across a field.'

'What!!' Anna was intrigued.

'He ran into a barn and I followed him and beat him up until he gave me the address of that dreadful place where he had left you. I spoilt his looks before I finished with him. It gave me great pleasure to cause him so much pain—I only wish I'd killed him for what he'd done to you.'

'Oh, Josh—but your thumb? You didn't do more damage to that, did you?'

'To tell you the truth, I forgot about it while I was knocking him about. I went mad when I got hold of him and went on punching his face until he told me where to find you. I passed the police coming to get him as I drove away.'

'And then I wasn't there. I wish it had been you who had found me. I kept thinking you would come. I knew you would never stop looking for me.'

Josh put his arms around her and held her tight. 'Thank God, someone found you. I saw that awful place for myself. They should put him in there and forget about him. That would be a better punishment than prison, in my opinion'.

'That reminds me, Josh. I want to send the two students who rescued me some money, as a reward, and the girl, Lulu, who called the police. Students are always short of cash and I've got plenty, despite Harry losing a million in the fire. You don't think they'd feel offended, do you, Josh?'

Josh smiled. 'I doubt it. They can always send it back if they do! They'll be hoping to find more ladies in distress to help pay their college fees in future, is my guess.'

Anna was thoughtful. 'I've been thinking while I've been sitting here. It was Harry all along, wasn't it, Josh? I thought it was him under that horrible mask, but I was never absolutely sure.'

'Oh yes; it was Harry all right, but forget about him now, my love. He's gone for good. No more nightmares on his account—promise?'

'I promise,' she said, kissing him, fondly. The next day the hospital were only too pleased to let Anna go home after the doctor had been in to see her and pronounced her fit, as long as she continued to treat her cuts and bruises with the ointments they had given her. Josh wheeled her out to the car, with a basket of flowers on her lap.

'I've told your parents we are on our way, and they have let my aunt and uncle know so there will be a great welcome awaiting you.'

'I hope they won't make too much fuss,' said Anna. 'I'd just like a nice cup of tea. I used to long for a cup of tea. I got so thirsty.'

'You can have as many cups of tea as you like,' said Josh. 'Just state your preference. Your every wish is my command from now on.'

'You might have cause to regret that remark,' laughed Anna, giving him a sidelong glance. The family had all gathered to welcome them back, including Josie, who had taken a day off school for the occasion and Reg had some bottles of champagne on ice, to celebrate.

'She only wants a cup of tea,' Josh told them.

'Too bad,' said Reg. 'It's champagne today, or nothing,' and he poured out a glass each and handed them round.

'I'd like to give us a toast,' said Josh, raising his glass. 'To Anna, my wife to be.' Everyone was only too pleased to drink to that, and another toast was drunk to them both. Mollie brought a letter over to Anna, which had arrived while she had been away. She had a feeling it was good news. Anna opened it. It was her decree absolute. She waved the paper above her head.

'I'm free—I'm free,' she shouted, joyfully.

'That's another good reason to drink a toast,' said Reg, happily, who had never liked his daughter being married to Harry, and he filled up their glasses to the brim. Mary Hardy became quite overwhelmed, drinking so much champagne, and burst into tears of happiness, to add to the joy and relief they all felt. On this occasion Mollie raised no objection to Josh staying at The Rows with her daughter. Josh had become a hero in her eyes, and was soon to become a member of the family. They planned to be married just before Easter, when The Old Priory gardens would be a mass of daffodils, primroses and violets. It would be a joyful time for a joyful celebration. In the meantime they would have time to arrange the interior furnishings in The Priory Stables, so all was ready for them to move in. Sack loads of letters arrived at The Rows for Anna after the story of her abduction hit the headlines of all the daily papers. The most unlikely people spoke to the press of their involvement in her release, hoping for some financial gain from her ordeal. A spokesman for the hospital gave a brief report on her condition on arrival, and of her release. There were photographs of the inside of the flat, in lurid colour, and photographs of the students who had rescued her. Someone had obtained copies of her wedding to Harry on Saint Lucia. There was no end to it, and the papers had a field day. Josh thought it best if the papers were kept away from Anna, but she wanted to see them for herself, if only to threaten to sue if the reports were incorrect.

'It will be a nine days wonder,' said Josh. 'Next week something else will happen to whet the public's appetite and they will forget you. It's only because Harry is a lord that makes people so interested in the story. It will soon be forgotten, that is until his trial and when he is locked up in prison; after that he will be a non-entity'

'But all these letters!' complained Anna. 'Most of them are begging letters. Now people know about the lottery win they seem to think they have a right to a share of it. Some of them sound so genuine too. I find it heart breaking to read them.'

'It's best to ignore them all,' said, Josh, sensibly. 'Once you start, where do you finish—but perhaps you should read them—some are from people who really felt sorry for your plight.'

'Oh, yes, that reminds me -I'd almost forgotten -I found some letters in a drawer.'

'Letters?'

'Yes, love letters to Lady Letitia. I only looked at a few of them -it didn't seem right to pry. Especially as they concerned a child she gave birth to out of wedlock – anyway they were burnt in the fire so her secret will remain that – a secret, best forgotten.'

'The more I hear about it the more I'm glad The Old Priory burnt down. We'll start anew, you and I and make it a happier place than it was in the past,' said Josh, and Anna was only too happy to agree.

CHAPTER 28

The days had flown by in a whirl of intense activity and excitement. Chantelle kept an eye on all the preparations until people wished she would leave them alone to get on with things in their own way. For Chantelle her special day was to be perfect. The day before the wedding was to take place the florists arrived with vanloads of flowers and transformed the chateau with their magnificent white arrangements. The hair-dresser took up residence, ready for the great day, and the chefs were already busy in the kitchens. Chantelle expected Harry to appear at any moment. He had told her not to expect him to contact her while he was away. His business needed to be completed before their wedding so their future was assured. The truth was quite different. He had to remain incognito to avoid the possibility of the police tracing him, should anything go wrong with his plans. As he had turned up unexpectedly one day, because he had missed her, she hadn't worried about him returning in time for their wedding. Now she was not so sure. His absence on the eve of their wedding had alarmed her, especially as his last words to her were of returning in good time. Her father felt the same concern, while trying to calm her fears.

'The police came to question Harry, Papa, after he had left for England the first time. They said they would return to speak to him later, once he had come back.'

'What did they want to speak to him about?' asked Jacques LeBrun, wondering if this had anything to do with Harry's absence.

'I don't know. They didn't seem very concerned. I told Harry about their visit when he came back to see me, and he thought it might have been about that drugs party he had been taken to, when he had been attacked.'

'The one I reported, you mean.'

'Yes, Papa. Harry wasn't at all bothered about their visit. He said he would sort it out after our wedding. They probably wanted him to tell them what happened.'

Her father had other ideas. The police visit could have been about a far more serious matter, in which case Harry might never turn up to marry his daughter. The family would lose face if his darling child was left waiting on her wedding day. She would become a laughing stock amongst her society friends, and he must avoid that at all costs. Chantelle was becoming weepy as the hours ticked by without Harry putting in an appearance and even Marie looked sad and disconsolate. It was more than a man could stand having these two miserable women around him, on what should have been a joyous occasion. Monsieur LeBrun telephoned his friend, the Chief of Police, to see if he could throw any light on Harry's absence. He was soon put in the picture. They had a Bernard Le Valet in custody for admitting to tampering with the brakes on Lord and Lady Charlesworth's car, causing a fatal accident. Monsieur LeBrun remembered it happening. The accident was reported in the newspapers at the time as it was so horrific, but no one had been charged and the case had been closed. But that was not all; their son, Harry, had been blackmailed by Le Valet ever since, having paid Le Valet to cause the death of his parents.

'Surely not—we find Lord Charlesworth such a charming man. You will have to prove that Le Valet is telling the truth.'

'Not so difficult, Jacques; we have proof of the payments.'

'But why would Harry want to do such a terrible thing to his parents, even if you have this proof?'

'To gain a title and inherit their wealth, perhaps. Why else would he want to kill them, unless there was a family vendetta?'

Monsieur LeBrun was speechless for a while. 'I can't believe this is true—I can't believe it—I know the man.'

'We have someone else in custody, Jacques, who knows him well; his mistress, Leonie, the model. You know of her—yes? She hoarded the drugs he sold on to his friends. She informed on him when we raided her apartment. He is a drug dealer, my dear Jacques, and maybe a murderer.'

'Where is he now? Do you know? He is supposed to be marrying my daughter tomorrow. He went to England and has not returned.'

'I will get in touch with the English police. They may know something about him, and I'll call you back. It is not my business but do you think it is wise to let the marriage go ahead under the circumstances? If your daughter is so lovesick over him postpone the wedding until we have questioned him.'

Jacques LeBrun went to find his daughter, hardly able to contain his anger. Chantelle and Marie were sitting together in the conservatory, comforting each other. 'Listen to me both of you.' Jacques demanded, angrily, forcing them to give him their undivided attention.

Chantelle had never heard her father address her in such a rough tone of voice before and her sobs ceased abruptly. 'Papa. Whatever is the matter?'

'Stop your weeping, you foolish women. There will be no wedding. He won't be coming here ever again. He is wanted by the police.'

'But why, Papa? What has Harry done?'

'I cannot tell you, my little one, as it has to be proved—but he is a very bad man—a villain. I'm sure you were in love with him but you must forget him.'

Chantelle's sobs began again, and Marie was almost as heartbroken as her stepdaughter. Jacques stormed out of the conservatory to answer the telephone call from his friend, only to learn that Harry had been taken into custody by the English police and was now in a remand prison awaiting trial for the abduction of his wife, and the attempts on her life.

'But he has no wife,' shouted Jacques down the 'phone. 'We understood she had perished in a fire at her home. We felt some sympathy for him when he told my daughter about it.' His friend had no knowledge of a fire, but he did know that Lord Charlesworth's wife was still alive.

'He would have married my little, Chantelle, bigamously,' shouted Jacques, in a fury. 'It is too terrible!' He put the 'phone down and stood staring at it, hardly able to take in what he had just heard when he noticed a letter addressed to Harry on the silver plate which was used for the incoming post. He picked it up and slit open the envelope with the silver letter opener. It was from Harry's solicitor containing his decree absolute, to take effect from the day after the wedding. His precious daughter would have had a bigamist for a husband, and none of them any the wiser. He picked up the letter and went to find, Chantelle. Perhaps, she would realise what a rogue she had almost married. 'If you want to know why the wedding is cancelled, look at this letter, Chantelle, and be thankful you didn't marry him.'

Chantelle scanned the letter. 'I don't understand, Papa. Harry told me that his wife was dead. Perhaps he thought that she had died in the fire at her home.'

'I'm afraid not, ma petite, she is very much alive. He was divorcing her to marry you. Your wedding would not have been legal.'

'Perhaps Harry had thought his divorce would have come through in time, Papa. It was only one day late.'

'Don't make excuses for him, Chantelle. He told you a lie about his wife, and has probably told you other untruths'

'But he loved me Papa. He didn't love his wife. I know he loved me.' Chantelle began to weep again.

'Maybe he did love you, ma petite, but he is a bad man. He is in prison in England for trying to kill his wife, to get her money.'

'But we have money, Papa. Why did he need money?'

'Everyone needs money, cherie. Perhaps he wanted it so he could be rich like us.'

'But I wouldn't have minded if Harry had nothing.'

'I know, cherie. I understand. You loved him very much but you cannot marry such a man. I must find you a good husband. You will soon be happy again.' There was a sudden cloud burst, which wrecked the silk arbour where the marriage was to have taken place. Chantelle looked at the mess outside, as the pieces of silk were tossed about in the wind.

'I won't need it now,' she said, sadly, wiping away her tears. Her father took her in his arms to comfort her. 'Both you and Marie can go for a long cruise on the yacht and invite your friends. Forget Harry, and enjoy yourselves, and please stop crying the pair of you. I can't bear any more of it. Just go away and leave me in peace.' Chantelle and Marie kissed him fondly, on both cheeks. He was a generous husband and a kind father, but they would both miss Harry. There would never be another, Harry.

Why did you cry so much, Marie?' asked Chantelle, when her father had left for Paris.

'I cried in sympathy with you, Chantelle. Why else should I cry? You were so upset that I felt sad too. I am soft hearted and I cry easily.' Chantelle put her arms round her stepmother, affectionately. 'I know Harry loved you, Chantelle. Why he told me so himself. Let that thought be a comfort to you.' The wedding forgotten the two young women packed to suit a hot climate and set off on a luxury cruise with their friends. By the time they had arrived at the Greek islands Marie had taken another lover with whom to pass the time, although she kept the affair a secret from Chantelle. She wasn't ready to part from Chantelle's father just yet. And Chantelle met a handsome, debonair, and rich marquis, of noble French lineage, whom her Papa had asked to join the cruise at the last moment, in the hopes that he would amuse his sad little daughter. Chantelle found the marquis a delightful companion, both in and out of bed—but there would never be a lover like Harry, she told Marie, when they were sharing confidences. Marie had smiled. She knew that only too well without Chantelle telling her.

CHAPTER 29

Two weeks later, on a beautiful spring morning, Anna and Josh were married at the register office in Chelmsford with only a few family members attending. After a modest reception at the Priory Stables they wandered, hand in hand, around their much loved garden. It was then that Anna told him she was pregnant.

'How long have you been keeping that a secret from me, sweetheart?' asked Josh, who was overjoyed by the news.

'Not long, darling. I just wanted to tell you on our wedding day, to make it perfect.' Josh sat her down on a garden seat and kissed her long blonde hair, his arm encircling her waist. 'You must take care of yourself, sweetheart. Promise me.'

Anna laughed. 'It's a perfectly normal thing for a woman to have a baby, Josh, and I feel really well.'

'When did you find out?'

'The doctor at Addenbrooks told me, after he'd given me a test which proved to be positive. He said the sick feelings I'd had in that terrible place might have been caused by my being pregnant, and he was right.'

Josh felt as if he was the happiest person in the whole world at that moment, and he kissed Anna tenderly. 'So when do we expect our baby? Do you know?'

'You remember the first time we made love, Josh -when you came back from New Zealand.'

'As if I could forget it!'

'Then I must be about three months pregnant, but I can't be absolutely sure.'

'And you kept this from me, all these weeks?'

'I didn't want to—I often wanted to tell you since I've known, but you know why I didn't—I kept it for today.' Josh swept her up into his arms and carried her, laughing across the lawn towards the house. Mary and Mollie, who had been tidying up after the reception saw them coming and slipped discreetly away as Josh carried his happy bride over the threshold.

CHAPTER 30

There was a comprehensive selection of law books in the prison library as many of the inmates studied them in their free time. Harry was one such prisoner. He was convinced that the more he understood the law, the more likelihood there was of finding a loophole in his defence, which would lessen his sentence. The police only had Leonie's evidence about his drug dealing. She was a woman scorned, as he would point out at his trial, and as such they should give no credence to the stories she had told them. The ransom for Anna's release had been burnt to a cinder in the car after the crash, and nobody could prove he was the one who had abducted her. She had never seen his face and the police only had a few smudged fingerprints to go on. Josh had behaved like a madman in the barn, and he should be sued for the damage he had done to his face, but the police would never see it his way. He would say he had made up the address in Cambridge to stop the beating Josh had given him. He hadn't been to Cambridge for years and no one could prove otherwise. As to the fire at The Old Priory—that could have been anyone. He had explained how the death of the limbo dancer had been accidental. For once, he had told the truth but no doubt that would be held against him too. In retrospect he regretted having ever mentioned it. His solicitor had told him the police had arrested Bernard Le Valet on a matter of blackmail. Harry felt confident that Bernard would never admit to cutting the brakes of his father's car on his orders. It would implicate Bernard in murder when he was out of the country. Harry decided to say he had lent Bernard the money as a loan to buy a garage, and had refused to pay him any more. Bernard was a tough character and used threats to get what he wanted. The more he thought about it the more

Harry thought he could wriggle out of the worst things he had done, and he studied the law books assiduously.

He had written to Jacques LeBrun to explain how he had heard of Anna's death in the fire at The Old Priory, and had been astounded to hear that she had survived. He had never willingly misled anyone and had immediately arranged for a divorce. It had seemed unnecessary to tell the family as he expected to be free in good time to marry Chantelle. He expected to be released from prison as the charges against him were entirely false. It had been a case of mistaken identity, which he was trying to prove. A letter from Monsieur LeBrun as to his good character and his desire to marry Chantelle, would be a great help in his present situation. Harry had also written many letters to Chantelle, begging her to ask her father to write on his behalf, but he received no replies from her. The prison authorities had received a request to suppress all of Harry's letters to the LeBrun family, and after a while Harry stopped writing.

Harry was an ideal prisoner, charming and affable to everyone. He asked if he could work in the prison library as he spent all his free time there, and offered to make an inventory of the books. His education at Eton was taken into consideration and what seemed to be a reasonable request was granted. It gave Harry the opportunity to order more law books, to be brought whenever the mobile library replenished the stocks, which was about once a month. Occasionally, old newspapers found their way into the library and were eagerly read by the inmates, especially those who wanted to read reports of their own exploits, as reported to the general public. Harry came across a short article about Anna's new marriage, after he had been inside for many months, awaiting trial. He read it with interest. There was a small photograph taken outside a building which appeared, on closer examination, to be the stables at The Old Priory. Her new husband, a Mr J Hartington, was unknown to Harry at first sight. The name meant nothing to him, yet there was something familiar in her bridegroom's cheerful smile. Looking closer at the muzzy photograph Harry suddenly realised it was Josh. He grew red in the face with anger and thumped the photograph with his fist, drawing attention to himself. He had always thought Josh had shared the same name as his uncle. His father had called them both Hardy, but presumably Hartington was his proper name.

'Is anything wrong?' asked the warder on duty. Harry controlled himself with difficulty and shook his head. So Josh had won the right to Anna's fortune: the fortune Harry had schemed so hard to acquire and now would never enjoy. Harry ground his teeth in anger. He had hated Josh all his life. Josh possessed the attributes his father had tried unsuccessfully to impose upon him, and Josh had been the stronger of the two when they had fought as boys, but Josh knew he had to give in or he would have been in trouble if Harry had been given a bloody nose. Harry would run away after taunting him to a place where Josh had been forbidden to follow, so he never got hurt. Harry would like to make him suffer for winning the greatest prize of all—his ex-wife and all her millions. Harry spent hours thinking about it. To escape, if such a thing was possible, would mean a longer sentence, and if he killed Josh, it would mean life for sure. Revenge was sweet, so the saying went, and Harry was hell bent on revenge. As the weeks passed Harry was allowed to choose the new books for the prison library from the mobile when it made an appearance within the prison compound once a month. He took requests for books from the prisoners, and suggested new titles, taking into consideration their tastes in reading which were mostly erotic and pornographic and not to be found on the library shelves. Such dedication to his post earned him the nickname of 'the professor' from the other inmates.

The law books which arrived at Harry's request each month gave him the chance to speak to the man and woman who drove the mobile library, although speaking to outsiders was strictly forbidden by prison rules unless at visiting times. Inside the van nobody could see Harry striking up a friendship with the two librarians who thought of him as an inoffensive and friendly individual. As the months passed they looked forward to their prison visits. There were two warders on the gate which closed behind the library van on arrival. Harry watched every move as he planned his escape, and noticed that one warder was attracted to the young lady assistant and often helped her with the trolley stacked with books, pushing it for her into the prison, while the man restocked the shelves in the van with the returned books and then followed behind, accompanied by Harry, carrying his books. One very hot day at the beginning of September the warder at the gate lit a cigarette surreptitiously and wandered a few steps along the wire perimeter, gazing out across the deserted airfield where the prison was situated. The sun beat down on the tarmac causing a heat haze in the distance. The warder watched idly, as if hypnotised, with his back to Harry. Harry dropped his books and stooped to retrieve them as the two assistants and the second warder made their way into the prison. Harry stepped quickly into the van and put on the baseball hat which had been left on the seat, pressed the switch to close the door and started up the engine. He turned the van round and was relieved to see the warder come out of his trance, stub out his cigarette and open the gates. Harry drove away at a dignified speed as the gates closed behind him.

A bright yellow mobile library van was not the best of get away vehicles, but Harry knew the area and kept to the route through the Suffolk villages along the way towards the Essex border where The Old Priory was situated. Nobody would think a mobile library was worth looking at twice as they visited all the villages weekly, and keeping to the usual routes was the best way to go for the first few miles, until the police came looking for him, which would be fairly soon. The van was slow and cumbersome and once he reached the small town of Clare he parked it in the High Street and made his way on foot. Outside the village he took footpaths across high fields of corn where he would be camouflaged if helicopters flew over, but he only heard police sirens wailing in the distance as police cars made their way along the twisting country roads. He kept to the hedgerows where possible, and lonely lanes on his journey until he found a bicycle leaning up against the wall of an isolated cottage, and then he took to the main roads. Nobody would be looking for a lone cyclist. A police car passed him at one point and disappeared quickly. Harry felt elated—he was free and unrecognised. The baseball cap he had tossed into a ditch and he looked like any other cyclist out to enjoy the summer weather.

It was evening before he reached The Old Priory gates and he cycled down the drive to the burnt out ruins of what had once been his home. He saw nobody as he passed The Lodge, and doubted that the Hardys would have recognised him if they had seen him. He had grown a beard since being in prison which fitted his new persona, as 'the professor'. Leaning the bicycle against the end wall Harry crept round to look at the stables. He was surprised to find an elegant house where the old buildings had been, and the lights on upstairs. So Anna and Josh were at home and his journey had not been in vain. He tried the back door which opened to his touch, and picked up a knife from the knife block on the dresser. He had thought the kitchen was empty until a small, yapping dog hurled itself towards his ankles, taking hold of his trouser leg. Despite all his efforts he was unable to throw the animal off and yelled as it bit through his ankle to the bone.

'What is it, Charlie? Who's there?' Anna came out of her bedroom and stood looking over the banisters. At the sight of Harry holding a kitchen knife she let out a piercing scream and called for Josh. Harry was amazed at the size of her. She looked as if she was about to give birth to twins.

'Call your bloody dog off,' he shouted. 'It's got my ankle.'

Anna's screams only grew louder. If Josh was around he would surely have arrived by now, thought Harry, trying to kick the persistent animal away. Josh was in the paddock, shutting up the pheasant chicks for the night, when he saw a police helicopter hovering low overhead, its lights sweeping the garden. Josh looked up in surprise. He presumed they must be looking for someone.

Then he heard Anna's screams and Charlie's barks and sprinted back to the house to see a man with his leg held firmly in Charlie's teeth, trying to shake him off. In his hand he held a knife and was obviously up to no good. Josh picked up a heavy wooden chair and hit the man on the back of his head. As the intruder slumped to the floor Charlie let go and crept back into his basket.

'Good dog,' praised Josh, to the excited animal, as he turned the man over and stared down at his face. Even with a beard it was obvious he was looking at Harry. Anna began to struggle down the stairs, calling to him. 'Go back sweetheart. It's O.K. I've knocked him out cold.' But Anna had seen Harry's face and began to scream again. The last they had heard of Harry's whereabouts he was in prison awaiting trial. On hearing all the screaming and barking from the stables, Joe picked up his gun and he and Mary ran down the drive to see what was happening.

'I've brought my gun,' said Joe, as they ran into the kitchen. 'What's going on?— My God! What have we here?' Mary went up the stairs and helped Anna back into the bedroom, where she had been resting from the heat. Anna was doubled up, clutching her stomach and moaning, as her waters broke.

'She's started the baby, Josh—poor girl. It's no wonder seeing who's lying down there. It's the shock.' Josh picked up the knife where Harry had dropped it and replaced it in the block. Then leaving Joe to guard the prisoner he ran outside, waving frantically at the hovering helicopter, which was already looking for a place to land, having seen Joe running up the drive holding a gun. Two men jumped out as the helicopter landed on the paddock and were soon in the kitchen, putting handcuffs on Harry, as he came round.

'We know him,' said Josh, breathless with exertion as he came through the door. 'It's Harry Charlesworth—my wife's ex-husband, and believe me he's dangerous.'

Harry sneered at Josh as he rubbed the back of his head. 'You bugger,' he snarled. 'I came to get you this time—marrying all those millions. You've no right—.' Harry was hauled to his feet and half dragged to the helicopter, still shouting obscenities at Josh as he was bundled inside.

'He won't get out to bother you again,' said Joe 'They'll keep him in a secure unit from now on. Broadmoor's the place for him. He's as mad as a hatter.'

Josh closed the door and ran upstairs two at a time to comfort Anna. 'The baby's on the way,' said Mary. 'Her water's broken and you'll have to ring for an ambulance.'

'Surely not—it must be a false alarm. It's not due for weeks yet.'

'She's so big, poor girl, and so uncomfortable in all this heat, it'd be a blessing if it is early in my opinion,' commented Mary.

'I must get to the hospital, Josh,' moaned Anna, with the sweat pouring off her. 'The contractions have started'

Josh phoned the emergency services and Anna was soon in an ambulance ready to be whisked away to the maternity unit. 'I'll follow in the car, sweetheart—see you there. You're in good hands now.' In the early hours of the morning Anna's son was born, screaming lustily.

'A beautiful boy,' said the midwife, 'a real bonny little boy, with a pair of good lungs by the sound of it.' She handed him to Anna to hold and the agony of his birth was forgotten as she held her child. He looked like her idea of a perfect baby, without the screwed up, puckered little face she had expected. She marvelled at his long eyelashes and blue eyes, and the tiny fingers which grasped hers, and love for him overwhelmed her. Josh gazed at him in wonder. Now he had a family that he could really call his own.

'His hair is dark,' remarked, Josh, stroking the soft down on the baby's head, as he held him.

'That usually rubs off in the first few weeks,' said the midwife, 'and then his real hair will begin to grow, although it takes some time with a lot of babies.'

'I didn't expect him to be so big. He's quite a weight. It's a good job he decided to come when he did or he would have been enormous in a few weeks time.'

'Consideration for his mother,' smiled the midwife, 'in all this heat. But he's an average size for a full term baby.'

Josh looked at Anna but she had closed her eyes. The midwife must be mistaken, he thought as the baby was placed back in the crib beside his mother. Perhaps, Anna had got her dates mixed up, but what did it matter; the child was healthy and Anna had looked radiant when her son had been placed in her arms. In this heat she would have had a difficult time being heavily pregnant for another three or four weeks and the baby would have been a monstrous size. It was better this way. And Josh gave the matter no further thought. Anna opened her eyes and he bent to kiss her.

'I'm just going to ring your parents with the good news, sweetheart. I won't be long.' As he walked down the corridor names for the baby came into his head. James Maximillian perhaps; they went well with Hartington. He would suggest them to Anna and see what she thought. He was filled with the joy of unexpected fatherhood and people smiled at his happy face as he passed them. When he returned Anna's heart melted as he put his arms round her and kissed her tenderly. There was nothing for her to worry about any more. All the money in the world could never buy such exquisite happiness. Josh already adored their handsome little son and she would never tell him the terrible truth she had realised as her pregnancy had advanced, for it would break his heart.

Lightning Source UK Ltd.
Milton Keynes UK
UKOW03f0709090514

231359UK00002B/35/P